"Is that a *baby monitor*?"

"What's he doing up?" Micah grumbled. "He should be napping."

"There's a *baby* in there?" Deirdre asked.

"How is it you don't know about my son? No one told you?"

"And who would have told me? I think there's been a misunderstanding."

"You've got that right. Why would anyone send a federal agent out here? You never said what you're here to ask me about."

"Your stepmother."

"I have nothing to say about *Ariel Porter*."

Deirdre startled at Micah's words, missing neither the alias nor that he'd ground out the words when he spoke them.

"I've flown from Washington to speak with you, so please give me a chance to tell you about my investigation."

"I'm sorry for your wasted trip. I don't want to talk about *her*. I haven't seen or spoken to Ariel in the more than fifteen years since Dad died. I can't help you, so I don't want to waste your time. Or mine."

"Just try to answer a few questions. I'm sure you'll be of more help

He shook his h

D1010420

Dear Reader,

I am thrilled to bring you my story in this exciting Coltons of New York series. It has been a privilege to collaborate again with such fine writers as we tell these exhilarating connected stories. I love the world of the Coltons! No matter what obstacles they face or dangers pursue them, these characters move forward with determination and the bond of family.

I had a blast writing Micah and Deirdre's story, which serves as a reminder that what we're really searching for in life might be far different from the picture we've painted in our minds. Or, in Deirdre's case, might be far away from the bustle of the city and found in a place where prairies stretch for miles and where neighbors are not strangers but friends. I loved sharing Micah's journey from the scars of loss and betrayal to the realization that the person who can fill the empty place inside him just might be a special agent who breaks the rules.

I hope you have enjoyed the first few books in this series and are looking forward to the next seven as I am. Please join me in rooting for each of these Colton siblings and cousins as they search for answers to bring the guilty to justice, collaborate and face danger throughout their journeys, opening themselves to the hope of lifetime love along the way.

Happy reading!

Dana

AGENT COLTON'S SECRET INVESTIGATION

Dana Nussio

HARLEQUIN

ROMANTIC
SUSPENSE

Special thanks and acknowledgment are given to Dana Nussio
for her contribution to The Coltons of New York miniseries.

HARLEQUIN®
ROMANTIC SUSPENSE™

Recycling programs
for this product may
not exist in your area.

ISBN-13: 978-1-335-73838-7

Agent Colton's Secret Investigation

Copyright © 2023 by Harlequin Enterprises ULC

For questions and comments about the quality of this book,
please contact us at CustomerService@Harlequin.com.

Harlequin Enterprises ULC
22 Adelaide St. West, 41st Floor
Toronto, Ontario M5H 4E3, Canada
www.Harlequin.com

Printed in U.S.A.

Dana Nussio began telling "people stories" around the same time she started talking. She's continued both activities, nonstop, ever since. She left a career as an award-winning newspaper reporter to raise three daughters, but the stories followed her home as she discovered the joy of writing fiction. Now an award-winning author and member of Romance Writers of America's Honor Roll of bestselling authors, she loves telling emotional stories filled with honorable but flawed characters.

Books by Dana Nussio

Harlequin Romantic Suspense

The Coltons of New York

Agent Colton's Secret Investigation

The Coltons of Colorado

To Trust a Colton Cowboy

The Coltons of Grave Gulch

Colton Nursery Hideout

The Coltons of Mustang Valley

In Colton's Custody

True Blue

Shielded by the Lawman
Her Dark Web Defender

Visit the Author Profile page at
Harlequin.com for more titles.

I dedicate this story to my readers, who make this career of storytelling possible. Thank you for allowing me into your lives and for connecting with the characters who escape from my mind onto the page. I so appreciate you for sharing their pain, their hopes and their triumphs and for smiling along with me when they earn their happily-ever-afters. I am grateful to those of you who ask bookstores to stock my books, place them on your online preorder lists and leave reviews when you've finished enjoying them. This one's for you!

Chapter 1

Deirdre Colton shielded her eyes as the dust her rental car and the wind had kicked up on the ranch's ridiculously long driveway smacked her in the face. She elbowed the door shut, kicked the dirt with her new cowboy boots and brushed off her mouth with the back of her hand. Great. She'd already seen more of the desolate Wyoming countryside than she'd hoped to in two lifetimes during the drive from the airport in Casper. Now that she'd reached her destination, just outside Laramie, she could taste that parched earth, too.

Shivering, she zipped her jacket up to her throat, convinced that the weather app had skipped a few details when it predicted a high of nearly seventy degrees. That wicked wind made it downright chilly for May.

"Deirdre, you're not in DC anymore."

She adjusted both her sunglasses and her attitude.

Even if everything she'd seen so far in the Cowboy State made her long for the constant activity around Capitol Hill, for morning jogs through the National Mall and for the black-mud coffee in the DC FBI field office—well, not that—she had a job to do. This time it involved more than just an investigation, even if this lead could help her assist a team of Colton cousins in solving a missing-persons case *and* allow her to capture an alleged serial killer. It was critical that she be the one to make this arrest. Her future with the bureau might depend on it.

The property that spread before her looked nothing like the location she'd pictured for this career-defining moment. But then, she'd had no reason to expect something like Harmony Fields Ranch, a place that appeared from nothing around it like those occasional crusty peaks that jutted from the miles of flat land along the interstate. The massive log-and-stone house itself could have been the centerfold in one of those snazzy home and garden magazines. It held court above the property with two sparkling walls of windows peering out over the ranch buildings and a raised deck that hugged the whole second floor.

At the trunk, she unlocked her .40-caliber Glock 22, stowed it in her FBI cant holster and positioned her jacket to cover it. Then she carefully scanned as much of her perimeter as she could see without binoculars or a rifle scope. Whether the place appeared deserted or not, she planned to follow at least some of her protocols.

A collection of newer wood outbuildings stood in the distance with letters *HF* woven into the patterns of their green shingles. Beyond those, fenced fields stretched in all directions, cattle grazing over them looking like black specks on the straw-colored ground. The sign out front even said there was a petting zoo here, too, but someone had to be exaggerating there.

The whole display proclaimed that Maeve O'Leary's long-lost stepson had found success out West.

Just as Deirdre's gaze shifted to the open doors of the largest barn, a cowboy stepped away from the building, a stereotype in hat and boots. Her muscles immediately tightened, senses on alert, as she tucked her phone in her pocket and tugged her jacket to cover her weapon. The man observed her for several annoyingly long seconds and then sauntered her way. No, *swaggered* was more like it, given the slight bow in his legs and his unhurried approach. As though he had nowhere else to be. Only his scuffed boots, well-worn jeans and the flannel shirt—rolled sleeves straining above his elbows—countered any assumption that the guy lazed around all day. And with that wary look beneath the brim of his hat and the handgun holstered at his hip, he appeared anything but relaxed.

Deirdre pressed her left elbow against the holster at her hip, her senses on alert. Though she'd planned for only a witness interview today, like always, she needed to be prepared for situations to change faster than the speed of pistol fire. Especially here in the Wild West, where she worried that her quick-draw skills were a bit rusty.

The cowboy stopped a few feet in front of her, standing taller, his shoulders broader than the impression he'd given from across the lot. With that closely trimmed beard and mustache, he could have ridden out of one of those fifty-year-old Westerns she'd become an expert on during her bouts of insomnia, which were too frequent lately. Good thing she didn't go for the young-Clint-Eastwood shtick, she decided, as the man squinted back at her, his eyes gray rather than Clint's blue. That flutter in her belly had to be indigestion from airplane snacks, though she couldn't explain the Ennio Morricone spaghetti Western score playing in her head.

"Good afternoon, ma'am."

The music cut, and her stomach settled into a hard lump. Yes, she was supposed to be in her work zone, but who had the guy just called *ma'am*? At thirty-three, she didn't look a day over thirty, in her opinion. Could manage twenty-seven if she bothered with powders and creams. Which she didn't. The cowboy blew right past her affront, anyway, yanking off the hat and giving that sweaty crop of chestnut-brown hair a brisk rub before repositioning it.

"May I help you with something?" As his gaze dropped from her face to her feet, skipping the whole part in the middle, a smile spread on his lips. "Directions to a Western outfitter in Laramie, perhaps?"

Deirdre frowned. Why she'd thought buying those boots would make her look like she fit in on a ranch, she couldn't say, even if they were the cutest pair, with traditional round toe, cowboy heels and fancy stitching. The jeans and waffle Henley top didn't seem like good ideas now, either. She *didn't* belong on this ranch or in this part of the country, though she could say the same about most places in her life. But after hours in planes, shuttles and automobiles just to reach this destination, she wasn't in the mood for the man's pithy comments, either.

"This is the Harmony Fields Ranch, isn't it?"

The cowboy's smile disappeared, his eyes narrowing. He shot a glance at the house before looking back to her again.

"That's what it says on that enormous arch you passed," he said, his words clipped.

"Good. Then I'm at the right place. I'm looking for Micah Perry."

His chin lifted slightly. "You've found him. I'm at a disadvantage here, though. You know who I am, but I don't know…"

He gestured to her and then lowered his hand to his side, keeping it relaxed but within easy reach of his firearm. She couldn't help wondering if everyone in that part of the country greeted visitors with such suspicion.

"I'm FBI Special Agent Deirdre Colton."

She slowly withdrew her badge from her jacket pocket and held it out to him. He stared at it a few beats and then nodded.

Though he tucked his thumbs through his belt loops in a casual pose, his gaze flicked to the house a second time, and he shifted already-dusty boots in the dirt. "How can I help you, Officer? I mean, *Special Agent.*"

His unease shouldn't have struck Deirdre as odd. Guys she met in social situations seldom said things like "that's cool, so pass the pretzels" when she told them where she worked. Their reactions usually fell more under the category of How to Scare Off a Guy in Sixty Seconds. Her ex, Brandon, would have made his exit in less than thirty, which had only made applying to the bureau more appealing to her after their Big D.

Something about Micah's response struck her as different than any man she'd met, though. As though he'd been expecting her to show up at Harmony Fields. Had someone at the field office gotten wind of her plan and tipped him off? Had she miscalculated the risk in conducting her cross-country, not-quite-sanctioned investigation?

"Is there someplace we can talk? I'd like to ask you a few questions about—"

"Can't you just take your report out here?"

He sneaked a third peek at his home, and this time the tiny hairs at Deirdre's nape stood on end. Who or what was inside that house? She steadied her breathing while calculating her next move, her eyes trained on his hands in case he went for his weapon. Sure, she'd made the rookie mistake of going in without backup, but he was supposed to be a witness. A *victim*, even. Not a suspect. Her failure to consider that he might be harboring a fugitive could turn out to be only one of her mistakes today, but it would be the biggest. And the deadliest.

"I think it would be better if we spoke inside."

Deirdre braced herself for him to demand a search warrant, though that would be the *least* problematic action he could take. She reached for her phone to make the pointless call to 911, since the authorities would never reach her in time to assist, but Micah's confused look made her hesitate. As she started to demand to know who was inside the building, a strange sound, like a cry, startled her. She clicked her teeth shut. The odd noise seemed to have come from Micah's belt. He unclipped a little receiver and stared into the even tinier screen.

"Is that a *baby monitor*?" She pointed to the device, but since he didn't look up, she lowered her arm.

Without answering, he stomped toward the house, still watching the screen. She had to jog to keep up with him, her left foot smarting from the blister already rubbing at her heel.

"What's he doing up?" Micah grumbled to himself as he walked. "He should have napped another hour."

"There's a *baby* in there?" Why had she even asked? She pretended not to notice the incredulous look that Micah gave her. The sound of crying. A baby monitor. *Napped.* Of course there was a baby, the existence of whom hadn't popped up in any of her research. With investigative skills like hers, no wonder she was on thin ice with the bureau.

He stomped on until he passed one of the six-by-six deck pillars and opened a slider on the ground floor. "Why'd you think I wanted to talk outside?"

Micah had just gestured for her to precede him inside, but now he stepped in front of her to block her entrance.

"How is it that you don't know about my son? No one told you about him?"

It was Deirdre's turn to squint. "Your son? And who would have told me? I think there's been a misunderstanding."

"You've got that right. A big one. Why would anyone send a federal agent out here? Especially one from the East Coast."

"How did you know—" she began, but she didn't bother finishing. Whether or not his words made sense to her, she couldn't have been a bigger fish out of water on this land, more than a thousand miles from both the Pacific and the Atlantic. Even the cowboy realized that.

"You never said what you were here to ask me about."

"Your stepmother," she blurted and then pressed her

lips together. What was wrong with her? She could go toe to toe with any of her fellow special agents—male or female—so what was it about this cowboy that unnerved her? Could the fact that she needed his help so badly be crippling her effort to secure it?

The rancher stared back at her as though he'd seen a ghost, his jaw slack. He closed his mouth just as another cry poured from the monitor still in his hand. He held up an index finger. "If you'll excuse me."

Without waiting for a response, he stepped through the open doorway and closed the slider. It wasn't a bad place to be dismissed, with her choice of chaise lounges and patio dining and conversation arrangements, but she had no way of knowing if he would even return. That was one way of avoiding an FBI interview, she supposed, and a new one to her. On the other hand, she'd done a lousy job of starting this conversation, and now she would have to come up with another plan to get him to speak with her.

Just as she'd started back to her car to regroup, the sound of the door slide brought her back around. Micah stepped outside, and a toddler with sweaty dark hair and a red, tearstained face peered out at her from his dad's arms.

"This is Derek." Then he gestured to her. "And this is Special Agent Colton."

Deirdre pasted on a smile. "Hi, Derek."

The toddler buried his face in his dad's chest, another reaction that didn't particularly surprise her. She'd never had the touch with kids. They probably realized she was more frightened of them than they were of her, so they wisely kept their distance. After a few seconds, though, this particular little boy turned his head and peeked back at her. Automatically, Deirdre covered her face with her hands and opened them like a pair of doors. What made her do that, she couldn't say, but it worked for others who had success with children, so she gave it a shot. The child's eyes widened, and a smile disturbingly similar to his father's spread on his lips.

"I have nothing to say about *Ariel Porter*."

Deirdre startled at Micah's words, and she shifted her attention back to him, missing neither the alias he'd mentioned nor that he'd ground out the words when he spoke it.

"Now, Mr. Perry, I've flown all the way from Washington, DC, to speak with you, so please give me a chance to tell you about my investigation."

"I'm sorry for your wasted trip. As I said, I don't want to talk about *her*. I haven't seen or spoken to old Ariel in the more than fifteen years since Dad died. I can't help you, so I don't want to waste your time. Or mine."

"Just try to answer a few questions. I'm sure you'll be of more help than you think."

He shook his head. "Thanks for stopping by."

Deirdre's thoughts raced. Her only witness—and possibly her only chance to save a career that dangled by a thread—would be gone in seconds. Her heart thudded as she scrambled for something to say that would, if not stop him, at least slow him down before he returned inside and locked the door.

"Don't you mean Maeve O'Leary?" Deirdre hated the desperation that had sneaked into her voice and hoped he couldn't hear it, too.

"Who?" Micah had just opened the door again and

stepped across the threshold, but he jerked his head to look back at her.

Her lips pinched. "Maeve—"

"I heard you. I just don't know who you're talking about. Look, it sounds like you've received some faulty information, but now I *know* I can't help you." He shook his head when she started to interrupt. "We're not even talking about the same person."

"Unfortunately...we are."

The cowboy turned to fully face her and waited for an explanation. If his arms weren't already filled with a wiggling toddler, she figured he would have crossed them, too.

She began carefully, well aware that her words ripped new holes in his already tattered memories and that a victim would be forced to relive a tragedy made worse with new revelations. "Ariel Porter Perry is an alias of a woman whose real name is Maeve O'Leary. One of several aliases, our investigation is beginning to show."

"Is your investigation also revealing that she *murdered* my father?" Micah lifted his chin as though daring her to contradict his claim.

"Yes, we believe that O'Leary was responsible for the death of Leonard 'Len' Perry."

He slowly lowered his chin. "Took you long enough to figure it out."

Deirdre accepted his criticism with a nod, though she didn't deserve to be its target. She needed answers from him, and she would do whatever it took to get them. "Yes, we have found some problematic areas in the original investigation."

"That's what you call not following up after she drained my father's accounts, sold the house and vanished? Wonder how anyone could have overlooked something so insignificant."

At that, she shrugged, though she couldn't help drawing her shoulders closer to her ears. Sure, someone had made mistakes, but she couldn't help the temptation to come to the defense of fellow peace officers. The blue wall of silence was a thing for a reason.

"We also believe there is at least one more victim. Another *husband*. Possibly more."

Micah opened and closed his mouth twice, his shock obvious in his rapid blinking. She should have delivered those bombshell details in smaller, more digestible bites, but he wasn't exactly being a cooperative witness, and desperation made her spill the whole story.

"A *black widow killer*? You're saying that Ariel—I mean this Maeve…"

"Yes." She nodded for emphasis. "Now would you be willing to answer a few questions?"

The cowboy took two steps backward, as if he wanted to put distance between himself and the woman who'd just set fire to his past.

"I already said I don't know—"

"Are you unable to help? Or just *unwilling*?" Her accusation hung heavily between them as she stared up at him in disbelief. After everything she'd just told him, how could he still be reluctant to help her?

"Want juice," Derek announced, breaking the silence.

The toddler reached up and splayed his pudgy hand over his father's whiskers.

Micah covered the child's fingers with his own and slowly slid the hand from his face. "Just a minute, buddy. Let me—"

"Juice!" The word came out as a plaintive whine this time, and the child wiggled, trying to get his father to put him down.

"Looks like someone needs some juice," Deirdre said. The distraction probably wouldn't be enough to convince her potential witness to change his mind, but it gave her a moment to scramble for another plan. Only she was running out of ideas. And hope.

When Micah lowered his son to the ground, the child shot off for the stairs and then scrambled up the steps in a hands-and-feet approach.

The cowboy yanked off his hat and then waved with it at the staircase.

"Guess you'd better come inside."

Chapter 2

His breath coming in short gasps that had little to do with the stair climb, Micah caught up with his son in the kitchen. Already, Derek was busy adding fresh handprints to the collection always present on the bottom third of their stainless steel refrigerator. Though the child could reach the handles on the side-by-side doors, at least he hadn't mastered opening them yet.

"Juice. Puleeze." The child drummed his hands on the refrigerator door as if his dad needed help locating his favorite drink.

"Just a minute, kiddo."

Micah needed a moment himself to digest the information their guest had just dropped on him. He'd barely had time to register the news so far, and his whole body shook from the resounding clash of suspicion and truth. His heart pounded in a plot for escape from his chest, and his hands were so sweaty they would have slipped off the handle if he tried to open the refrigerator door.

His father really *had* been murdered? He was right all along? Though Micah had known it in his heart, the agent's announcement had sharpened the truth to a wicked point, and her revelation that Ariel—*Maeve*—might be a black widow killer as well pierced the layers of nearly healed scars.

Dropping his hat on the quartz countertop of the island, he bent at the waist and gulped mouthfuls of air. He had to get control, for Derek at least. Straightening, he closed his eyes and opened them again, hoping to clear the fuzzy edges of his new reality. It didn't work.

If only learning that law enforcement officers were finally pursuing the woman who'd destroyed his family could give him some relief. He wouldn't get off that easily. The regret he carried for fleeing west instead of fighting harder after the county coroner had listed his father's death as from natural causes pressed down on him now, heavy and damning. The police might have failed at their jobs, but he was Len Perry's only son. He'd let his father down and allowed his stepmother to get away with murder.

He shook his head, trying to force the thoughts from his mind. Nothing he said or did could make up for his choices then, anyway. And right now, he couldn't afford to look at past mistakes when he needed to focus on the current threat to his ranch, and, more importantly, to his own son. Dread formed a knot and settled heavily in his gut. Would he fail to protect Derek as he once had his father? He ground his teeth, jutting out his chin. He would never let that happen. Whoever was sabotaging Harmony Fields would have to get through him first.

"Daddy!"

Micah blinked, pulled from his dark thoughts to glance down at Derek. The child clung to his jeans just above the knees now, a tantrum already building toward an impressive crescendo. His own self-flagellation would have to wait. His son's needs came first. Always. He chose not to consider whether his father had ever believed the same about him.

"Almost there, buddy."

He scooped up Derek and deposited him in the highchair. The toddler started pounding on the tray before Micah could lock it in place. Soon, he had the child settled with a firefighter sippy cup filled with juice, and he'd scattered a handful of O-shaped cereal over the tray. Only then did he glance over to find their uninvited guest standing in the kitchen doorway. He'd let her inside downstairs before he'd edged off his boots, but he couldn't wait for her while she'd struggled to remove hers. Not with a frustrated two-year-old running loose in the house.

Now the special agent leaned against the wood in her stocking feet, one set of toes rubbing against the opposite heel.

"Guess you found the kitchen."

"My advanced FBI investigation skills at work there," she said dryly.

Her hazel eyes appeared to take in every detail of the room, from the black farmhouse sink to the fancy pecan built-in pantry and range hood cover that Leah had insisted on during their home construction. Strange how those upgrades seemed even more frivolous as he viewed them through the stranger's eyes.

"And I guess *you* averted a crisis." Deirdre pointed to Derek, who was mowing down his snack as quickly as his chubby hands could grasp the O's. When she waved at the child, he lifted his grimy hand and opened and closed it to wave back.

The fist that had gripped Micah's chest since they'd come inside loosened by degrees. At least the agent hadn't immediately leaped into her list of interview questions, which she probably assumed he'd agreed to by letting her in the house. He couldn't help with her investigation. He'd run as far as he could from New York City after his dad's death and buried those memories so deep it seemed as if they'd happened to someone else. With just a few words, the FBI agent had reopened the Earth, forcing him to see and feel it all again.

To delay the conversation, Micah sprinkled a few more pieces of cereal on his son's tray. "A snack can make a lot of things better."

"I have to agree with Derek on that." She watched him for a few seconds longer and then shook her head. "I don't know how you parents do it."

"What? Hand out snacks? We do it fast."

Until that moment, the agent had reserved her smiles for his son, but she turned one on Micah, her full, rose-colored lips curving and her heavily lashed eyes crinkling at the corners. For a flash of a moment, he forgot why they were even together in his kitchen. Warmth spread beneath his rib cage, his mouth so dry that he was tempted to steal Derek's juice. He turned his head to short-circuit the strange connection. What was that all about?

Appearing to have missed the jolt of electricity altogether, the agent stepped around the L-shaped bar that formed two sides of the kitchen's perimeter and then past the wrought iron bar stools that lined it and into the great room. As she smoothed her hand over the buttery leather sofa he'd chosen himself and her gaze moved from the floor-to-ceiling windows to the stone fireplace that stretched nearly as high, Micah couldn't help watching *her*.

Weren't female FBI agents supposed to be buttoned-up middle-aged women with no makeup and their hair in tight buns? Didn't they blend in with dark jackets, sensible shoes and an everywoman diligence? If those things were true, then Special Agent Colton had clearly missed the memo.

To be fair, she'd tied her dark blonde hair in a knot of some sort. She didn't appear to be wearing cosmetics, either. But nothing could have prevented her oval face, heavily lashed eyes and flawless light pink complexion from making her stand out in a crowd. Her fitted shirt and those curve-hugging jeans probably didn't fit the agency dress code, either. And, for that matter, no one would have referred to those sexy boots that she'd left on the mat downstairs as *sensible*.

Deirdre stood at the base of the staircase, her gaze moving from first the baby gate at the bottom and then the wooden handrail and metal balusters that led to the balcony above. Unfortunately, her position offered him an unobstructed view of her perfect, round behind. To his mortification, she swung around and caught him appreciating said benefit.

He didn't miss her crossed arms and pursed lips as he averted his gaze, suddenly needing to check on his son. As if she would ever buy that. What was wrong with him, anyway? That his senses were out of whack after the news the agent had dumped on him was no excuse for gawking at her. He didn't gawk. He didn't even *date* these days, since the women he'd met couldn't accept that he and Derek were a package deal, and his son deserved a stepmother who actually wanted him. Anyway, if he were interested in female companionship, an FBI agent tracking his father's murderer would never be his first choice. Or even his twentieth.

"You have a beautiful home," she said after a long pause.

"Thanks. We like it." He turned her way but stared at his hands folded in front of him. That the agent had still offered her inane compliment instead of telling him where to stuff his wandering eyes demonstrated just how desperate she was for information about his stepmother. Details he probably couldn't give her, even if he wanted to.

"Do you live here with your son and your…partner?"

"Just my son," he answered automatically over her politically correct inquiry. "My, uh, *wife*—that's Derek's mother—passed away two years ago."

His throat thickened with emotion as it did whenever he shared his sad story. Deirdre shot him a questioning look, but her focus moved on to his son in the chair. She drew her brows together as though weighing the child's age against the information he'd supplied.

"Car accident. Derek was only six weeks old when it happened." He would tell his son the gentlest version of that story when he was older.

"I'm so sorry." Deirdre grimaced, her investigator's

impassive expression falling away briefly before she put it back in place.

"Thanks." He nodded his appreciation as he'd done with dozens of friends and even more strangers in the past two years. No one knew what to say, and he knew even less how to respond.

"Do you have a babysitter or a nanny to help with him while you work on the ranch?" She gestured to the windows and the fields beyond them.

"I have off and on, but they keep leaving for better opportunities in town. I do have a cook, who comes in once a week, and a cleaning service once a month. And the neighbors help out when they can."

"Still, it must be hard."

The muscles at the back of his neck tightened, her pity harder to take than her earlier disdain. "It's not perfect, but we do the best we can."

He lifted his chin and glared at her the same way he had others who'd dared to question whether he could care for his own child. "He's my son."

She nodded and cleared her throat. "Apparently, my intel about you wasn't nearly as good as I thought it was, either, since I didn't know he even existed."

"Don't you hate it when that happens?" He'd meant it both as a joke to lighten the tense moment and a quick step away from memories where grief and betrayal were bound together with an unforgiving rope. Some of those details from the time of his wife's death no one needed to know.

"I'm not wrong about Maeve O'Leary. And I'm not wrong about your father. Or *you*."

"Me? What does this have to do with me?"

"You might be Maeve's only surviving victim."

"I'm not a—" He shook his head, the term ill-fitting, yet the truth of it squeezed in his chest. He'd been just a kid, an adult only by a few days along with eighteen candles on a birthday cake.

Suddenly, the timing of the agent's arrival and that of all the acts of sabotage to the ranch seemed less coincidental as well. Could they be connected? Could the suspect behind all those crimes on Harmony Fields be none other than his step*monster* herself? The idea was absurd. If Ariel, aka Maeve, was a black widow killer, he wasn't another husband she could strangle in her web. But the possibility of connection still niggled at the back of his mind. Could this smart, lethal adversary have found out about his success out West and followed her insatiable need for money right to him and his son? And if she had, could he stop her before she killed again?

"I really could use your help," Deirdre said, breaking the long silence.

He shook his head. "Look, I appreciate your confirming what I already believed about my dad. And I'd like to see my stepmother pay for her crimes as much as anyone, but I've already told you I don't know anything—"

"About Maeve O'Leary," she finished for him and then sighed.

"I'm sorry. Really. I wish I could help. I'm also tied up with problems of my own around here." He tried to ignore the truth that he was failing his father again, but with Derek's safety at stake, he had no choice. "In fact, when you pulled up, I thought you would be—"

He stopped as the sound of crunching gravel filtered in from outside. The agent must have heard it, too, as she immediately crossed to the wall next to the windows and peered outside. "Were you expecting someone?"

"If I'm guessing right, that's Sheriff Richard Guetta." He stepped behind her and glanced down at one of the familiar white SUVs from the Albany County Sheriff's Office with black and yellow lettering on the side.

She jerked her head to look back at him. "You called the *sheriff*?"

"That's what I was trying to tell you. I was waiting for him to come by and take a report. *Another* report on whoever's been sabotaging my ranch." He shook his head, smiling over his confusion at her arrival. "Sheriff Guetta had agreed to come out himself this time since so many things kept happening, but I thought it was overkill for him to send the FBI."

Her expression tight, she kept watching the vehicle on the driveway below. After the sheriff's recognizable mop of prematurely white hair appeared over the top of the SUV, Deirdre turned back to Micah.

"I get what you meant now." She sighed and then pushed her shoulders back. "This isn't going to go well."

"Why is that?"

She'd slid another look at the window, but now she met his gaze directly. "Because I'm not exactly supposed to be here."

"What do you mean 'not exactly'?"

"Not at all."

Chapter 3

Deirdre shifted in her seat as Sheriff Guetta turned the kitchen bar stool sideways so that he faced her instead of the countertop, his black uniform slightly rumpled but the seven-pointed star above his heart shiny. Her face felt hot. Her chest tight. She'd had no choice but to give a quick overview of her story, and she now sat stuck like a convict, waiting for the guillotine blade to drop. Okay, maybe not that extreme, but the sheriff now had the power to end her career, and she was sweating while awaiting sentencing.

The law enforcement officer didn't seem to be in any hurry to continue his questioning, watching her instead with unnerving pale blue eyes. He took a sip from the iced tea glass that Micah had rested in front of him. No way would she be able to swallow if she took a drink from hers. She recognized his tactic. She'd used it herself dozens of times to keep her interview subjects off balance. It was equally effective on her, she decided, pressing her shoulder blades against the metal back of the bar stool.

Guetta leaned forward and rested his elbows on his knees, his fiftysomething spread spilling slightly over his fully outfitted duty belt. Finally, he spoke.

"Now let me get this straight." He paused again to flick his lollipop stick from one side of his mouth to the other, hinting at an attempt to beat a tobacco habit. "You have exactly *zero* approval for this cross-country journey you made to get a witness statement. In fact, you're not assigned to this case, or *any* case, because your boss benched you for coloring outside the lines."

Deirdre shot a look to Micah, who stood next to the highchair, wiping his whining toddler's hands and face and pretending not to listen to every word she and the sheriff said. His rapid blinking gave him away. She didn't owe the rancher any answers, even if he probably had as many questions as the sheriff did. Micah could have given her the heads-up that law enforcement was on the way, after all. And, though she'd at least tried to tell him about her investigation, he still hadn't agreed to help her.

She purposely turned her stool away from him to focus on the sheriff. "My issue with the bureau wasn't as bad as you're making it sound. My superiors and I just had a disagreement about my approach in pursuing a suspect. Someone wanted for heinous crimes, I might add. And one we were able to detain without any further loss of life."

"Well, that's something," the sheriff said.

At least someone understood that, since no one in

the DC field office had appreciated her efforts. *You're welcome.* If she'd come out and said those words that had been burning on her tongue at the time, she probably wouldn't have a job to save right now.

"Sounds like a suspension to me," Micah pointed out.

"I wasn't *suspended*."

Deirdre shot an annoyed look at Micah, surprised to find him standing on the other side of the bar now, holding Derek, instead of across the room near the refrigerator. As the toddler wiggled in his arms, again trying to get his father to put him down, Micah trapped her with a condescending look. Who was he to judge her? Had he never made a mistake before? Had he never had a wonderful idea that turned out to be not so great? Even if she'd gone a little off book by taking a side trip to Wyoming, at least she'd been tracking his father's killer, which was more than officers from any other agency had done on this cold case in a long time.

"What do you call it, then?" Guetta asked.

Her cheeks burned, but if she had any hope of weathering this situation, she had to come as clean as possible.

"My superiors referred to it as 'forced leave' while I remain under investigation. And, technically, this trip is a *vacation*."

"Sounds like splitting hairs to me," the sheriff said with a chuckle.

"But you know how important that distinction is." At least she hoped he did.

The sheriff gestured to Micah as if to include him in the conversation. "A *suspension* would have required her to forfeit her badge and weapon. And she still seems to have those."

Deirdre pressed her elbows to her sides to feel the reassuring presence of her holster, but it offered no comfort now. With one call to Washington from the sheriff, her badge could disappear. She stared at her hands as all that work she'd put into her job for the past three years—and the two years of testing and training before that—floated away like smoke through an open window.

Micah pointed to the holster nearly concealed at her hip. "You carried that thing on the plane?" He waited for her nod. "How did you even do that when you're supposed to be on 'vacation'?"

"By jumping through a lot of hoops, I would guess," Guetta chimed.

Deirdre gestured to the sheriff. "What he said. But also, FBI special agents are technically always on duty, even when traveling for personal business and even when the bureau isn't paying for the flight. If I had checked my weapon and something happened on the flight that I possibly could have prevented, there would be hell to pay."

The sheriff held both hands up, palms out and fingers splayed, an incredulous look on his face. "What's funny is you put yourself in the doghouse for not following orders, and you plan to get *out of trouble* by conducting an off-books investigation and single-handedly bringing down a serial killer."

When he put it that way, it did sound ridiculous. The sick feeling in her gut confirmed that suspicion. But since she'd already flown across the country and driven over even more of it while searching for information, she had to at least try to defend her plan. Her only hope was the lawman's pity, and she would be naive to depend on it.

"Anyway, I'm also helping my cousin Sean Colton, of the NYPD Ninety-Eighth Precinct, and his team with *their* investigation."

"Your cousin?" the sheriff asked.

Though she understood that he was trying to rattle her, she couldn't seem to avoid the blur. "Second cousin. His late dad, Kieran Colton, and my father, Eoin, were *first* cousins."

She waited, her throat tight, wishing she'd avoided specifically identifying the two men. Maybe this far from Virginia no one would recognize her high-profile politician father's name, but she couldn't guarantee it, since he loved publicity almost as much as the womanizing that kept him in the news. Good thing she caught no recognition in either man's gaze. Today was already bad enough without bringing dear old Dad into it.

Micah gestured with a circular motion for her to get on with her story, and then he started it for her. "You said this team you're helping is trying to find a missing person, who happens to be their family friend."

She narrowed her gaze at him. What had changed? Had the rancher decided to support her now, instead of just judging her? She couldn't decide whether to be grateful or suspicious, but since distrust better fit her DNA, she went with that. She adhered to the Benjamin Franklin quote that "God helps those who help themselves," and in her experience, people never lifted a finger for anyone else without something in it for them.

"Yes. The prominent psychiatrist Humphrey Kelly," she said, clarifying his comment, anyway. "If he hadn't stepped up after Kieran Colton's death, the four siblings wouldn't have been able to stay together."

The sheriff planted his elbows on the counter, folded his hands and turned his head to look right through her.

"So, when you found a link between that case and a potential serial killer that you could make a splash by arresting, you agreed to help your cousins out, even if that meant going rogue."

She held her hands wide and blew out a breath. "You're right. I didn't think it through. But since I'm here—"

"Since you're here," he repeated, "we'll have to deal with the FBI agent who just can't follow the rules. That'll mean having a little chat with your superiors back in DC."

Her gut clenched as her last bit of hope flitted away. Her career, the only thing she'd ever done without her father's express direction and approval, was over. *He's my son.* As Micah's words from earlier replayed in her thoughts, she wondered if her own dad had ever felt that kind of vehement bond with her. He certainly wouldn't now.

"That's enough, Richard."

Micah's stern voice shocked her as much as his stance. With his arms folded over his chest, he stood staring down the lawman as though he had no sense at all. He couldn't talk to a police officer like that. He'd even called him by his first name. She braced herself, looking back and forth between them, waiting for one to throw a punch. Or, worse, draw a weapon. She didn't know what to make of Micah clearly taking her side this time—or her temptation to appreciate it just a little. The last thing she needed was a cowboy with a hero complex coming to her aid and getting one of them shot.

Guetta threw his head back then and laughed in a full-belly way that would have been great to share if she weren't the butt of his joke. When Micah's lips lifted as well, a sign that the men were friends, she ground her teeth hard enough to unsettle years of orthodontia.

"What is this? I don't have time for your jokes." That she couldn't turn her rental around now and drive back to Casper, ignoring posted speed limits, frustrated her even more.

The sheriff chuckled for a few seconds longer and then wiped the corners of his eyes.

"Look," he said, when he finally stopped laughing, "I manage a department with forty-five officers covering nearly five thousand square miles of land. To say we're stretched pretty thin is an understatement. You think I have time to waste tattling on a rogue agent whose work is outside my jurisdiction?"

"You mean you're not going to contact the special agent in charge?"

"Why would I do that when I have an allegedly competent investigator, who's on vacation and has decided to be a *volunteer* to help us out on a case?"

"I haven't volunteered for— Wait." She stopped as some of the puzzle pieces fell into place. "I'm already here on an investigation. Two, really. You don't expect me to assist on one of yours, too, do you?"

She looked from the grinning sheriff to the rancher, who watched the other man with a guarded look.

"You're not serious," she said, though he clearly was. "You're attempting to blackmail a federal agent into doing free investigating for your department?"

"Will you be reporting *me*, then?"

Deirdre opened her mouth and closed it. She couldn't go to the agency about him without falling on her weapon and figuratively pulling the trigger. And if she didn't agree to work as an unpaid investigator for the sheriff's office, he could still report her. She swallowed, feeling the squeeze all the way down her throat as the jaws of a trap snapped around her.

"Besides, I'm not that big a fan of the feds," Guetta admitted. "Whenever we get a big case, someone from the Denver office charges in like the Lone Ranger to take over."

Her lucky day—now she was stuck in the middle of a turf war with someone who'd probably watched as many Westerns as she did. She'd dealt with officials from local agencies who bristled when she'd arrived to take charge of investigations deemed federal but never from a disadvantage like this.

"I don't think this is a good idea," Micah said.

Well, she agreed with him on that one thing. The sheriff turned to the rancher.

"Think about it for a minute, Micah. You've phoned in how many reports now? Half a dozen? A baker's dozen? I even agreed to drive out myself today because we still haven't figured out who's targeting your ranch. A fresh pair of eyes on the case couldn't hurt. I know how much you want to protect your son."

Micah immediately ducked around the end of the bar to check on Derek, who sat on the floor next to a toy box, pulling out a fire truck, then a xylophone, then a teddy bear and then a whole box of plastic building blocks and dumping them all on the floor.

"But she's an outsider," he said when he looked back

to them again. "She doesn't know Laramie from Colorado Springs. She doesn't know how things work around here."

Guetta pinched his chin, causing the few days' growth of white whiskers to flutter. "Could be a good thing. As I said, fresh eyes. And if Quantico did its job, she also should be handy with that firearm she's packing."

"I'm standing right here, you know," Deirdre said, crossing her arms.

The toddler raced back into the kitchen, awkwardly balancing a hard plastic pickup truck and a police car of the same material in his arms. He dropped them next to Deirdre's stool and kicked off his own demolition derby, complete with zooming engines and crash sounds.

Deirdre looked up from the child first, but when Micah lifted his chin and met her gaze, his worry palpable, something unfamiliar, tender even, spread in her chest.

"Maybe Richard has a good idea," he said.

She cleared her throat, pushing away emotions that had no place in her job. Or life. "You kidding? It's a terrible idea."

"Worse than your showing up on my property today without approval from DC?"

She answered with a shrug. Why did they have to keep bringing that up?

He rested his elbows on the counter and folded his hands as the sheriff had done before. "How about we make a deal?"

"Deal?" She wasn't exactly in a strong negotiating position.

"If you assist with the sheriff's investigation and help us find out who's targeting us, I'll tell you everything I know about my late father's wife."

She should have been happy. Though he'd agreed to give her the interview she'd flown across the country for, it had become an empty victory. "You've already said you don't know anything about her."

"I'll try to think of something." He gave her a close-lipped smile. "It's the best I can do."

She didn't answer, but he didn't need her to. They both knew it was an offer she couldn't refuse.

The sheriff stood up from his bar stool. "Remind me not to negotiate with you, Micah. You drive a hard bargain."

Again, Deirdre gritted her teeth. If the two of them fist-bumped, she would scream. She swallowed and then dived in. "I don't know anything about your case."

"That's because we just spent all of this time talking about yours," the sheriff pointed out. "It seems to be a campaign to frighten the Perry family off the land. At least so far."

He gestured from Micah to Derek in a signal that he believed the situation would escalate.

"Let me see. Someone cut the fences and released the horses from the pasture. Twice. They opened the doors to the petting zoo in the middle of the night, setting all the animals free." He gestured to Micah. "What am I forgetting?"

Micah started ticking off items on his fingers. "He ransacked our house while Derek and I were at the feed store. Several thousand dollars' worth of damage there. Then there was a suspicious fire in one of the storage sheds."

"We've been hoping to catch the trespassers in the act, but that hasn't worked out yet," the sheriff added.

Except for the arson and the breaking and entering at the house because of the amount of damage, most of the crimes could have been misdemeanor level so far. She would have said so, too, but she doubted it would go over well.

"Are you sure it's not kids messing around? You also said 'he.' Are you certain the suspect is male?"

"I'm not certain, but the buffet that someone turned over in the great room weighed a ton." Micah pointed to an empty space along the wall where the piece of furniture had probably been located before. "Still waiting for a new one to be shipped from the manufacturer."

He shifted his hand to point at the driveway. "The rabbit hutch in the petting zoo wasn't light, either. Whoever it was destroyed that, too."

She winced at the image of the scared bunnies scattering and hated to ask the next question. "But still no loss of life, right?"

"Not directly. But if you count that he locked all the dogs in my office and then set two of the rabbits free without protection against the foxes that prey on the defenseless around here..." He paused to shrug. "Well, it wasn't pretty."

Deirdre shivered involuntarily. What was the matter with her? She'd been on the scene of some fairly gruesome homicides, but just the thought of someone hurting those poor bunnies infuriated her. She hoped Micah would miss that, but the look he gave her suggested that he didn't miss much.

"And if you find that disturbing, just consider that

whoever is doing these things has been inside the house where my son sleeps."

Her gaze lowered to the child on the floor, oblivious to the possible danger around him as he played. She couldn't help it; she shivered again. Just the thought that someone who had a problem with Micah might target his child sent ice through her veins. The child looked up at her then and hit her with one of his cherubic grins.

"Dee-Dee!" he announced, pointing right at her.

"It's Special Agent—" Micah started to correct, but she waved him off.

"Dee-Dee is fine." A little too pleasant, she hated to admit.

She leaned far over, and of its own accord, her hand reached down to ruffle his baby-soft hair. An unfamiliar warmth started somewhere in her chest and spread down her arm to her hand and fingers. So this was what her coworkers meant when they talked about how easily children climbed inside their hearts. Of course, she couldn't let anything happen to that sweet little boy, but she needed to guard herself around him, too. If she lost her professional distance and became too attached, she would be of no help to either him or his father.

"It does sound like someone is trying to scare you away," she said, hoping Micah missed the lingering thickness of emotion in her voice. "Do you have any enemies? Anyone who would have a reason to take this land away from you?"

"Not anyone I can think of."

He glanced across the room to the staircase instead of looking at her. She was tempted to tell him that this would go a lot faster if he didn't lie, but she would mention that later.

"I'll need you to come up with a list, anyway. If you already gave one to the sheriff's office, you'll need to dig deeper. Look at anyone who might have a beef with you—the guy at the feed store who was angry because you took his parking spot. The high school classmate your girlfriend dumped to date you."

He met her gaze and looked away. She immediately regretted bringing that one up, since it sounded like she was looking for his dating history, but spurned lovers were classic suspects for revenge crimes.

"I'll make a list," he said, still not looking at her.

Ready to change that subject and unable to sit still any longer, she headed into the kitchen to retrieve her messenger bag from where she'd left it, next to the closed basement door. When she returned, she set it on a bar stool next to the one she'd been sitting on and pulled a notebook and pen from it.

"What report were you filing today?" she managed as she flipped the notebook open. Maybe if she put herself back in her regular routine for taking witness statements, she could escape some of the strangeness of dealing with this one.

"Someone cut the fence in the pasture, letting fifty head of cattle escape this morning before the first feed. My neighbors and I spent half the morning corralling them again. That's why Derek was late getting down for his nap."

"And he didn't sleep as long as you'd hoped," she said, recalling his words earlier.

He nodded. "He's going to be a pistol by dinnertime."

"Or before," Guetta agreed. "That's my cue to get out of here."

The sheriff crossed through the great room in several long strides.

"Wait," Deirdre called after him as he reached the front door. "Weren't you taking a report?"

"You can take notes and photos when Micah shows you the damage. I'll file the report later from my office." At her confused expression, he added, "We have computers there. Real internet, too. Not even dial-up."

"I never said—"

He lifted a hand to ward off her comments as he opened the door. "I'll catch up with you again tomorrow."

Deirdre's breath caught. "And you're expecting me to *be here* tomorrow?"

The sheriff held his hands wide. "How else are you going to figure out what's going on with this ranch?"

He pointed out the door to her rental car. "Let me guess—you planned to get your witness statement today and take off on a plane tonight."

"The red-eye," she said with a shrug.

"You were optimistic about convincing the witness to cooperate, weren't you?"

"I'm good at my job. Usually."

The sheriff grinned back at her. "Looks like you'll have to reschedule."

"I don't even have a place to stay. And the last hotel I saw was—"

"About thirty-five miles from here," Guetta finished for her. "Good thing Micah here has a ginormous house with plenty of empty guest rooms."

"That's not going to work." Even if she were okay

staying in the home of a cowboy she'd been checking out earlier, she'd already broken enough rules today without agreeing to be a houseguest of a potential witness.

"I have to agree with Special Agent Colton on that one," Micah said.

"Might as well call me Deirdre," she grumbled.

When Micah didn't answer at all, the sheriff chuckled. "You two appear to be capable adults. I'm sure you can handle being together in this house without turning into bags of hormones."

"That won't be a problem." Great. She'd just made it sound like it would be.

Micah shot her an uncomfortable look and then coughed into his elbow. "Of course, that wouldn't be an issue, but wouldn't your place be a better choice? Special Agent Colton—I mean, Deirdre—probably didn't bring any luggage. Maybe your wife and daughters have a few things she can wear?"

"Clearly, you haven't been to my house lately. With three teenagers grumbling around, I wouldn't wish that estrogen bomb on anyone. Even a disobedient FBI agent." Tilting his head to the side, he pointed at Micah. "Anyway, don't you still have a few things from your—"

"Fine. She can stay here," Micah blurted before the sheriff could say *wife*.

"We'll figure something out."

"I'm sure you will."

Guetta let himself out, and Deirdre could have sworn she heard him laughing as he strode along the deck to the stairs and the drive below.

Chapter 4

Micah was sure he'd been to libraries louder than the quad cab of his pickup as he drove with Deirdre to the north pasture to photograph the most recent damage. Derek's uncharacteristic silence in the car seat behind him hinted at a catnap that would only add to his grouchiness later. After a peek in his rearview mirror to check on his sleeping son, Micah frowned. He couldn't blame Deirdre for being less than talkative as well. She didn't care about the newest round of sabotage to his fence lines, no matter how many head of cattle had made a run for it that morning. And no matter what the sheriff had said, she was no volunteer.

Why he'd made the situation worse by ganging up on her and bargaining with his offer of help on her investigation, he couldn't say. The last thing he needed as he tried to determine who'd been targeting his family was an investigator who didn't play by the rules. Special Agent Colton found no gray areas off-limits when she tracked a suspect. For her, the ends always justified the means. But did they, really? She'd told him and the sheriff about the investigation that put her in trouble, but she hadn't said whether her unconventional methods had caused problems for that case when the suspect went to trial.

Was she really all that different from his stepmother or his late wife? Okay, maybe it wasn't fair to lump an investigator who broke some rules to stop a murderer to an *actual serial killer*. Also, since she still appeared to be breathing in the passenger seat, Deirdre clearly hadn't abandoned her husband and newborn only to die in a car accident during her grand exit. Still, whether their situations were exactly alike or not, he couldn't afford to rely on someone whose moral code offered as many offshoots as theirs had.

You have no choice. He squeezed the steering wheel as the truth washed over him. In their lack of options, he and the agent were the same. Already, the events of sabotage on the ranch had escalated since someone had first broken the latch on the corral gate and allowed the horses to visit his back porch and munch his flowers. He was fooling himself to assume that the situation wouldn't grow more dangerous until whoever had been targeting them got whatever they wanted. Only he had no idea what that was.

To prevent his sweet little boy from getting caught in the crossfire, he would have to do whatever it took. Even if that meant collaborating with an FBI agent whose definition of *right* stretched so far outside the right/wrong lane that it required escort cars with posted Wide Load signs and flashing lights.

His fingers tightened again, causing the steering wheel to bite into his palms. He might have to work with Special Agent Colton, but that didn't mean he had to trust her. Beautiful women had already wreaked enough havoc in his life and those of his whole family, thank you very much. He didn't bother trying to tell himself he didn't find Deirdre attractive. If that episode before the sheriff's arrival hadn't been proof enough, now his whole body hummed with nervous energy that had more to do with her nearness than today's sabotage incident or even the news about his stepmother. Whatever it was, it needed to stop right now.

"I'd prefer not to wear your late wife's clothes, if you don't mind."

As Deirdre's words fractured the silence, catching him thinking things that were so far out of bounds that the sidelines had vanished, Micah jerked his shoulders. He tried to play off his awkward move by including it in an even more graceless stretch, but as her words sank in, he pressed into the headrest instead. Leah's clothes.

"Good thing, because I donated them a long time ago."

Immediately, he regretted the words that escaped before he could stop them. Though he kept his eyes on the dirt road ahead, he could still feel her gaze, warm on the side of his face. Why had he put it like that? Did he *want* her to ask more questions about Leah? He couldn't blame her for being curious about him disposing of his wife's possessions so soon. Some widows and widowers clung to their late spouses' things, even holding on to items they couldn't justify—like socks—for years. His temptation to tell a stranger that the situation had been different with his late wife made no sense. How could he explain that he'd needed to purge rather than cherish basic reminders of her?

"I don't know why Richard even suggested it," he added when he couldn't hold still under her scrutiny any longer. "You're at least three inches taller than Leah was."

He forced himself to use her name and hoped Deirdre didn't notice the effort it had required. She resettled his extra hat that he'd loaned her earlier on her lap. It was too big, but she had to wear something out in the fields.

"Probably forty pounds heavier, too," she said after a few seconds.

"Much less than that," he said automatically and then frowned. He'd all but admitted that he'd sized her body up against his memory of Leah's. "It's not that. It's just…you know, your job. The fitness regimen. You're—" he paused, grasping for words "—sturdier."

Her laugh came out low, slow and more sensual than she probably realized. Parts of him weren't nearly as naive to that power.

"Now that's a descriptor every woman dreams that someone will use when referring to her," she said in a dreamy voice. "*Sturdy.*"

Micah dampened his lips, never letting his gaze leave the windshield. These waters were already too muddy for him to try to clarify further without risking getting lost in the soup. No way would he tell her what all that *sturdiness* did for him, either.

"I'm sure I can find you something to wear."

With a quick peek to the side, he caught her watching him, an incredulous expression on her face.

"You think *we* wear the same size?"

This time he blew out a breath. "No. I—"

Deirdre swiped a hand at the dash in front of her. "Aw, just kidding. You're probably right, anyway."

Not even close. Somehow he managed not to say it out loud this time. He peeked out the side-view mirror. Everything he said to her seemed to be a mistake. Not only had he drawn attention to the uncomfortable intimacy of her being forced to share his wardrobe, but now he'd also painted in his own mind the image of the agent's feminine curves brushing the inside of *his* clothes. She probably was wondering if the pants and shirts he would give her would even be clean. He hadn't missed her disdain as she'd spoken of her journey to his ranch. The agent was no fan of the West. And more than likely cowboys like him in general.

"We'll run into Laramie later this afternoon, so you can pick up a few things."

"At the Western outfitter?" At his side glance, she grinned. "You mentioned it earlier."

They both knew he'd been making fun of her when he'd suggested that. "I was thinking about Gary's Farm & Fleet. Closest big shopping mall is back in Casper. But if you still think you need more barn dance gear, we can—"

"No, no. Gary's it is."

He didn't even try to hold back his smile this time. "Great. You'll love the place."

Her silence told him how much she believed that.

They drove slowly over the last half mile of bumpy road, and then he pulled his truck to the soft shoulder.

He pointed through the windshield to the field off to the east.

"This is the area that received the damage this morning."

She glanced up and down the fence line, which, at least in this area, remained intact.

"How come I don't see any cattle out in the pasture?"

"Since there's a *gaping hole* in the fence, we had to move them to the weekend pasture. They do love to find a break in the fence line and head off on adventures."

She closed her eyes and shook her head. "Right. I didn't think about that."

Micah threw open the truck door and jumped down from the step. Deirdre hopped out as well, meeting him near the tailgate.

He couldn't resist a grin as he pointed down at her pristine boots. "I hope you don't mind getting those dirty. We're going to have to walk. Just a half mile or so."

"We have to *walk*?" She squinted until her eyes were tiny slits.

He pointed to tall grass along the fence that they would have to follow to reach the area of damage. "We could have taken the horses, but I wasn't sure you could ride."

"You could've asked."

"I'll remember to do that next time." He noted that she still hadn't said whether she had any experience sitting a horse. "Anyway, I thought city slickers were used to walking in your concrete jungle."

She gestured to the dry grass. "That doesn't look

like concrete, and believe me, I would never walk that far in *these* boots." Like earlier, she rubbed the pointed toe of one against the heel of the other.

"Blister?"

She lifted both shoulders and let them drop. "One of those, and a raw place on my calf where the top of the boot rubbed. I should have known better than to wear them."

He stared at her boots for several seconds, surprised that she'd admitted to her mistake. In her field of work, where male agents probably outnumbered females at least three to one, it probably didn't serve her well to admit any form of weakness.

"You'll break them in. If they're a great fit, you don't get blisters at all."

"Guess I didn't pick well." She kicked at the dust and then winced.

"Do you mind if I ask why…?" He gestured to her whole getup, reminding himself not to linger on his favorite parts of it. His memory adeptly filled in the blanks.

"Thought it would help me fit in better."

He tried not to smile and could tell how badly he'd failed from her frown.

"How's that working for you?" he managed.

"Other than the blister and the cowboy who thinks I'm a comedy skit, just dandy."

"I'm not laughing. Well, not really."

"Thanks." She pointed to the rear window of the truck cab, where the back of Derek's car seat peeked around the sides of the rear-seat headrest. "You don't plan to leave him in there, do you?"

"With an FBI agent right here watching me? Not a chance."

After lowering the tailgate and lifting the flip cover on the truck bed, he pulled out the child-carrier back-pack. He used the pack's kickstand to prop it on the ground outside the truck door.

Deirdre followed him around the truck bed, appearing to watch every step.

"You mean you would if I weren't here?"

"Well…" Grinning, he held his hands wide and then shook his head. "You're too easy. You know that?"

Her eyes widened. She had to know that he'd meant *too easily fooled*, but what he'd said sounded like something else entirely.

"No. I never leave him in the truck. Even when it's only going to be a few minutes and it's really tempting."

"That's good to hear."

Her question should have offended him more. Not for the first time that afternoon, she seemed to be evaluating whether he was a good parent. He couldn't help but to respect someone who had his son's best interests at heart, even if she'd admitted that she knew nothing about caring for children.

He pushed back his hat and stared up at the sky. "On a sunny day like today in the low seventies, the temperature inside that closed cab would climb to over one hundred degrees in about thirty minutes. There's not a job I can think of on the ranch that takes less time than that."

She nodded as though satisfied with his answer and then pointed to the backpack on the ground. "That looks like something you'd be wearing for a hike, not a day in the fields."

"Works in a pinch. We have to get creative sometimes on days when I can't find childcare."

He reached into the cab and unbuckled Derek's car seat. The child grunted and groused as Micah worked the harness straps to release his legs and arms.

"You said something about coming out here on horseback. You don't ride with him—" Deirdre stopped and pointed over her shoulder to her back.

"Why not?" Micah chuckled until her eyes widened with alarm.

He had to stop with the ranch jokes. She might have experience in investigating crimes and tracking serial killers, but here on Harmony Fields, she was greener than a spring calf still getting its footing.

"I don't do that, either."

"Then how…?"

She squinted at him as he lifted his still-lethargic son and propped him on his hip.

"It's been a little tricky, but the truth is there's no safe way to take a baby on horseback. Other than maybe a gentle circle around the corral."

"So what do you do with him when you have to go out in the fields?"

"My neighbors are always happy to watch him for a few hours so I can get some work done."

"Didn't you say they also helped you corral the cattle this morning after they escaped?" At his nod, she added, "I can't believe they do all that. I don't even *know* my neighbors in my condo complex outside DC."

"It's different around here. We're all so spread out.

We count on each other when something comes up. We're not just neighbors. We're friends."

"You're lucky to have that support system."

She stared off into the distance, making him wonder if she had one of those herself, or even any close friends.

"Sometimes one of the ranch hands will do babysitting duty when it's my turn to ride the fences, or lately, check out more damage," he said, trying to draw her back from wherever she'd gone.

She grinned when she turned back to him. "Now that I really can't picture."

"You kidding? Some of those guys are my best childcare providers." Swaying back and forth to comfort his child, Micah frowned at her. "You should know better than to discount a whole gender in possible performance on a certain job."

"I was thinking more about guys more comfortable roping a two-hundred-pound steer than diapering a twenty-pound human, but point taken."

"Make your steer about a thousand pounds heavier and I'll concede *your* point."

Until then, Derek had still been slumped against his shoulder, but as Micah glanced down, the toddler opened one eye as a test. Slowly, he lifted the other lid and studied Deirdre warily. Then he lowered his gaze to the backpack, stationed on the ground.

"No ride," he announced, clasping his legs around Micah's waist.

"Just for a little bit, buddy." Micah gently peeled Derek away from his side and aimed the child's feet at the two leg holes in the backpack. The toddler kicked his feet and shook his head, the game becoming an upside-down version of whack-a-mole, without the bat. Only by bracing the contraption between his legs could Micah prevent the whole thing from falling with his son inside.

"No!"

Even with his seat planted and his father snapping the harness straps over his shoulders, Derek still protested. He yanked off the New York Yankees baseball cap his father had put on him, held it out and dropped it on the ground.

"I wish I could get to ride around in that cool pack."

Deirdre's words must have surprised Derek as he let his tennis shoes touch the ground and peered between his dad's legs at her. Micah lunged for the hat and lifted the backpack, baby inside, onto the tailgate. He had to hold on to the contraption to prevent it from toppling over.

"I really like your fancy hat, too," she said.

"Yankees!" Derek announced.

When Micah plunked the cap back on his son's head with his free hand, Derek patted the top several times.

"Not the Wyoming...? Not the Cheyenne...?"

Realizing her questions were for him, Micah glanced up from where he was sliding his arms into the backpack straps. He grinned at her furrowed brow. "I'll save you from having to list every city. There isn't a single pro sports team in the state of Wyoming."

She leaned her head to look from the boy to his dad. "New York, then?"

Micah hefted the pack onto his back, securing the waistband first and then snapping and adjusting the straps at his sternum. "You can take the boy's dad out of Manhattan, but you can't take Manhattan out of—"

"The boy's dad," she finished for him. "But isn't the new Yankee Stadium in the Bronx?"

"Must you be so borough specific?" he asked with a grin.

"What about the Mets?"

"The *who*?" Even a former New Yorker like him knew that those team allegiances were formed in the crib and held until the grave.

She shook her head. "Never mind."

He shouldn't have made her smile. Certainly not laugh. When she turned both on him, the force connected like a sucker punch. His throat tightened and warmth spread across his hips, right where he'd anchored the backpack. Then lower. Worse than even that, his knees buckled, and he practically dumped his precious cargo.

Deirdre shot over to him and gripped his upper arm, compounding his humiliation. He could have sworn he'd never looked at a beautiful woman before.

"You sure you got that?" she asked after a few seconds.

He flexed his biceps, both so she would release him and because he hated hoping that she wouldn't. She did, slowly lowering her arm to her side.

"I'm fine. I just tripped." He looked past her, hoping she wouldn't call him on his lie.

As she started to step away, Derek reached out and grasped the short ponytail that Deirdre had tied her hair in before their drive into the fields. She pulled back, surprised, but the toddler only continued to stare at his hand, where her light-colored strands had spilled through his fingers. Micah tightened his jaw. Whatever statement it made about a man's character that he could be jealous of his own two-year-old, Micah had to admit that all those negatives applied to him. He shoved his hands in his pockets, wishing his fingers didn't ache to feel all that softness for himself.

"I want Dee-Dee," Derek announced.

Deirdre's gaze flicked to Micah's and then away, her cheeks pink. And though he'd worn a hat all day, his face still felt sunburned. In advocating for himself, the child had unknowingly spoken of his father's wants as well—the kind that Micah had no business having.

"I'm carrying you, buddy," Micah said when he found his voice. "Deirdre will be right there with us."

"No. Dee-Dee can carry me."

"You're *my* little boy. It's my job to take care of you."

Hoping if they got started that Derek would be distracted enough to forget his demand, Micah marched into the grass toward the fence corner. Deirdre fell into step beside him.

"You see. We'll all be there in no time," he assured his son.

"I sure hope so," Deirdre answered for them all.

Since she was pretending not to be in pain as she walked, he tried not to notice her tight expressions every time she stepped on a rock.

"Dee-Dee, carry me. Dee-Dee, carry me."

"She can't do that. You're much too heavy—"

"Too heavy for whom? Me?"

Micah winced as he realized he'd said the exact wrong thing to this woman, who probably had often experienced others questioning her strength and abilities.

"I'm sure you could do it. There's just no reason to. You're already doing so much for us. You don't need to prove—"

At her glare, he forgot whatever he'd been about to say.

"Here. Hand me the pack." She reached out her arms and waited.

"You know, it's not always good to reward a child for making demands."

Instead of answering, Deirdre, who had to be the most stubborn woman he'd ever met, continued to stretch out her arms. Finally, he unbuckled the chest strap.

"You're going to regret this decision."

"No more than anything else I've done today."

She had a point there. He unbuckled the belt and allowed her to help him out of the backpack straps. Once she'd settled the pack on the ground, kickstand open, she turned away and let him slide the contraption over her arms. She widened her stance to accept the weight when he released it and then buckled and tightened the waistband and cinched the side straps.

Derek giggled the whole time, but he seemed to know better than to thrash his head around and unbalance her.

"Ride with Dee-Dee," he called out with glee.

"Hope you're ready for this." Forcing himself not to look back and risk the temptation to help her, Micah started off again.

She marched along beside him, her shoulders back, her chin lifted.

"Just show me where to go. We need to get this handled so we can move on to the other case."

"Up there. Past that hill." He pointed to an area that he knew from experience was farther away than it appeared.

Deirdre didn't wait for him to lead and marched ahead, her slight limp from earlier barely perceptible now. She had to be in pain. His aching shoulders knew how much that pack and the toddler inside it weighed. But she would never admit to what she probably thought of as weakness, even if she had to crawl back to the truck. As she powered on, Micah grinned and tried to keep up. He couldn't help but like Special Agent Colton a little more.

"Now that's an interesting new development."

Crouched low in a conveniently located stand of trees, the spectator shot a glance around to see if the words had been overheard. A chuckle replaced the silly gasp that preceded it. No need to be concerned. There were no humans around for miles besides that rancher and his guest, who traipsed together across the field to examine today's damage.

The newest gift. The freshest warning.

Good thing local police had bumbled every bit of this investigation so far, like a collection of circus performers squeezing into a clown car without doors. *Investigations*, plural, the viewer corrected with a grin. And this new officer, whoever she was, would probably be just like them, complete with white makeup and a red nose.

Sinking back to ensure that the brush provided an effective cover, the viewer adjusted field glasses that were showing their age and watched the pair's progress across the field through the scratches. Earlier, the sheriff couldn't get his squad car off Harmony Fields fast enough. He'd left clouds of dust and rock in his wake as he made his escape.

The sheriff must have left the case in the hands of this newcomer, but she'd already proven herself a simpleton by letting Micah trick her into hauling his kid on her back. The rancher had always been too clever for his own good, but on this, he didn't seem to be able to take a hint.

At least his success would be of benefit soon.

Harmony Fields. Even the name was laughable. There would be no harmony on that land until Micah Perry packed up the kid and rode away as fast as one of those horses could carry them.

But his time was running out. Polite hints could only work for so long. Then people just vanished. Without a forwarding address. Or a proper goodbye.

Chapter 5

Deirdre dumped several packages on the overly ruffled bed in a guest room, which featured lace or doilies on every available surface. If she weren't so worried that she would sleep right through dinner, she would have taken a swan dive into that mess of pillows, too, even if the room looked like the top of a '60s wedding cake.

"You're going to regret this decision." She repeated Micah's words from earlier and made a mean face in the dresser mirror.

Oh, she regretted it, all right, but no way in hell she would admit that to him. Just like she hadn't gushed with gratitude when he'd reclaimed the backpack and his son so that she could take notes and use her phone to photograph the crime scene. She rubbed the back of her neck, the aching muscles at its base still nothing compared to her burning feet, and then started pulling items out of the shopping bags.

Gary's Farm & Fleet had met her expectations for fashion shopping à la feed store, but at least now she had a couple of outfits to get through the next few days, and she wouldn't have to wash out her panties and sports bra and go commando every night. The pink fuzzy slippers that she'd also found in that miniscule lingerie department and the pair of slip-on sneakers from the closeout display near the checkout were bonus buys.

A knock at the door caught her attention just as she set aside the fleece shorts and T-shirt that would serve as her pajamas.

"Yes?" she called out.

Micah pushed the door open and leaned his head inside.

"I just wanted to make sure you're comfortable. Is the guest room okay?"

She nodded, though she suspected he hadn't selected a single item inside it.

"Is there anyone you should call to let them know you won't be returning tonight? Boyfriend? Girlfriend? Spouse? Or boss?"

Deirdre crossed her arms but shook her head. "No boyfriend. *Ex*-husband doesn't care where I am. Never did."

She squeezed her arms tighter, not sure why she'd told him so much. Or why he'd asked. Beyond being utterly pitiful, her personal life was none of his business. "And you already know I can't tell my boss."

His lips lifted, though he appeared to straighten uncomfortably in the doorway.

"Then you have everything you need?"

"I think so."

"I would *hope* so."

He grinned as he gestured to the new Resistol hat and the huge pile of clothes and toiletry items she would never use again after this trip, even if she'd bought a cheap duffel to haul it all home. Ranch chic just wasn't her vibe. Still, she appreciated his sacrifice in joining her on the shopping spree. He'd spent the afternoon chasing Derek down aisles, past everything from horse feed to beekeeping gear to tractor parts while she'd picked through the limited selections. He'd even been forced to intervene during an impressive toddler meltdown while she'd tried on a few boxy shirts and some pants, all before he had to hurry back to the ranch to help with the cattle's dinner feed.

He cleared his throat and pointed to the insulated rubber work boots she'd set next to the bed.

"You're going to love those boots. More comfortable than the ones you've been wearing. We wear those instead of the Western style for a lot of our work." He held his hands wide. "Well, except for anything on horseback. They don't fit well in the stirrups."

She couldn't help grinning over his rambling, but she couldn't blame him for being uncomfortable standing at the door of her assigned bedroom for the next few days. She wasn't feeling superconfident herself. How are they supposed to stay in the same house when she couldn't help watching him every time she thought he wasn't paying attention?

"I still don't know why I needed them, though," she said, returning to the safe subject of her footwear. "I'll only be here a few days. And, technically, I'm not working on the ranch."

"Clearly you've never been on a ranch before. *Everyone* works here."

She tilted her head and studied him. "Why do I have the sneaking suspicion that the sheriff blackmailed me to stay here because you're short on ranch hands?"

As the low rumble of his chuckle tickled through her skin, she crossed her arms to protect herself from its intoxicating roll.

"Nah. Richard told you he needed extra manpower—er, *person* power—to help on this investigation. Harmony Fields is taking up more than its share of time and resources from his department. Your being here to offer an extra pair of hands on the ranch is a bonus."

She followed his gaze to the pair of leather work gloves he'd insisted she would need. Then, as she recognized that they were both staring at the bed she would sleep in, the room becoming a little too cozy, the air too warm, Deirdre pivoted to glance past Micah's legs, looking for his son.

"What happened to Derek?"

"Why? Haven't you seen him? I thought you had him." Micah looked over his shoulder, his eyes wide when he glanced back.

Just as Deirdre shot toward the door, Micah grinned.

She planted her feet and crossed her arms. "Funny."

"I'm a good dad, you know. At least, I try to be." He gestured over his shoulder and then twisted his arm to peek at his watch. "I have a show on for him in the family room. I figure I have about thirty minutes. Forty-five, max."

"For what?"

"Before the witching hour."

"Witches? Not knocking on anyone's religion, but I didn't sign up for a conversion."

"No conversion involved. It's that late-afternoon period where toddlers are too hungry, too tired, too *everything*, and their world implodes."

"Sounds like a blast."

"Clock's ticking. You have enough time to hit the shower." He pointed to the guest room's attached bath. "Towels are in the cabinet. Water heater's generous. I'll get started on dinner."

Her whole body was already melting with the idea of hot water pouring over her head and her sore muscles when his last words sank in. As if it weren't bad enough that she would be staying at the home of a potential witness, now he planned to *cook* for her, too.

"Oh. I figured we'd just get something delivered."

He'd started to turn away, but now his head swiveled back. "From where? Gary's?"

She pursed her lips. Obviously, she'd said something ridiculous again. Food delivery had to be a foreign concept out here. "I think Gary has gotten enough of our business for one day."

"I agree. Oh, I forgot."

Micah disappeared from the open doorway for a few seconds. When he returned, he stepped all the way inside and rested a box of adhesive bandages and a tube of antibiotic gel on the short bookshelf near the door. "Thought you might need these."

"I don't," she began but didn't bother finishing. He already knew about the blisters.

"Remember, *tick, tick, tick*." He pointed at his watch and closed the door behind him.

For several seconds, she stared at the first-aid products, not sure what to think about how he'd spent the afternoon taking care of her needs. She was supposed to be independent. Self-reliant. Strong. So she shouldn't have liked being taken care of that way. She didn't know what to make of the fact that she did. A little too much.

Delicious smells of basil and oregano and the clang of banging metal greeted Deirdre twenty minutes later as she headed down the stairs. She found the sources of both scent and sound in the kitchen, where something wonderful simmered on the stove and the little musician on the floor banged another saucepan with its lid and a serving spoon.

Despite her plan to behave as if she'd turned the homes of every witness she'd ever interviewed into bed-and-breakfasts, she couldn't help hesitating in the kitchen doorway. She hated conceding the upper hand in any situation, and Micah's advantage here was several arms, legs and a few torsos above that. She braced against the doorjamb, waiting for him to rub in that point.

Instead, Micah, who'd changed into a brown University of Wyoming T-shirt with gold letters and a bronco-riding cowboy on the front, glanced over from the stove and smiled. He appeared more relaxed now that they weren't speaking in her bedroom, and she could agree with him on that.

"Feel better?" Micah called out over his son's drum solo.

"Yes, thanks," she shouted back.

Only Derek chose that moment to cut his performance, and her words reverberated off the walls. Both

Perry guys stared back at her, one with curiosity, the other with mischief.

"Glad to hear it," Micah said.

His gaze skimmed over her T-shirt and shorts more slowly than necessary, and just as they had when she'd caught him checking out her butt earlier, nerve endings that had no business reacting at all sizzled and popped.

"Nice slippers," he said after a long pause.

Humiliation washed over her as even her toes tingled under his notice, but she planted her hand on her hip and frowned to cover her discomfort. If only this were as effective as the slippers had been in masking the bandages on her feet. "Hey, these are my recovery shoes."

He gave her footwear another glance but lifted his gaze just as the shivers started working themselves up again.

"Hungry?"

"Starving." She didn't bother denying it. Those airplane snacks hadn't exactly stuck to her ribs, and if she didn't eat soon, she might cry louder than the toddler had in his toughest moment of the day.

She pointed to the two pots on the stove. "What is that? It smells amazing."

"Just spaghetti."

"Basghetti! Basghetti! I'm hungry!"

Derek leaped up from his pans, letting the lid and spoon clang to the floor. Then, with a moan that could have kicked off an acting career, he wrapped his arms around his father's legs. Pressing his lips together as if holding back a smile, Micah shuffled toward the counter, his son still clinging to him like a koala on a branch.

"Here, let me handle this," he said to Deirdre. "We're on borrowed time."

He swung his son up on his hip and deposited him in the highchair, positioned at the head of the rich wood table in the alcove dining area. The table was already set for dinner with casual dishes, paper napkins and two huge red wineglasses, all out of reach of the highchair's occupant.

"It's almost ready, buddy." He reached down to brush back Derek's hair.

Once he'd wrestled wiggling legs into the safety strap and reluctant arms into a pocketed bib and locked the tray in place, Micah used his foot to straighten the plastic beneath the highchair. He hurried back to the stove to dump cooked pasta into a colander in the sink.

"Witching hour?" she couldn't help asking, using his term from earlier.

"It arrived early today." With efficient movements, he doled out a small portion of noodles on a cowboy plate. "Thought he'd make it to the end of the program. Not so much."

Though Micah wouldn't see it as he stirred the pot of sauce, Deirdre nodded, aware that her arrival had been at least one of the things that had thrown the child off his schedule.

The cowboy moved around the kitchen with the deftness of a short-order cook, chopping up his son's pasta, mixing in a tiny bit of sauce and delivering it to the table, along with a toddler-size fork. Derek went to work on his plate, using the utensil and sometimes his hands to guide food to his mouth. Red streaks quickly appeared on the tray, a few stray noodles landing on the mat.

"Anything I can help with?" Deirdre asked, not entirely sure she wouldn't eat with that same gusto and mess when her plate finally arrived.

"I have it under control. You can take a seat if you like."

Soon, Micah had two plates of pasta and sauce on the table, both topped with freshly grated Parmesan. Deirdre eyed the food, trying to hold back attacking at least until the cook took a seat. Manners were of no concern to Derek, who'd already finished his dinner and sat sated, smearing drips of sauce in circles on his tray.

Micah pursed his lips and then shrugged, signaling he'd picked his battles and would let that one go. Taking his son's plate with him, he slipped back into the kitchen and returned with two small plastic cars and an already open bottle of Sangiovese. He dropped the cars on Derek's tray, right into the mess, and then held out the bottle.

"I forgot to ask if you drink wine, if you drink at all or if you'd like some of this."

She looked from the bottle to his face and then back to the bottle. Now wine, too? She'd already broken so many rules today that any witness statement she obtained from him could only be used as background, since it wouldn't be admissible in court. Having a drink with him now would only add to her tally of shame, so what the heck.

Decision made, she lifted her oversize glass. "Yes. To all three."

"Well, set that down if you expect me not to spill this everywhere."

Once she followed his instructions, he tipped the

bottle, giving her only a stingy restaurant pour despite the promising size of the wineglass. Not that even a generous home version would have helped to calm her nerves, anyway. She doubted that anything could.

"Looks like you're an expert," she said as he filled his own glass, twisting the bottle to avoid the drip.

"Surprised I even remember how to do this."

"You don't usually drink?"

"Not wine. More a beer guy if I have anything." He set the bottle aside and brushed his hand over the smooth wood tabletop. "Can't remember the last time I even sat here. Derek has his own chair, and I eat most of my meals standing at the bar."

"You're still standing now, too," she pointed out. "But you also seem to be a busy guy. I don't see how you ever find time to sit down."

"Occasionally, I do."

Micah pulled out his chair and dropped into it, rolling his shoulders, as though this had been a long day for him, too. He glanced from his plate to Deirdre's and then to his son, playing contentedly in his chair. "Hey, this is nice."

"Yeah, it is," she admitted before she could stop herself.

That was the problem. It was *too* nice. Cozy, like it had been in the guest room. More intimate without the necessity of a bed. Like a sweet little family dinner where she'd cast herself as the wife and mother. She blinked away that ridiculous daydream, her lungs tight, as if someone had vacuumed all the oxygen from the room. Her face felt hot, the wine only responsible for part of it.

She focused on the thick wood beams that created

the dining area and suspended the balcony above them. When she'd taken in every inch of those, she lowered her gaze to her plate and lifted her fork to twirl it in the pasta. Anything to delay having to meet Micah's gaze again.

Where had that vision come from, anyway? She wouldn't have recognized a real family dinner if one popped up and took a big bite of her spaghetti. Now, photo-op dinners staged for campaign ads, she knew all about those, since they were the best family photos Eoin and Georgina Colton ever took with their only daughter. More than that, she didn't have dreams of domesticity and biological clocks. And if she hadn't already declared a moratorium on dating since marriage hadn't worked out for her, and motherhood didn't seem to be in the cards, either, she would never choose a family member in a murder case she was investigating for her prospects list.

"Thought you said you were hungry."

Deirdre startled at Micah's words, her head and fork coming up at the same time and a bit of sauce flinging across the table. It splatted on the silkscreened cowboy centered on Micah's T-shirt.

"Bull's-eye," he said with a chuckle.

"Oh, no. Sorry. Here, let me clean that up." She popped up from her seat, napkin in hand, and leaned over the tabletop, intending to do that.

Micah held out a splayed hand. "I've got it. No harm. No foul."

Continuing to chuckle, he cleared it away with a few quick swipes with his napkin. If only she could dispose of her humiliation as quickly. The ship had already sailed on her plan for looking like an in-control agent, but she would appreciate it if she could stop making a fool of herself around him.

"Sorry," she said again. "I got a little lost in my thoughts."

"Hey, I'm used to food decorations on my clothes. I have a two-year-old. I just wasn't expecting them from your side of the table." He pointed to her plate. "Now, could you eat some of that instead of teaching my son how to start a food fight?"

He twirled spaghetti on his fork and lifted a big bite but paused before putting it in his mouth. "It's really good. I promise."

"I'm sure it is."

Deirdre took his cue and twisted a bite onto her fork but found she wasn't as hungry as she had been. Clearly, she was the only one feeling a little uncomfortable with their cozy meal, she decided as Micah put away his dinner with enthusiasm. As she took her first bite, she realized why. The savory mixture of flavors burst on her tongue and filled her mouth.

She sighed, her appetite returning. As she took another bite, her eyes fluttered closed. When she opened them again, she caught Micah watching her with something unreadable in his eyes. Though he quickly looked down at his plate, she couldn't help wondering if he was more bothered by their private little meal than she'd assumed.

"Told you it was good." He slid another bite in his mouth and smiled as he chewed.

She quickly cleared her plate and then set her fork aside. "If you tell me you just whipped that up in the past twenty minutes, I will skulk out of here in shame.

I have had endless time to cook lately, and I've still barely touched the microwave."

"Being suspended probably doesn't inspire you to get creative in the kitchen."

"I'm never an inventive cook." She paused, frowning. "And, as I already told you, I wasn't suspended."

"I know. Just a forced vacation. Whatever you say."

Wanting to avoid that topic and needing time to come up with a better one, she sipped her wine and then set down the glass.

"Your crystal is beautiful. You're lucky whoever ransacked the house didn't find these." She gently rubbed her finger over the delicate rim, and then her breath caught as she realized what she'd said. While trying to steer clear of a topic that made her uncomfortable, she'd introduced one that reminded Micah of both his dead wife *and* his fears for his child's safety. Zero for two on that one.

"Yeah. Lucky."

His sad smile was bad enough, but the raw look in his eyes went beyond just contradicting his words. It touched a place inside Deirdre that she usually shielded better than her body behind a Kevlar vest. Her throat felt so thick that she had to concentrate to swallow. This had to be the same sensation someone felt after running into an active crime scene with neither weapon nor protective gear, and yet she was still tempted to step around the table to Micah, cradle his head against her and tell him everything would be all right. He knew that wasn't true. Already, he'd lost two people he loved, and now he was terrified he couldn't protect a third.

"I'm sorry. That was so insensitive."

"No worries."

But rather than take another bite, he moved his pasta around on his plate, as lost in his thoughts as she'd been earlier.

"I didn't, by the way," he said when he finally looked up.

"Didn't what? Think what I said was insensitive?"

He shook his head. "I didn't cook the sauce. I just warmed it up."

His smile returned, and Deirdre found she could finally breathe normally again.

"Remember when I said I have a cook a few days a week?" He waited for her nod before continuing. "She's a grandma and a chef wannabe. She prepares a few things fresh and then bulk cooks at home and loads my freezer."

"So, you and Derek definitely aren't starving out here on the ranch."

"We wouldn't starve without her help. We would just eat a lot more mac and cheese and frozen pizzas."

"A family after my own heart."

Micah's gaze flicked to her, and she straightened in her seat. Though she hadn't wanted him to know what she'd been thinking about earlier, she'd all but announced it by burying it in a joke. He didn't seem to notice as his attention turned to his son, who'd begun to nod off in the chair next to them.

"I'd better get someone in the bath and into a fresh diaper before he has to go to bed as a big orange monster. Have another glass of wine, and I'll be back in a few minutes."

His father's words having awakened him, Derek shook his head. "No bath."

"Yes, bath. Sorry, kiddo." Micah removed the tray

and reverse-wrestled his child out of the chair and bib. "You're too dirty."

"No bath." Derek started running the moment his father set his feet on the ground.

"Wait. I've got an idea," Micah called out.

The child stopped and looked back curiously.

"Maybe Miss Deirdre would like to help with your bath?"

Micah tilted his head and lifted an eyebrow. She could only guess from his grin that her own expression showed pure panic.

"I haven't ever—"

She didn't get the chance to finish as the toddler ran full force to her, not stopping until he rammed the side of her leg. He lifted his arms over his head.

"Up."

Unable to resist those sad eyes and those chubby little hands, she reached down and hauled the little boy into her lap, sticky fingers, dirty face and all. As he snuggled against her, she couldn't help but to wrap her arms around that tiny body and lean close to breathe in his hair. An unfamiliar warmth spread in her chest and all the way to her fingers.

"Think Miss Deirdre might need another bath now, too," Micah said.

Despite his light words, he had that same sad look in his eyes, and this time she was tempted to carry the toddler to his dad and hug them both. She held herself perfectly still, hoping the impulse would pass. Worried that it wouldn't.

"So you want Miss Deirdre to help with your bath?" Micah asked his son.

Derek nodded. "Dee-Dee helps."

She stiffened as the little boy turned in her lap and touched her face with a sticky hand. *Help.* That was what she'd come to Wyoming to do in the first place. By assisting her cousins with their investigation to find missing person Humphrey Kelly and tracking and arresting black widow Maeve O'Leary, she hoped to help herself as well by proving her value to the bureau. Now that the threats against the rancher and his son had become part of the equation, she hoped to help them, too.

Only she couldn't do that if she became too close. If she'd learned nothing else in her training, she'd understood that keeping a professional distance was critical for both cases and witnesses involved. Yet, already enjoying herself as the houseguest of a witness, now she would be headed to bath time, too.

It was a mistake. She could feel it. If she got too close to them, then she might miss a clue and fail to protect either the sweet little boy or his father from whoever had been threatening them. And if emotions became involved, someone could get hurt. She worried it just might be her.

Chapter 6

Nearly an hour later, with Derek's bath and bedtime ritual completed and the clean saucepan and pasta pot drying in the sink, Micah dropped into the same seat where he'd eaten dinner earlier. He gestured for Deirdre to take the chair across from him, though this part of their to-do list promised to be more awkward than even sitting with a child between them in a big-boy bed for two whole stories.

No way would he admit just how relieved he'd been when his son begged Deirdre to read a second book to him before he drifted off into dreamland. Micah wouldn't have been able to get any words past the golf ball that had wedged in his throat while their house-guest read *Good Night Moon*, anyway. As Deirdre had sat close enough that her new floral shampoo flooded his senses and her surprisingly sweet reading voice tickled his ears, the truth had pressed on his heart that his son would never hear a story from his own mother, and there wasn't a damned thing he could do about it.

He drummed his hands on the table edge to clear his mind of those melancholy thoughts and then pointed to the empty space in the middle.

"I should have left the wine on the table." He would definitely need something to calm his nerves if he planned to work with Deirdre tonight, especially if she interjected questions about his stepmother between those about the recent events at the ranch.

Deirdre waved him off as he started to stand. "I'll get it."

She headed around the corner into the kitchen. Sounds of clinking glass and the closing of cabinet doors filtered from the room. When she returned, she carried a bottle of craft beer in each hand and had a pair of hard-plastic cups tucked under her arm.

"Best I could do." She pointed to the plastic when she'd set everything on the table, even pulling a bottle opener from inside a cup. "I couldn't find any beer glasses."

He shrugged. "Casualties from the buffet in the living room."

"I figured."

"You don't have to switch to beer on my account. But thanks for this." He pulled one bottle closer to him and reached for the opener.

"You never said you had IPAs, ambers and American lagers in there." She gestured in the direction of the refrigerator. "Right up my alley."

"What'd you expect me to have? Bottled river water?"

Her small smile hinted that her assumption hadn't

been far off from that. Ignoring the cups, he drank directly from the bottle.

"Or cans." She opened her own beer and took a long pull from it.

Again, Micah pointed to the seat across from him, but instead of sitting in it, Deirdre moved to the counter and returned with the notebook and pens he'd given her earlier. She rested those on the end of the table where Derek's highchair had been stationed during dinner and lined up the chair in that spot.

When she finally sat, she lowered her shoulders and let her head hang forward. The temptation to step over and rub her neck took Micah by surprise. He gripped his hands together and stayed in his seat to avoid the impulse. Okay, he might have had as long a dry spell as one of his three bulls in the off-season—well, longer—but that didn't give him an excuse to be trying to get his hands on the special agent. For any reason. Their lodging situation was already awkward enough without having to include any of *that*, no matter how tempting it sounded.

Deirdre reached back and rubbed her own neck, briefly closing her eyes. Then she lifted her head.

"You go through that whole routine every single night?"

"Well, most nights. Sometimes when we go into Laramie for supplies, and Derek falls asleep in the truck, I just brush his teeth and tuck him into bed." He gave her a sheepish look. "One time I even put him to bed without teeth brushing. You won't report me, will you?"

She crossed her arms, tapped her lips with her index

finger and stared up at the ceiling as if pondering his question.

"Well, not yet. But if I see any concerning evidence—like mismatched socks—I'll be all over that."

"Then I'll be sure to keep you far from the laundry room."

"Good idea." She pulled the notebook closer to her and clicked the pen, indicating that it was time for them to get serious. But as she tapped the pen on the paper, creating a random decoration of dots, she slid a glance his way. "I wasn't expecting Derek to ask me to read *both* stories. I didn't mean to invade on your bedtime routine."

He could admit—to himself, at least—that he'd had a twinge of jealousy, but it had passed quickly. His thoughts about how sweet she'd appeared next to his son—he didn't need to think about those.

"Can't blame him. He was just excited to have someone other than boring old Dad to read to him. Some stories probably sound better coming from a female narrator." He paused before adding, "Particularly the princess ones."

Earning the exact sour expression he'd been expecting from her, he grinned. She probably dealt with a lot of gender issues in her work, but he couldn't help suspecting there might be more to it.

"Since I would know so much about princesses, of course." She lowered the pen and used both hands to crown herself with an imaginary tiara. "Particularly ones with task-force experience and active-shooter training."

"There definitely should be more kick-ass heroines in fairy tales."

She shot a glance his way, her eyes narrowed, as though checking to see if he was joking. He must have convinced her as she returned her attention to the notebook, where she doodled tiny circles that became entwined in ink tornadoes.

"Thanks for helping with Derek's bath, if I didn't tell you that earlier. And for helping to clean up the kitchen."

"You didn't let me do much." She shook her head. "At first, I thought you were asking me to bathe Derek, not just monitor the splashing from a seat on the bathroom throne."

"Why would I expect you to do that? Because you're a woman?"

"A few of my fellow special agents might have said that. Some people think those mothering instincts are bred into us." She appeared to consider the premise for a moment. "I'm not sure I believe that."

"I don't."

Micah swallowed as Deirdre's curious gaze told him he should have moderated himself better or said nothing at all. He sat still, not ready to give more away. But she kept watching him until he either had to explain himself or run out of the room.

"I just believe that caring for a child isn't about gender," he said. "It's about determination, character and heart."

She nodded. At least she'd accepted that explanation. If she hadn't, he would have struggled to come up with a better one without telling her the real reason he believed as he did.

Deirdre pointed to the list again. "We'd better get

started on this or we'll have nothing to say when the sheriff checks in on us."

"You think he'll be checking in?"

"Why wouldn't he?"

"With a competent investigator handling the situation for a few days?" He held his hands wide. "He'll probably take a quick vacation to Cheyenne or Denver."

At her shocked look, he grinned.

"Seriously, he'll probably try to catch up on his backlog of other duties. Like ordering ammunition and office supplies, overseeing receipts for patrol car maintenance, and checking to see if all the *i*'s are dotted and *t*'s crossed on police reports to be sent to the county prosecutor."

"Wow, his job sounds as glamorous as mine does."

"You mean that FBI work isn't all showing up with search warrants in your blue jackets and taking in bad guys?"

"Hardly," she said with a chuckle. "Most of the job is meticulously following the evidence and documenting everything so that we get a conviction when the case goes to trial."

She pointed to the notebook, but when she glanced down at the page, now covered with doodled tornadoes, 3-D cubes and stars, she flipped to another sheet of paper. "I still need your list of enemies, if we're ever going to get to *my* case."

"That's just the thing. I don't have any."

Deirdre started tapping the pen again, her jaw tight. "There has to be someone who doesn't like you. Someone who didn't get as good a deal as you did on a seed delivery. Or resented that you were late getting your cattle to market."

"Really, there's not a lot. That's part of what's been

so frustrating during the investigation from the sheriff's office." He took a drink of his beer and shook his head as he swallowed. "In fact, a lot of people around here appreciate me for setting up the petting zoo."

She squinted at him as if he'd suddenly grown two heads.

"You mean that sign was real? You really have a *petting zoo*?"

"Of course it's real. Why would I have a sign if there wasn't one?"

She shifted her shoulders. "It just didn't seem, you know, possible. Out here in the middle of nowhere."

"First of all, we're here, so it's *somewhere*." He tried to keep the annoyance from his voice but didn't quite succeed. "And, yes, this is a rural area. That's the point. I built the petting zoo so the area children, including my own, would have a place to enjoy nearby. Admission is also free, so it's pretty popular."

"Forget appreciating you. I bet you're a local hero for that." She appeared to consider it further and then tilted her head. "But don't children who live on ranches already have a lot of exposure to animals?"

"Not everyone around here lives on a ranch. Those who do are around a lot of livestock but not *these* animals. You'll see tomorrow when you help me clean cages and pens."

She immediately shook her head. "But I'm not—"

He held up an index finger to interrupt her.

"*Everyone* works on a ranch," they said together, one with a grin, the other frowning.

What surprised him most was that she'd agreed to go along with his plan. Even if the sheriff had blackmailed her into helping with his case, Micah couldn't force her to help out with his ranch chores.

Deirdre puffed up her cheeks and blew out a breath. "When I finally get the information I need around here, I will have earned it."

"You never know. You might end up liking the ranch and even southeast Wyoming far more than you think. All that sky. And those amazing mountain ranges in the distance."

"All that *wind*. And mucking out stalls."

At that, he laughed. "You might appreciate a breeze when you're doing *that* job."

She pointed to him with her pen. "Names. Please."

When he didn't answer, she added, "You've got to give me something. You must have had the sheriff's office look into a few people. Let's start there. Maybe it will spark some ideas."

"Guess we started with my exes."

"Okay," she said, stretching out the word. "Exes, as in plural?"

He frowned. "There've been *a few*. Mostly before I married Leah." He shot a look at her and then away. "Davis was her maiden name, but I don't think you need to put her on the list. I had to identify—" He stopped himself, shivering at the memory. No one should have to die like that, whether she'd left him or not. "You get it."

Deirdre looked up from where she'd written his late wife's name. "You said you don't have any enemies, but since your late wife can't tell us, we have to look into anyone who might have held a grudge against *her* and wanted to exact revenge on her widower or her child."

"Guess I never thought of it that way."

"Did anyone take a closer look at—" she paused and glanced down at the paper "—Leah?"

"Not yet."

She made one of her fancy stars next to his late wife's name. "When did you get married?"

"Three and a half years ago." He hated that he was tempted to tell her that the marriage had been rocky from the moment the justice of the peace's signature dried on the marriage license. She'd announced that she was pregnant within weeks. No one needed to know any of that.

Deirdre looked up at him, her pen poised in her hand, her lips slightly slack. "But you said she passed away…"

Her words trailed off as she seemed to be calculating the dates again.

"Two years ago," he filled in for her. "Everything happened pretty quickly for us. Marriage, baby, then the accident."

"Such a short time. I'm sorry."

"Barely had time to finish the house." He didn't know why he'd said it, but he regretted it even more as she lifted a brow.

"Where was she from originally?"

"Cheyenne, but I met her in Laramie when I went to get supplies."

She jotted another note in her book. "Okay, who else can we look at? Other exes? Was anyone particularly upset when you dumped her?"

"I rarely broke up with anyone. Usually, I was the dumpee."

Again, she watched him with unmasked curiosity, and this time he straightened in his seat. He had to be careful what he told her. She interviewed crime suspects for a living.

Finally, she returned her attention to her list. "But there were a few, right?"

He shrugged. "There was Lila Nichols. I only dated her for a month or two in my early twenties. Though the ranchers weren't ready to accept me as a local even after I'd bought land and started adding cattle, their daughters weren't as reluctant."

She bent her head lower, but he caught her rolling her eyes.

"Why did you break it off? Did you have a line of successors waiting in the wings?"

"No." He waited until she looked up again to answer. "I had to back away from her because she reminded me too much of my stepmother."

"Oh."

Deirdre had deserved a little pushback for asking that nasty question, but he regretted answering that way if it made her so uncomfortable. He already had a few questions about her, and now he wanted to know about the creep who'd hurt her. What he couldn't figure out was why anything about her mattered to him.

"She slashed my tires right after that."

"That's something. Maybe she was a little like Maeve." She placed a star next to the woman's name. "Do you have any idea where I could find Lila now?"

"Right in Laramie. She's Lila Westerfield now. But she prefers people to call her Mrs. *Gary* Westerfield."

She started to write and then looked up again, her lips lifting. "You don't mean Gary of *Gary's*, do you?"

"That's the one."

"Then why did you take me to that store?" she asked. "Does she work there? Is it awkward seeing her there?"

At that, he couldn't help but to laugh. "She does stop in to see her husband, and I've seen her there, but she ignores me. Figures she got the better end of the bargain, I guess."

"So not much of an enemy." She scribbled out the star next to the woman's name. "Did you break things off with anyone else?"

"One. Kara Sullivan. The first woman I went out with after Leah's death. She was pushing for marriage from the second date, but she never seemed to want Derek around when we were together. Then, when I broke it off, she told me she hoped my son would choke and die."

Deirdre planted her hands on her hips, her mouth gaping open. "You're kidding."

"Nope. It definitely put me off dating for a while."

"Where is Kara now?" After putting a star next to the woman's name, Deirdre lifted both shoulders close to her ears and winced. "Let me guess. She's married to Sheriff Guetta now."

"She's a little young for him, but she married his deputy Jerry Jackson." At her shocked expression, he added, "It's a small town."

"And I suppose that the two of you are best friends now."

He shook his head. "She pretty much still hates me. But she's probably too busy with her new baby and a couple of stepkids from Jerry's first marriage to have time to sabotage my ranch. Besides, she likes to bring her crew to the petting zoo."

Shaking her head, Deirdre put a question mark next

to the star by Kara's name. "We're back to square one. Isn't there anyone who despises you enough to make you want to leave Harmony Fields?"

"Clearly, there is, but I don't know who it could be. Now do you see why the sheriff's office has had such a tough time with all the incidents?"

Deirdre didn't answer, frowning down at the list instead. "What about when you bought the land? Did you outbid anyone?"

"No. The man who used to own the small plot of land I bought first lost it to foreclosure. But he died ten years ago. All the other adjacent pieces I purchased at a fair price from neighbors, who were happy to sell so they could retire to Florida or Arizona."

She stared at the list again and shook her head. "Other than a quick check on your late wife, we've got nothing."

"Here, let me take a look at it." He held out his hand until she passed the list over to him. "I'm really reaching here, but I'll give you a few more."

He jotted down some names, each sounding more far-fetched than the last. The businessman in Laramie who freaked out over the scratch on his pristine new SUV from Micah's pickup door. The lady at the property tax office who swore Micah hadn't paid last year's tax bill though he could produce both the receipt and the canceled check. They were little things and hardly worth the effort of sabotaging his ranch or threatening his family.

Only a single possible suspect stood out as one who might want something from him—more money—and had no scruples about taking whatever she wanted. The evil stepmother. But for some reason, he couldn't bring himself to write down the names Ariel Porter Perry or Maeve O'Leary. Inscribing either name in ink would make that threat real, and he still wanted to believe that his ridiculous suspicion was just that.

As he pushed the list back to Deirdre, his stomach knotted with the truth that his stepmother had killed before. If she believed she'd found another way to line her pockets and he stood in her way, she wouldn't hesitate to kill again.

"You can't think of anyone else?" Deirdre asked.

He shook his head.

She studied him with a narrowed gaze, as if she didn't believe him.

"You're sure?"

He pushed back his shoulders and met her gaze, forcing himself not to look away.

"No one," he somehow managed, his mouth so dry that he craved another beer.

"Then I guess we'll have to go with this. I'll stop in the sheriff's office tomorrow and get a copy of all the reports to date. Investigators must have missed something."

He swallowed, hoping she didn't notice. She had to be right that they'd overlooked some details. He could only hope that the information he'd held back wasn't the critical missing piece to the puzzle. And that he wasn't risking his own child's life in fear of fully reopening the Pandora's box that was his past.

Chapter 7

Deirdre could barely sit still on the leather sofa, even if it was so soft that if she dozed off on it, she would probably sleep until the next afternoon. She snuggled closer to one of the couch's rolled arms as a precaution. No way she could risk being distracted if Micah took a seat there instead of the matching armchair when he returned with the coffee. Not when he finally might be ready to give her details about Maeve O'Leary. And she didn't want to kid herself about the reality that *he* was a supreme distraction.

In the kitchen, Micah continued to arrange items on a wooden tray with handles. His coffee machine must have been the slowest one ever invented. Since she should already have been given an award for her patience in waiting for the interview for *her* case, this delay pushed her to the edge. If he returned with the announcement that he wouldn't share any information until the police had captured the sabotage suspect, she couldn't be held accountable for how she would use the self-defense skills she'd acquired at Quantico to persuade him.

She leaned forward over the quartz-topped coffee table to take another look at her notebook. Only a few stars stood out next to the names on Micah's suspect list, and those were the dim kind of stars that barely peeked out of galaxies billions of miles away. How could the guy have no enemies? But unlike her dad, who had so many political foes that the family home in Virginia and his apartment in DC both required extra security, Micah said his neighbors generally liked him. Strange how she was inclined to believe him.

With a dearth of leads like this, the local investigation would progress even slower than her team's search for Humphrey Kelly. And if Micah insisted on using her progress on the case here as a benchmark on his trade for information, she might never get the chance to go home.

"Cream? Sugar?" he called from the open refrigerator.

"Black." Not that she usually took her coffee that way, but she wanted to appear all-business now. She needed information and was tired of waiting.

He carried the tray, holding two steaming mugs, a porcelain bowl of sugar cubes, a cream pitcher and napkins, into the great room only a moment later and set it on the coffee table.

"Really? I like mine so sweet that it makes my teeth ache," he said, continuing their conversation.

Justifying her earlier worry, he sat on the other end

of the sofa. He lifted both mugs, setting one closer to her and one in front of him.

"Thanks."

She pulled the mug to her, warming her suddenly freezing hands. What if he was right? What if he had no information that would help her locate Maeve? Could the best lead she'd been able to locate, the one good idea for which she could claim credit, end up another dud? How could she go back to the team empty-handed? Worse, how could she return to the DC field office with nothing to prove her value?

Micah added a sizable dollop of cream to his coffee and used mini tongs to add four sugar cubes.

"Now you're making *my* teeth hurt."

He chuckled as he stirred. "And you're making me cold. I don't even have the air-conditioning on. If you're uncomfortable, I can start a fire."

Her gaze scaled the protruding rounded stones of the real-wood fireplace and then lowered to the open area at the center, a few logs already positioned on the grate, and her cheeks warmed as though he'd just lit the flame. Nope, a fire wasn't a good idea.

"The temperature's fine," she managed.

She stuck with specifics since she refused to admit how flustered she'd already felt sitting alone with him at his dining table after those sweet, unsettling moments reading bedtime stories with Derek. Though she'd hoped that the great room would give her more space to breathe, they'd only moved closer to the wall of windows with the near-complete darkness outside holding the house in its opaque grasp. If she were doing anything other than interviewing a witness, she would call this a romantic cocoon, but it felt more like a tempting trap.

After resting the mug on the table as he had, she considered for a moment and reached for the cream.

Micah smiled knowingly and stirred his own coffee again before setting the spoon on a napkin. "I suppose you want to talk about Maeve O'Leary."

"How did you guess? I've just been waiting all day for it, so maybe."

She grabbed her notebook and flipped to a clean page, writing Micah's name and the date and time at the top. Then she lifted her pen and waited.

"Do you mind if I ask you a few questions first?" he asked.

"Are you serious?" She couldn't help wondering if this was a delay tactic or a plan never to answer her.

"I've just had to tell you all about my marriage, and now you want me to share about a subject I haven't discussed in fifteen years. One I'd hoped to avoid forever, so—"

"Fine," she said with a huff. He had a point. For her, this was just a search for information to close an investigation, but her questions involved one of the darkest and most heartbreaking points in his life. So if she planned to dig through that fragile graveyard, she needed to use a garden trowel, not a backhoe. "What do you want to know?"

"Why did you become an FBI agent?"

She frowned. This would take a lot longer than she'd planned. "Why does anyone become one? To protect the American people and uphold the Constitution."

"Did you read that off a brochure? I don't want to hear the company line. I want to know why *you* did it."

Her jaw tightened. She might have been tempted to pin the guy to the floor earlier, but now she had a whole different motive for doing it. One that would put her in the back of Sheriff Guetta's patrol car. But she needed information, and he had it, so she shared the abbreviated version.

"It's pretty simple. I didn't love practicing law as much as I thought I would, I was at a point in my life where I was ready for a big change, and I wanted to help people. So after more than two years of background checks, physical testing and training, I earned my badge."

She tilted her head and studied him. "Now, is that enough?"

"One more thing. If you want me to tell you everything I know, I think you should tell me more about this investigation first."

She sighed and returned the notebook and pen to the table. Of course he would want to know more than the abbreviated version she'd offered the sheriff earlier.

"I'm not supposed to give away details on an active investigation. I can get in trouble—"

"More trouble than you'd already be in just for coming here to question me?"

Deirdre shrugged. That heaviness she'd felt with each questionable decision she'd made that day pushed her shoulders forward. She reached for her mug and took a long sip before returning it to the table.

"Guess if I'm already going to hell, I might as well take the freeway."

He squinted and shook his head. "What do you mean?"

"I'm going to tell you."

He offered the kind of toothy grin that probably had women from all over southeast Wyoming sashaying to the gate of his ranch. "Should I get popcorn?"

Whether or not she was tempted to swish a bit herself, she glared at him until he tucked his grin away. He gestured with a swipe of his hand for her to begin.

"Like I said earlier, my cousin Sean Colton asked me to join a team he formed to investigate the January disappearance of Humphrey Kelly. His sister, Eva, a rookie cop, and his twin brothers, Cormac, a PI, and Liam, an NYPD informant, are also on the team. He even invited my half brother, Aidan, who's a US marshal."

"So, you and your *half* brother agreed to this plan to help out a group of *second* cousins?"

"We did it because we believe in justice." Deirdre frowned, his question rankling her as much as him picking up on her label for Aidan. Why she'd included Aidan in her comment about police work, she wasn't sure. She had no idea what her only sibling believed.

"At first, the team just kept me in the loop in the event that they would need me, but then the cases became more and more interesting. Last month, Eva called to ask me to take an assignment in the investigation."

She considered for a moment and then added, "And, yes, I was available since I'd already started my *vacation* and had the extra time."

Micah held both hands up in a sign of innocence. "I wasn't going to ask."

"You might want to remember that I'm trained to tell when people are lying."

"I'll keep that in mind." He stared into the beige liquid in the mug he held and then looked up. "You said *cases.* And more interesting how? Were they able to track down Kelly?"

She shook her head. "But they figured out that he may have engineered his own disappearance."

He set his coffee aside. "Okay, I'm intrigued."

Deirdre turned toward him on the sofa, warming up to telling the story. "Then, alongside Kelly's DNA evidence, found at his last known location—a supply closet in a Manhattan criminal courthouse—they discovered someone else's DNA. It created a strange connection between his disappearance and what should have been an unrelated murder investigation."

"Really? This is good."

"It gets even more interesting," she said. "The murder investigation just happened to have been Sean's case. One he had to pass off to another detective so he could look into Kelly's disappearance."

"That seems a little coincidental."

Dipping her head, she glanced at him from beneath her lashes. "I don't believe in coincidences."

"Me, neither."

His stark expression told her he no longer spoke about her investigation, but he blinked several times, and his smile returned.

"You should have let me get popcorn." He crossed one leg flat over the other, planted his elbow on his knee and positioned his chin in the L of his hand. "You can't make this stuff up."

"I could, but this truth is better than fiction. The DNA turned out to have come from a female relative of Wes Westmore, a New York suspect charged with the strangling death of his girlfriend."

He pursed his lips and closed one eye. When he opened it, he shook his head. "I don't get that connection. Other than maybe it had something to do with the Kelly case. Like that someone didn't want your cousin to be assigned to it."

She nodded, impressed that he'd not only followed along but also had remembered the names of those involved in the complicated web.

"You're good at this. Should I be concerned that you'll take *my* job?" Her throat tightened that she'd just joked about her position, which couldn't have been less stable these days.

He waved away that suggestion with a brush of his hand. "Just a cowboy playing some criminal armchair quarterback in the NFL off-season."

"Well, you had the right idea. We weren't sure what the connection was, either, until a psychiatric evaluation suddenly materialized in Westmore's case file, signed by Kelly and dated the day before he vanished. In the document, both digital and in the physical file, Kelly declared the defendant 'incapable of committing murder.'"

"Incapable?" Micah scoffed. "How can he say that? Depending on the level of desperation, *anyone* is capable of taking a life."

Though there were several legal definitions and a whole spectrum of motives in play with what he'd said, she nodded, agreeing with him on that basic truth. As fiercely as he appeared to love his son, she had no doubt that Micah would do whatever was necessary to shield him. No matter what it cost him.

"We believe the document was fabricated. Or at least heavily suggested. *Someone* got her hooks into Kelly to get him to write that evaluation to help in Westmore's defense."

"Westmore's female relative?"

"Yeah. The *relative*. She likely also paid another individual to sneak the document into the file." She cleared her throat, realizing she was the one stalling now.

Pushing her shoulders back, she took a deep breath and continued. "DNA analysis on the sample taken from the courthouse connected it to Westmore's mother, a widow who vanished off the face of the earth about twenty years ago."

She paused and then added the rest. "After Westmore's father died under suspicious circumstances."

Deirdre watched him, waiting for him to assemble the parts of her story. When he did, his eyes widened, and his mouth fell open.

Still, she laid it out for him. "Westmore's mother is—"

"Maeve O'Leary," he finished for her. "The black widow."

Their gazes connected, and then he looked away, leaning forward and lacing his fingers at the back of his head. After a silence that stretched so long that Deirdre could feel her heart thudding in her chest, Micah lowered his arms and looked up again.

"That's how you came to me," he said.

He slid a guarded look her way, appearing as distrustful as he had when Deirdre arrived at the ranch hours before. That she wished she could rewind their conversation to where her story had yet to involve him bothered her more than she wanted to admit.

"In a roundabout way, yes," she said. "That's how I located you."

She expected him to ask more questions, but he only watched her, waiting. When she couldn't bear the intensity of those gray eyes any longer, she began.

"I was supposed to find out anything I could about Maeve. Already, we suspected that she'd murdered Joseph Westmore, a man with a known allergy to shrimp who had an 'accidental' exposure."

Micah rolled his eyes. "Something the police at the time failed to investigate, right?"

Deirdre nodded. "Anyway, the team had also begun to suspect that she might be a black widow, so we were trying to figure out if she had other aliases and also track her down. We figured that once she no longer needed Kelly, she would kill him, too."

"What did you do to find out about her?"

"That was the hard part. We started with no photos of her, and Westmore refused to provide any. But in February, one of Kelly's former patients reported a sighting of him in Morningside Heights. He was with a woman, and both of them were in disguise. The team had the witness view footage of Westmore's female jail visitors. He was able to ID the woman as the same one he'd seen with Kelly, based on her huge eyes, even though she'd worn vivid green contacts instead of brown."

"Someone saw Maeve in New York?"

Deirdre blinked, surprised that Micah had pulled that one detail from all that she'd said. She pretended not to notice the strain in his voice, but from his worried look, she would have sworn that Micah, instead of the witness, had seen that ghost from his past.

"Her eyes were brown when I knew her." He took another sip of his coffee and stared at the grate as though he'd lit a fire after all.

Mentally recording the detail about her eye color to put in her notes later, she continued her story. "Beyond that ID, the team hit a lot of dead ends in locating her. Even an NYPD tech expert came up empty. According to the internet, Maeve O'Leary, or even Maeve *Westmore*, no longer exists."

"But you were able to find out some things about her. How did you do it?"

He appeared to have returned from wherever he'd traveled in his thoughts, and now he shifted his legs to face her and folded his hands between his knees.

"We went to the dark web."

"We?"

"The tech expert from the DC field office helped me—secretly and off-hours—using his advanced dark web know-how and some facial-recognition software," she said. "We were surprised when the biometric tool matched the photo from the jail with an older, blurry picture of a woman named Ariel Porter Perry. But we finally had an alias and were able to connect that name to a death certificate for Len Perry."

Why did she have to keep referring to the man in such sanitized terms? She was talking about Micah's *father*, someone he'd lost when he was barely old enough to vote and still too young to buy a beer. Couldn't she at least call him his dad?

"And through a search for him, you found me."

Deirdre blinked, Micah's words sounding as if he'd read her mind, but then she retraced her own comment. "Yes, we found you. We also figured that since your father's death was fifteen years ago, there might be several more dead husbands."

She braced herself for questions she couldn't answer. Already, she'd told him too much about the investigation. Far more than she ever should have shared with a crime victim. Now that he knew the truth, that she'd only stumbled upon his father's cold case while hunting for a suspect in a different investigation, he would be less inclined to help her. No one had looked into Len Perry's murder case in a decade, and even now, she wasn't focused on justice for him. Even if those answers might be a byproduct of her case, it seemed woefully inadequate.

"So Maeve's still on the run." Micah shook his head. "It still doesn't seem right calling her that."

As Deirdre reclaimed her pen, Micah tilted his head, watching her.

"Ever notice that you call her by her first name and all the other suspects by their last? Is that because she's female?"

"I don't think so," she said, shifting uncomfortably. "It's more because she's a black widow. Spiders get first names. Like Charlotte in *Charlotte's Web*."

She pulled her notebook into her lap and pointed to the page with her pen. "You can refer to her as Ariel, since that's how you knew her."

The humor vanished from his gaze.

"I *never* knew her. Neither did my dad. Her name is *Maeve*."

As Micah cradled his coffee cup and stared into the liquid that was cold now, something tightened in Deirdre's chest. She'd interviewed witnesses with sad stories before. She'd even had those moments when human emotion sneaked up to fill her throat, forcing her to stall while conducting an interview. But now she was tempted to tell him it was okay not to share his story. She couldn't do that. The team relied on her to gather this information—she was counting on herself, too—and she couldn't become soft. She had a serial killer to stop.

"Just tell me anything you can," she said instead, assuring herself again that this was the right thing to do. "Places she liked to go. Where she might feel comfortable hiding. Any detail, no matter how small, might lead us to her whereabouts."

"I don't remember any places, but I'll tell you what I can." He took a visible breath and let it out slowly. "I guess I wasn't shocked when my dad brought her home. He'd been lonely since Mom died from cancer three years before that. I knew there would eventually be someone. I just wasn't expecting *this* woman. Blonde. Tall. Slender. Beautiful—and *young*."

Lowering his head, he tightened his jaw as if gritting his teeth.

"I was a seventeen-year-old boy. Believe me, *I* noticed. She was just ten years older than I was."

She nodded, her eyes burning at the thought of his shame over his teenage hormones. "She did appear attractive, even in the few photos we have of her. As I said, Westmore refused to give us any."

"Sorry. I don't have any pictures of her," he said before she could ask. "It wasn't a period I wanted to remember."

Disappointment settled in her gut. Maybe Micah was right that he wouldn't have any information that would be helpful to the team.

"Though I found her attractive, I remember that I immediately didn't like her. It was as if she met Dad at a bar and instantly showed up with her suitcases."

"Was she mean to you?" she asked, to keep the conversation going.

"Just the opposite. She was syrupy sweet. And somehow cold at the same time. Sugar and ice. She and Dad were so different, too. He was a quiet, successful businessman, while she was—I don't know—loud and always needing to be the center of attention.

"I tried to tell him that something didn't seem right about her, but he wouldn't listen. She seemed to have him under a spell."

"How long before he married her?" she asked.

"Just two weeks after he first brought her home to meet me, they eloped. No prenup. Nothing. I wasn't even invited to the wedding. Wouldn't want to ruin Ariel's perfect getaway by having a stepson there."

"Did you at least get along after they were married?" she asked to return him to his story. The question had no bearing on the case, but she just had to know. Had to understand how he'd survived that time. She'd believed that nothing could have been worse than growing up with her parents in what had amounted to a mausoleum, but now she knew better.

"We got along as well as you could with anyone who thought you were in the way. Just a fly at her picnic. And my father always took her side. I just needed to be more understanding. More welcoming."

"That had to be hard," she said before she could stop herself.

"It was what it was," he said with a shrug. "She, on the other hand, seemed to be having the time of her life with daily shopping sprees for designer clothes, jewelry and fancy scents. Things that only benefited her. Never Dad or me. Or our apartment on the Upper East Side."

"Your dad didn't see what she was doing?"

He shook his head. "Not even during the meetings with the attorney. To make sure she and I would be cared for, *just in case*."

"He was probably just so happy that he blocked out every hint that didn't fit with his perfect picture." She wasn't sure why she felt the need to defend a man who'd failed to put his child first, just like her father had. Both men were responsible for the choices they'd made while chasing after women.

"Maybe." Micah picked at his nails as he considered her words. "He was still in an infatuation bubble. A twentysomething who told him he was sexy despite the mid-forties dad body. As an adult, I recognize how intoxicating that had to be."

The situation Micah described matched with the cases she'd been studying of other black widow murderers. Beautiful. Fawning. Deadly. But she didn't mention that truth. He seemed to need to share more of his story, and after asking him to unlock his past, the least she could do was listen to the whole thing, no matter how uncomfortable it made her.

"Dad kept telling me that his new wife wanted to make a home for us. He used the example of how much work she was putting into my eighteenth birthday party. If she didn't like me, why would she go to so much trouble? I wanted to believe it, too, and what teenager isn't excited to turn eighteen? To be a real adult."

He took on a faraway look, staring past her to the wall of windows. Deirdre hated realizing that she'd stirred up the images he saw on that inky backdrop. Suddenly, her search for information didn't seem so important. Micah had moved clear across the country to escape the past and start a new life, and she'd followed him there to drop it all back in his lap.

"You don't have to—" She stopped herself. As much as she wanted to, she couldn't let him off the hook. She needed answers, and she owed it to him to gather information that might help bring his father's murderer to justice.

Micah didn't seem to hear her, anyway. He continued to stare, remembering.

"The party was nice," he said. "Intimate. Just *family* and a few friends. But nice."

Her heart squeezed, and her nose burned. She blinked away the emotions rolling inside her before she shed embarrassing tears right there on his sofa.

"At least you had that," she managed.

"Then, a week after my birthday, Dad suffered a massive heart attack, and he was gone."

His words struck her so much like a punch to the gut that her shoulders curled forward. Again, he didn't notice. He focused on his hands, gripped so hard in front of him that his fingertips had turned red.

"I told the police that she'd poisoned him. That it could have been from one of those flowers and plants she grew in her plot on the building's roof or the balcony. Oleander. Foxglove. Lily of the valley. Or maybe it was one of those teas she brewed for him at night. *Something.* I knew it in my gut. But the coroner looked at Dad's heart disease history and had no trouble ruling his death as a myocardial infarction. Natural causes."

"You're probably right about the poison." She didn't

know how to tell him that there was a possibility that even if his father's body was exhumed now, after all this time, testing might not show evidence of poisoning.

"What happened...after?" she asked when he didn't say more.

"We met with the attorney two days after the funeral, and he presented me with the copy of the will. Dad had left everything to her. The house. His stocks. *Everything*."

"Didn't the attorney recommend that you fight it?"

"He did. Then my stepmother assured him everything would be okay, and she had every intention of taking care of 'my love's son.' But by the time I made it home from my first day back at school, the house was empty, sold to a real estate conglomerate for cash, the bank accounts had been drained and she was gone."

"How could she do something like that?" She grimaced over her own words. People did heinous things all the time. But somehow it was worse knowing that it had happened to Micah.

"Without a look back," he grumbled. "I had nothing except two boxes of clothes and stuff from my bedroom. She left them for me out front. Guess I was lucky to get even that."

"The bitch," she breathed and then shot a look his way, a shiver scaling her spine. What was she doing?

He didn't move, as if he hadn't heard her. Releasing her breath in a slow stream, she forced herself to record some of the details he'd given her. If she were truly investigating Len Perry's death, she would have planned to speak to the coroner, local law enforcement and the attorney who'd let them walk out of the office that day. But no one could ever make this right for Len Perry's son.

When Micah pounded the side of his fist on the coffee tabletop, causing the dishes to rattle on the tray, Deirdre jerked to lift her head.

"Six months," he said, more to himself than her.

"What do you mean?"

Micah glanced over, surprised. "Sorry." He rubbed his hand. "It's just that he'd known her for less than six months, and she killed him."

"I'm so sorry for your loss." She eased to the center cushion, no longer able to hug the couch's arm.

Seeming not to notice her movement, he nodded in the frozen way of survivors trying to bear all those offers of condolence at a funeral.

"And I didn't do a damned thing to save my *dad*."

As Micah's voice broke on the last word, something fractured inside Deirdre as well. Without stopping to consider whether she would be crossing a line of professional distance that already had so many breaks that it should have been a message in Morse code, she reached over and rested her hand on top of his. She froze, her pulse pounding, her throat scratchy. The right move would be to pull away, but the message refused to filter from her brain to her hand. She didn't even want it to.

For several breaths, Micah sat staring at their hands as well. Then, when she would have finally pulled away, he rotated his wrist and laced their fingers. His wasn't a sweet and tender touch but a squeeze that, while it wasn't painful, hinted at some of the pain he'd probably buried for years.

"We won't let her get away with it," she said.

Micah released her and, gathering the coffee mugs on the tray, escaped to the kitchen. She closed the notebook and turned to watch him pour out the warm cream, put away the sugar bowl and load items into the dishwasher.

He didn't believe her, and she couldn't blame him. The law enforcement officers after his father's death hadn't given him confidence that anyone cared about justice for him or his father. Micah's experience offered insight into his fierce determination to protect *his* son.

Well, he might not know this about her yet, but she kept her commitments, even when others didn't. She'd pledged to help him figure out who was sabotaging his ranch and endangering him and Derek, and she'd assured him she would get justice for his dad. If it was in her power at all, she intended to keep both promises.

Chapter 8

As Micah finished filling the pygmy goats' trough and shut off the water the next afternoon, the melodic sound of Derek's laughter drifted from the outside of the enclosure. He couldn't help but grin as he opened the gate and closed it securely behind him. Around the building, past the visitors' entrance, Deirdre knelt next to his son by a section of the wood-framed hog-wire fencing that offered more secure viewing for timid petting zoo visitors.

Deirdre looked the part of a regular ranch hand now, if someone who made even work jeans, a dusty Henley and muck-baptized rubber boots look sexy could still be called *regular.* She must have left her hat somewhere again, as her twin blond braids bobbed every time she turned her head.

"Booger!"

Playing tour guide, Derek pointed to the brown-and-white-spotted goat that had pressed its snout through one of the six-inch squares right next to them.

"Are you sure his name is Booger?" Deirdre gave the child a skeptical look, not noticing that they had an audience in the barn doorway. "That doesn't sound like a nice name for a respectable goat."

The toddler nodded his head. "Booger."

"I hope he isn't offended that someone picked out a name like that for him."

"'Fended," Derek repeated with a nod.

Micah couldn't help grinning at their serious conversation. Though Deirdre said she knew nothing about kids, she was great with his son, talking to him as if he were a small adult instead of a toddler. If only she could be as comfortable with him as she was with Derek and even the goat that nibbled her fingers when she rubbed its snout.

She laughed, something she hadn't done since they'd had that intense conversation the evening before, and she'd reached out to take his hand. Her relaxed expression was a welcome change as well.She'd been cautious around him all day. How they'd managed to complete their share of chores and examine locations of prior damage around the ranch while she'd maintained a social distance and treated him like a contagious co-worker, he wasn't sure.

On the other hand, he couldn't blame her for dancing cautiously around him after he couldn't accept her gesture of kindness without clinging to her like a lifeline or something. If anyone should have been embarrassed after that conversation, it should have been him. He'd shared more than she'd needed to know for her investigation.

Strangely, he wasn't sorry. As if someone had lifted an anvil off his neck, he could finally breathe. And whether or not she was actively working on his dad's murder case, with everything else going on around the ranch, he appreciated her for giving him that moment of lightness.

"If he is offended, we can just give him some extra snacks," Micah called out. "He'll forgive us."

Deirdre startled and turned her head toward the sound at the barn door. The goat chose that moment to push its head all the way through the fencing to nibble her braid. She squealed but laughed again as she stood. After swiping at the damp ends of her hair, she secured the band the animal had managed not to eat.

"His favorite snacks are watermelons or pumpkins, but hair will do in a pinch." He grinned as he approached her and his son. "But I wouldn't give him too much of that. It's not good for his diet."

"Thanks for telling me." She brushed her fingers over the bottom of her braid again. "We indentured servants need all the information we can get."

"Sure a lot of whining for someone who's serving her indenture by playing with animals in a petting zoo."

"It's a tough job, but somebody has to do it."

While Derek ran back and forth, pausing to pet any of the pygmies that poked their snouts out to greet him, Deirdre reached over the top of the fence to rub the same goat's head. When Micah realized that in that moment he would have happily traded places with that lucky animal, he turned to his task list mounted on the wall and checked off the last few items. He had to be careful around this agent or he would do or say something else that would send her rushing off to her bed-room the way she had the night before.

After he'd finished checking off items and had re-claimed his good sense, he crossed to the fence and stood next to her.

"His name is Booker, not Booger, by the way. As in Booker T. Washington."

She turned to him, surprised. "An *educated* goat that just happens to snack on hair?"

He nodded. "Has my son introduced you to any of the others?"

"Not yet."

He pointed to the black adult female, attempting to get her teeth on the bill of Derek's cap through the fencing. "She's Jane Austen. The brown one with the white dot on top of his head is Alexander Hamilton. The doe eating from the hay bale—" he paused to point to a goat with tan, white and black markings "—that's Harriet Tubman."

"What about the really pregnant one in the corner? I like her spots."

"She's Anne Frank, of course."

Her hands on the wood railing atop the fence, she glanced over at him. "Your petting zoo provides his-tory lessons as well?"

He shook his head. "Not really. They all just have special names. When kids want to know about them, I say they can ask their parents to help them look up those names on the Internet. Learning is just a bonus."

"I thought people didn't name farm animals."

"That's because those go to market. I don't name any of the cattle." He gestured to the goats on the other side of the fence. "But these guys are pets."

"You were right that these animals wouldn't be ones that children regularly saw on the farm. Pygmy goats and miniature alpacas. Now, those look like real-life stuffed animals."

"They're not like cuddly stuffed animals, though. A few of them don't even enjoy being touched that much. And they live in a *petting* zoo."

"Must not have understood the assignment," she said with a chuckle.

"Guess not. And I might not have made the best selection for the zoo when I chose them. But they're here." He shrugged and then tilted his head, studying her. "Have you been over to see the mini lops?"

"I've been putting that one off."

"I get that. But I need to clean out the bunny hutch and enclosure before lunch, so I can take you there now." He turned back to Derek. "Let's go see the lops."

"Lops. Lops. Lops," Derek chanted as his father put him on his back and marched over to the enclosure.

Deirdre trailed behind them, clearly reluctant to visit this spot. As they approached, the tiny tan, brown and black domestic-breed rabbits with long, lopped ears skittered on both sides of the divided hutch and the equally segregated covered play yard.

"They're so adorable." She bent at the waist and peered into the fencing on top of the yard.

"Now these are the real stuffed animals," Micah told her.

After lowering his son to the ground, he unlocked a gate on the does' side of the play yard, pulled out a wiggling tan bunny and locked it again. He let the animal settle in his arms and then lifted his elbows, offering her to Deirdre. "This is Amelia Earhart. Get it? *Ear*hart."

"I get it, but I don't—" She stopped and took a step back.

"Come on. You can't be afraid of a floppy little bunny. You're a tough, highly skilled FBI special agent."

She pushed back her shoulders, as though she'd just remembered that, but finally, she accepted the animal into her arms.

"She's so soft."

When, after she'd petted the rabbit for several seconds she buried her face in the animal's fur, he couldn't help but smile. There were so many things to like about Deirdre Colton. Too many for his own good.

"Mini lops are one of the cuddliest breeds. They love to be held and brushed. Good thing, since they aren't low-maintenance pets like the goats."

Derek scooted closer to her and tugged on her pant leg. "Dee-Dee, I see Milla?"

"Of course you can see her. Do you like bunnies?"

He nodded enthusiastically. She asked him to sit crisscross on the ground and then lowered the rabbit into his arms. For several seconds, she watched him, a small smile playing on her lips, and then she stepped closer to the hutch that Micah had fashioned like a pair of side-by-side bunny hotels. She peeked into the screened windows and then rounded the perimeter of the play yard, examining it.

"This enclosure looks perfect. I don't see any damage at all."

"Can't you smell it?"

She wrinkled her nose. "Well, now that you mention it…" She shrugged.

"I don't mean the farm smells. Those are expected here. I mean the fresh wood."

With a dubious look, Deirdre inhaled. "Yeah, I smell it."

"The whole structure had to be rebuilt after someone destroyed it. This is a replica of my first hotel."

"Where you lost—" She stopped and stared at the bunnies playing in the yard.

Her melancholy touched him. He'd been pretty upset about those as well, but, like when it happened, he tried not to dwell on it.

"We added a few new friends recently. Abraham Lincoln and Mary Todd Lincoln." He pointed to a pair of bunnies in the corner of the yard.

Her sadness sliding away, she grinned, and the disconcerting thought struck him that he would do almost anything to keep her smiling like that.

"If you're inviting in married couples now, you might want to build a bigger enclosure."

"Not this time. You saw that both of them are on the left side of the enclosure, right? The *does'* side. Does to left and bucks to the right, just like in *Rudolph the Red-Nosed Reindeer.* Anyway, those two turned out to both be *Mrs.* Lincolns. A mistake from the breeder."

"Oops. Not going to change their names?"

"Why would I? They like them."

Micah stepped over to Derek and crouched down to lift the bunny.

The child tightened his hold, causing the animal to squirm in his lap. "I keep Milla."

"Remember, buddy? Gentle." He carefully loosened

the child's arms. "We can't hold her too tight, or it will scare her."

Deirdre crouched next to them as well. "She sure is sweet. You're lucky that she lives right at your petting zoo, and you get to see her every day."

"See her tomorrow?" Derek asked. "Dee-Dee, too?"

She shot Micah a glance and dampened her lips. "Yes, tomorrow."

Neither of them knew how long she would be at Harmony Fields. If she were focusing only on her own case, she already would have been at the airport and maybe all the way back in DC. But as long as they still had questions on the ranch, she might be around a few more days. He should have wanted them to find all those answers right away, so he hated the truth that he hoped the investigation didn't go too quickly.

Micah finally lifted the bunny from his son's arms now that he'd loosened his grip. That served as a reminder to him: it would be a mistake for either of them to hold on too tightly to their guest.

"Right now Amelia needs a chance to go have her lunch and get a drink." He gathered the animal into his arms. "And after we're done cleaning their home, we get to have lunch, too. We're having a picnic."

"A picnic!" Derek clapped his hands, his loss of contact with the bunny forgotten. "Dee-Dee, too?"

"Of course she can come to our picnic."

Deirdre shook her head. "You don't have to go to any extra trouble for me. Really."

He carried the rabbit back to the enclosure and released her back into the play yard on the female side. "No trouble."

She followed him over to it and spoke in a low voice.

"I can just make a sandwich or something. Well, if there's anything in the house to make one with, I mean. Or I can drive into Laramie to get groceries."

After locking the enclosure and checking it again, just to be sure, he held up his hand as a signal for her to stop rambling.

"It's just lunch, Deirdre, okay?"

She opened her mouth as if to argue, her shoulders lifting, but then she lowered them. "Okay."

He sent her a sidelong glance and then winked. "Around here, even indentured servants get lunch."

Chapter 9

Deirdre took the last bite of her sandwich and wiped her mouth on a napkin, able to pause for the first time since she'd sat down to eat. She stretched out her legs on the quilt Micah had insisted they should spread on the grass under the plains cottonwood tree, though two perfectly good picnic tables sat empty nearby.

Across from her, the only one remaining of her two lunch dates lay back on the blanket, his face directed to the trees' leaves and the near-cloudless sky that peeked through it. He appeared to be asleep. The other one, finished with his lunch, chased a ball not twenty feet away, kicking it every time he caught up with it and laughing as though it came as a surprise.

This wasn't a date, she corrected her earlier thought, even if it more closely resembled a date than any of the working lunches she'd nibbled through over the past three years. It couldn't happen, anyway, no matter how tempting the idea and the company. But since Micah's eyes were closed, and he would never know, she couldn't resist watching him a little longer. She couldn't shake the tightness in her chest over that moment between them the night before, but she liked seeing him at ease like this, without the worry that creased his forehead when he spoke of his son's safety or the sadness in his eyes when he shared his father's story.

His relaxed expression was a smile, she noted, her gaze tracing the slope of his jawline to his chin and around to the other ear. The temptation to follow that same line with her fingertips and the risk that he could catch her staring made her avert her gaze. Her cheeks and neck heated as she had to fight to keep from taking another look.

Micah lifted up on his elbows and glanced over at her, but seemed to miss it all.

"Did you get enough to eat?"

She gestured to her empty plastic plate, which had once been covered with a peanut butter and jelly sandwich on white bread, baby carrots, apple slices and a prepackaged snack cake. The classic school lunch for a third grader.

"Yes. Thanks. I was starving."

"Nothing fancy." He reached for her plate and wrapper, tucking them inside the open cooler. "A good day of work outdoors will make you hungry."

"Something did. When did you even have time to pack all that?"

He closed the lid and grinned over at her. "This morning while you were still peeling your eyes open and drinking coffee with a straw."

"It's not my fault you wanted to work before the sun even crept out."

"Welcome to ranch life."

She pointed to the cooler. "Do you often have picnics out here with Derek?"

"Not often enough."

He didn't meet her gaze as he said it, and she couldn't help being pleased to think that he'd made that special lunch because they had a guest. Leaning back on her elbows, she brushed her hands over the cool cotton quilt top with a pattern of brightly colored and interlinking circles.

"What's the story with this blanket? Isn't it too new to be used for picnics?"

Sitting up, he brushed some crumbs off the cloth. "My neighbor said quilts are supposed to be used. She made it as a wedding gift. Called a double wedding ring pattern or something."

"I doubt she meant that you should throw it on the ground." She glanced away, rolling her lips. Clearly, this wasn't meant to be a special outing for her if he'd brought along the quilt meant to represent his wedding vows. Why did she have to keep bringing up subjects that reminded him of his late wife, anyway? She traced the connected circles with her fingertip, wondering if anything on the ranch *didn't* bring back memories of her.

"You're right. She probably didn't mean that. But, hey, it's a picnic, and you've got to have a blanket." Micah turned his head just as Derek barreled toward them, his ball forgotten. "Incoming."

He held out his arms, but just before impact, the

toddler swerved and collapsed on Deirdre's straightened legs instead.

"Now *that* I wasn't expecting." She reached down to brush the little boy's sweaty hair from his forehead as he rested his cheek against her denim-covered knee.

"He likes you."

"I like him, too." Deirdre slid her fingers over those soft strands again. When she glanced up, she caught Micah watching her. Though her mouth went dry, her hands did just the opposite, becoming so damp that she had to brush them off on her jeans. She liked Derek, all right, but she wasn't immune to his father, either, and it scared the hell out of her.

"I like how you talk to him," Micah said after several seconds. "No baby talk nonsense. You have real conversations."

She lifted a brow. "What do you mean? How are people *supposed* to talk to kids?"

"I don't know about supposed to, but they coo at them like they would puppies."

"I don't even know how to *coo*."

"As I said, I like the way you do it."

Their gazes connected, and a butterfly dance party started in her belly, wings tickling her insides as the sensation spread from her core to her shaky extremities. This was ridiculous. He'd offered only the tiniest bit of praise, but she'd warmed as if he'd given her a medal of honor.

Needing to escape the intensity of the moment, she lowered her gaze to the child, who now cuddled against her legs. He looked so sweet, a thumb in his mouth, eyes glazed, lashes brushing his cheek as he fought the heavy weight of his lids.

"They do have a way of winning your heart, don't they?"

At Micah's words, she lifted her head and smiled. "Guess they do."

"Then they throw up on you or throw a fit at the feed store and you remember just how hard parenting is."

She shook her head. "I can only imagine."

"And…he's out."

The child in her lap had indeed given up the fight against sleep. As she watched him, her own words replayed in her head. *I can only imagine.* The problem was she *had* started daydreaming again about what it would be like to experience all those wonderful and terrible moments of parenting. Here. With Micah and Derek. She had to stop. She needed to make some progress in the local investigation and glean any remaining information Micah could offer on her case while avoiding more of these sweet moments with him and his son.

"Should we try to take him to his bed in the house?"

"That works in theory but not in practice. He never gets back to sleep. We're better off to let him rest here so he doesn't end up like yesterday."

So much for avoiding sweet moments. If only she could have been less giddy about having to spend more time with present company in a scene so picturesque that even a Renoir painting couldn't have done it justice.

She couldn't have been more grateful for the distraction when a pickup pulled up the dirt road near the petting zoo picnic area. A gift to get her back on track. Micah waved as two of the ranch hands drove by on their way to the main gate. Deirdre lifted her hand as well, pretending not to notice the strange look on the driver's face.

"How many ranch hands do you have working on Harmony Fields?"

Micah glanced back at her. "Just five. All men. Why do you ask?"

"Do any of them stay on the property full-time?"

He shook his head, answering her question, though she hadn't responded to his.

"All part-time. You've already met Rob and Kevin." He gestured to the dust of the disappearing vehicle. "They all have other jobs, so working here is bonus money. I'd like to get some full-time workers, but I need to have a bunkhouse built before I can do that. Now, if they have to be here overnight to help pull a calf, they sleep in the barn."

"Not the house?"

"I offer. They never accept." He studied her for several seconds. "Why are you asking all this? You don't think—"

"I just wondered why you hadn't mentioned names of any past or current ranch hands when we were putting together the possible suspect list."

He lifted a shoulder and lowered it. "You asked for enemies."

"You're telling me that you've never had an argument with a current employee or one who left with bad blood between you?"

"Sorry to disappoint you. I've only had a few leave at all, and they did for the chance to start their own small cattle operations. The others—" he paused, spreading his arms "—they still work here."

"You must be a great boss."

He chuckled at that. "Or their tolerance for my crap is awfully high."

She doubted that explanation. Those men probably were lucky to have the chance to work for Micah Perry.

"You don't trust easily, do you?"

She jerked her head to meet his gaze. "What do you mean by that? We're talking about *you* here. You're the one who has someone targeting your ranch. Not me."

"Maybe. But you're still a little sensitive, aren't you? Makes me curious."

Deirdre shifted, disturbing the child sleeping against her legs. She sat frozen for several seconds, hoping he wouldn't awaken.

"Is it because of your dad that you have a tough time trusting?"

"What do you know about my—"

"Eoin Colton," he said to interrupt her. "It's not exactly a common name. That's *Virginia representative* Eoin Colton, right?"

Deirdre blew out a breath. "I *knew* I shouldn't have said his name. But I figured it out here nobody would recognize it."

"You mean way out here in the wilderness? Believe it or not, we get TV here. Satellite mostly. Cable coverage is shoddy." He grinned. "Usually, you would be right that I wouldn't notice it. I don't even follow politics. Takes too much energy. But you remember certain names—"

"Like those involved in sex scandals," she finished for him.

"Whew! Thanks for saying that." He made a show of brushing sweat off his brow. "I was trying to figure out a nice way to say it."

"There is no nice way."

"Well, he's had a long and successful political career despite those *moments*."

"Long enough to build quite a résumé that has nothing to do with proposed legislation," she agreed.

Micah lay back on the blanket but turned on his side this time and propped his head up with his arm. "That had to be hard on you. But aren't your parents still together? Seems like I remember seeing that."

She considered for a moment. This had nothing to do with their cases and only took time away from finding answers for either of them, but she found herself answering anyway, somehow needing him to know.

"That's part of the story. Long-suffering Georgina, standing by her man while Dad made the rounds during the legislative session." She scoffed. "The gossip rags don't even report anymore that Mom was the socialite my father had an affair with when he was first entering politics. He left his first wife, Caroline, to marry *her*."

"They don't need to bring up the old stuff when he's regularly given them new material to report on. Are you their only child?" He squinted, thinking. "Oh. Right. You mentioned a half brother."

He extended his index finger, shaking his wrist. "Wait. Didn't your dad have a child with a famous model?"

"That's Aidan. His mother is Kara Dean."

"Guess that's not the first time that happened to a political leader."

She shrugged. "My father legally acknowledged Aidan, paid child support and even gave him the Colton last name, so I guess that's something."

She paused, the thought that always left a bitter taste

in her mouth souring again. "But that was because Aidan was the son he always wanted."

"I'm surprised he didn't make Aidan's mom Wife Number Three."

Micah watched her for so long that she couldn't help squirming. Derek groused in his sleep, shifted into a new position and snuggled against her again.

"I always wondered why he didn't," she said. "Well, when I learned about it. I was pretty little when it happened."

"How little?"

She brushed her hand over Derek's back. "Younger than him. Aidan's thirty-two. Just a year younger than me."

The truth that still hurt after all these years pressing down on her anew, Deirdre lowered her head. She couldn't look at Micah. Not now. She didn't want to see the pity in his eyes. Or let him see the pain in hers.

"Oh. That's tough," he said simply.

Deirdre continued to brush back the sleeping child's hair, grateful that Micah had given her a moment to collect emotions too close to the surface. As Micah shifted on the blanket to sit crisscross, she finally looked up again.

"I don't have any siblings, so I don't know what that would be like, and your situation has to be different from others', but are you and your brother close?"

His question made her smile, even if Micah had only shifted slightly from the earlier subject. She welcomed the break from discussing the skeletons her family had never been able to hide in any closet.

"We try," she said. "But we didn't grow up together.

Aidan lived with his mom and stepdad, and I lived with my parents."

"But you're able to work together. You even said he's part of your team."

"You don't forget much." She grinned. "Yes, he's on the team. He's a good US marshal. He's been with the agency nearly ten years now. An asset to the missing-person team."

"An asset, huh? Sounds like something you would write on a press release."

"It's also true," she said, frowning.

"I bet your dad is really proud of his two law-enforcement kids."

"You would think, wouldn't you?" She made a sound in her throat like a chuckle, though that truth had never been funny to her.

"What are you saying?"

Beyond the awkwardness of the conversation, she was becoming uncomfortable sitting in the same position on the hard ground to avoid awakening Derek. To ease some of the pain, she leaned back on her elbows. After a few seconds, she answered his question.

"He's proud of Aidan, anyway."

"But not you."

Since he didn't pose it as a question, she didn't answer. Anyway, there was something that she wanted to know.

"If you recognized my dad's name when I first said it in front of Sheriff Guetta, why didn't you say anything then?"

"I figured you already had enough to deal with in trying to convince Richard not to report you to the bureau."

"Then I guess I should say thank you."

He only smiled, waiting.

"Thank you." She rolled her eyes.

"How can anyone sit this way?" He unraveled himself and rubbed his calf muscle. "That feels like a torture method."

"Guess you have to be a kindergartner to appreciate it."

"It's been a while." He lay on his back again and stared up at the foliage and possibly a bit of sky.

She tilted her head back uncomfortably toward the blanket but couldn't manage the same position as his.

Micah gave her a sidelong glance. "I can move him if you like."

"It's okay. Really." She paused to watch the rise and fall of the child's chest. "I don't want to disturb him."

"You'll regret that when you have to limp all the way back to the house."

"I'll take my chances."

For a few minutes, they rested companionably without words, the only sounds coming from the rustling leaves above them and the bleating goats from their enclosure not far away. Deirdre didn't bother telling herself she could get used to lazy afternoons, just the three of them. She already had.

"That had to be really hard," Micah said, breaking the silence.

"What do you mean?"

"Growing up in that family."

Her throat immediately clogged. Few had acknowledged the truth that there were victims other than spouses in her parents' histories of infidelity, but now that Micah had said it, she felt the need to soften her version of the past.

"It's nothing like what you experienced, losing both parents by the time you were eighteen. Then the awful way it happened—"

He shook his head until she stopped. "This time, we're talking about *you.*"

"No one feels sorry for the little girl who has the best of everything," she said. "Amazing house. The opportunity to attend the best private schools, university and law school. A political family and the chance to follow in their footsteps without breaking a sweat."

"And parents who embarrassed you again and again, expected you to willingly be a part of their Stepford family, and had and still have zero interest in ever really knowing you."

Deirdre blinked, the leaves above her moving in and out of focus. "I never said all that."

"No, but I'm not that far off, am I?"

He wasn't, and she didn't know what to make of it that he'd come so close to the truth. "I must not have thought it was that bad. I married a guy just like my dad."

As soon as the words were out of her mouth, she regretted them. Why did she keep volunteering information to this man, telling him things he had no business knowing? She was like a suspect, who was stopped for a broken taillight and ended up confessing to murder. She had a right to remain silent and should use it. For some reason, though, she just couldn't help herself. Had a near stranger touched on feelings she'd pretended didn't exist and betrayals she'd never before admitted out loud?

"You know, that's the least surprising thing you've said to me," Micah said.

She popped up from her reclining position. "How can that even be?"

"The same reason that children of drug addicts become involved with drug addicts. You do what you know."

His words made sense, but she couldn't accept the easy excuse he offered.

"Well, I should have known better. Brandon and I were both political staffers. My dad was his hero, and I ridiculously thought it had to do with his actual office activities. Not extracurriculars." She shook her head, shame she'd thought she could no longer feel settling heavily on her chest.

"He knew what I would be willing to put up with. The worst part? He was right."

"That sounds terrible. How long were you married to him?"

"Three years. The whole time Brandon had a conga line of lovers trampling all over the marriage."

He rubbed his eyes, "That's a vivid image. But, hey, your marriage was *twice* as long as mine."

"That's not a fair comparison, and you know it. Yours didn't end voluntarily. It was an accident."

Micah straightened and then turned on the blanket, suddenly interested in the goat enclosure about two hundred feet away from them. "Whoever said life was supposed be fair?"

At Micah's solemn words, Deirdre's chest squeezed. His pain became hers, his loss an open sore on her heart. She glanced at his hand, so tempted to reach for it again that she had to lace her fingers over her abdomen to resist. She'd stepped back, and she needed to stay back.

"Want to hear a really sad one?" She paused, waiting for him to turn back to her. He didn't, but she continued telling her story anyway, needing to share her shame. "*He* left me. All those affairs he had, and if he asked me to, I *still* would have stayed."

Now Micah swiveled back to her, a stark look in his eyes.

"I'm sorry he did that to you."

She needed to stop, but she couldn't. The words kept coming and would keep coming until she had nothing left to say.

"Brandon probably thought I was like my mother, who built herself a life filled with the good things and wouldn't let something insignificant like more infidelity mess that up for her. He was wrong about me, though." She shook her head to emphasize that point. "I would have stayed because I believed in marriage. And I'd promised I would."

"Your determination is admirable," he said. "Not everyone would have been able to stick it out. But he didn't deserve your loyalty."

"I know that now. Believe me, I know it."

"Maybe there's honor in staying. Maybe not. But you have to be grateful that he saved you from having to make that choice."

"Are you serious? You want me to be grateful to *him*?" That word caught in her throat. "After everything I've said—"

Micah shook his head to interrupt her. "Not *to* him. Just that he chose to leave. He didn't make the decision for you. He did it for himself. Some people can't think beyond their own wingspan, and there's nothing the rest of us can do to change that."

Deirdre squinted at him, his words strange. Though his description of Brandon wasn't so far off, Micah had never met the man. He didn't seem to be talking about her loser of an ex-husband at all. *Nothing the rest of us can do to change that?* Why did he include himself in her sad story?

"How do you know—"

"They don't care who they hurt," he said, interrupting her. He looked away. "Or who they leave behind."

Her suspicion deepened, but before she had a chance to ask Micah more, the child next to her wiggled and then roused. The toddler came up on his hands and knees and rocked back and forth, his face pinched.

"No nap," he whined.

"Naptime's done, kiddo," Micah said.

The child whined again, his lips forming a pout.

"Better get him back to the house," Micah said.

He dumped the rest of the plates and trash into the cooler and checked around for any litter. Then, lifting the cooler by its handle, he bent to pull his son onto his hip.

"Could you bring the quilt?"

At her nod, he started away, walking quickly up the drive toward the house. She grabbed the blanket, looped it over her arm and hurried after him. She caught up with him just outside the slider.

"What aren't you telling me?"

"What do you mean?"

But his tight expression suggested he knew more than he was willing to say.

"You said, 'they don't care who they leave behind'?

Is this about Maeve? Did you remember something else about her?"

Micah rolled his eyes as he opened the door. He stepped inside and toed off his boots, waiting for Deirdre to follow him.

"This might come as a surprise to you, but not everything is about Maeve O'Leary."

He turned and strode off with Derek. She let him go as what she suspected was the true meaning of his words sank in. This wasn't about her case. Or even his. He was hiding something about his wife, and when he was ready, she would convince him to tell her the truth.

Chapter 10

Deirdre took the chair in the corner of Sheriff Guetta's office two days later, the space so tight that her knees hit the desk when she sat. The sheriff glanced at her from over his desk, stacked high with case files and who knew what else, and shrugged.

"I don't usually do suspect interviews in here, and we needed to squeeze in another chair." He pointed to the empty one. "We usually conduct those in the interview room down the hall."

"But you agreed we should speak with her here since this is just a casual, voluntary conversation," she reminded him. "Just to rule her out."

He laughed. "Did you make sure the security cameras outside didn't get any footage of you visiting my office as well? Wouldn't want anyone in DC to know what you were doing on your spring vacation out West."

"Are you going to spend the whole time making fun of me, or do you want to get this thing over with?"

She tried to cross her legs in the same pair of jeans she'd already worn for too many hours this week, but she couldn't accomplish it. If she had to conduct more potential suspect interviews, she would need a second shopping trip. And hopefully not another visit to Gary's.

"Did you tell Micah that in addition to picking up records, you asked me to call Kara in?"

She shook her head. "It's not *his* investigation, but no, I didn't. And we have to start somewhere." Not that they'd had any real conversations since yesterday when it had been too easy to share with him. Now she felt far too vulnerable that she had.

"Has anyone already interviewed her?"

"I have to say no," he said with a grin.

"Then let's see if we can mark someone off the list."

Richard reached for his desk phone and pushed a few buttons. "Liz, could you send her in, please?"

About thirty seconds later, someone knocked at the door.

"Come in, Mrs. Jackson."

"Mrs. Jackson?" A petite brunette opened the door slightly, a quizzical look in her striking blue eyes.

Clearly, she'd been on a first-name basis with the sheriff before that morning. She pushed the door wide and squeezed inside, lugging a handled infant car seat. She balanced the carrier precariously as she pushed the door closed with her hip.

Deirdre immediately wanted to abort the whole interview, not just because the room didn't feel big enough to share with a woman Micah Perry had dated and kissed and with whom he'd possibly even been intimate. Not because she was jealous of the woman or any of those other things, either. With a fine-boned frame like that and those manicured hands, Kara Sullivan Jackson was about as likely a suspect to have completed those strenuous acts of sabotage as Micah himself.

"Here. Let me help with that." Deirdre leaped up from her seat but found no way to maneuver over to assist the woman.

"I've got it," Kara said through teeth grinding with effort, as she wrangled the seat into the one bit of open space between the door and the desk. The baby inside, probably a girl, given the abundance of pink ruffles on the carrier and clothes, somehow slept through the whole ordeal, a blanket tucked up under her chin.

Task completed, Kara dropped into the chair next to Deirdre. "I'm stronger than I look."

Not that strong. She still couldn't picture the woman pulling over an enormous wood cabinet or cutting through huge sections of cattle fencing. At least not without help.

She looked back and forth between the two law-enforcement officers. "My husband said you wanted to see me."

"Thank you for coming, Kara." The sheriff stood up behind his desk. "I'd like you to meet FBI special agent Deirdre Colton.

"Special Agent Colton, this is Kara Jackson."

As the two women shook hands, Guetta sat again.

"You have a beautiful baby." Deirdre paused to admire the sleeping child.

"I do, don't I?" Kara stared down at her child and

then looked back at the sheriff expectantly. "Jerry said you needed help with a case. Happy to do what I can, but I can't stay long. Babysitter's with my two stepkids, so I'm on the clock."

"Special Agent Colton is helping investigate the series of suspicious incidents at Harmony Fields Ranch," the sheriff told her.

The woman's head jerked, and her jaw tightened. "What are you talking to me for?"

"Now, Kara, relax," Guetta said, gesturing downward with his hands. "We're not accusing you of anything. There's just been quite a few cases of malicious destruction of property on the ranch, and we're having a chat with a few individuals on a list of those who might have had a problem with Micah in the past."

"And you're talking to *me*? I don't have a problem with Micah Perry. I had my stepkids over at his petting zoo two weeks ago."

Deirdre leaned forward to take control of the interview, shifting the notebook in her lap. "Mr. Perry mentioned that you dated at one point."

"*He's* the one that put me on that list? That son-of-a—"

Kara managed to stop herself, but not before the sheriff and Deirdre exchanged a look. Micah's one-time girlfriend was a hothead, all right.

Deirdre twirled her pen in her fingers. "Do you remember a comment you made about his infant son?"

"He told you that? That's just ridiculous. He had no business—" Again, she stopped. This time, her gaze narrowed. "Do I need to have my lawyer here?"

The sheriff shook his head. "I don't think so."

"Look, I was angry, and I said some awful things,"

Kara said, folding her hands in her lap. "But I haven't done anything at Harmony Fields."

Deirdre nodded. "And whatever was between you two is in the past, right?"

"Oh. Absolutely. I'm a married woman." She gestured to her wedding band and then to the baby in the carrier next to her.

Deirdre stood then, resting her hands on the desktop. "That's all we'll need. Thank you so much for coming in."

She shook the woman's hand and waited as she wrestled the car seat out of the room. Once Kara stepped down the hall, Deirdre closed the door.

The shocked look that Guetta gave her probably matched the one on her own face.

"Hell hath no fury like a woman scorned," he said.

"Micah was right to say she hates him, but do you think she should still be considered a possible suspect regarding any of the sabotage damage?"

He shook his head. "I'm pretty sure that was all bluster."

"Yeah. Me, too."

"Still, if I were Micah, I would avoid meeting that one in a dark alley."

Though she recognized that the jocular sheriff was only kidding, she still couldn't laugh. Maybe this potential suspect wasn't threatening Micah and Derek, but someone still was. Even if she could find the answers for her own investigation, suddenly the idea of leaving Wyoming before stopping whoever was targeting them sent a chill up her spine. How could she walk away without knowing they would be safe?

* * *

The darkness no longer seemed so suffocating, Deirdre decided with surprise, as she and Micah tromped toward the petting zoo later that night, their two flashlights providing twin cones of illumination on the dirt road before them. She appreciated the night sky's generosity in providing hundreds of brilliant pinpoints on its canvas, but she suspected that a person could get used to even the nights where cloud cover veiled all the stars, if she chose to. And if she were in the right company.

She tucked her hand in her jacket pocket, her fingers coming into contact with her holster. Though she'd changed back into ranch gear after returning from the sheriff's office, she'd kept her weapon with her. Even if there'd been no evidence of new vandalism on the ranch since she'd been there, after meeting with Micah's unusual ex, she was convinced that they would all be safer if she remained armed.

"Do you think the animals will mind having night-time visitors?" With the flashlight in her other hand, she pointed in the direction of their destination. "They have to know it's not regular zoo time, and they might demand overtime pay for having to entertain during off-hours."

"I'm sure they'll cut us a deal if we give them snacks."

"Always works with me."

"I'll remember that." He patted his pocket, and the crinkling sound of cellophane filtered over to her. "I've been known to carry candy sometimes."

"I've been known to *eat* candy."

"Those two things just might go together," he said.

He was flirting with her. She should have avoided it, or at least tried not to play along, but she'd spent the past few days telling herself all the reasons she should keep her distance from Micah and his son, and she was tired. Tonight she just wanted to relax with him and take a break from searching for answers that had been harder to come by than she'd expected when she'd planned her little Wyoming getaway.

"So what shows do you think the animals will put on for us tonight? I'm on vacation. I need entertainment."

"You do realize these are animals, don't you?" He pointed the flashlight at her face. "You might get a little more than you're bargaining for with their nocturnal activities. Not that they always wait until nighttime."

"Right." She cleared her throat, her cheeks warm despite the drop in temperature after sundown. Were they really talking about animal mating habits while they walked, just the two of them, under a starry sky? She appreciated the darkness even more.

He redirected his flashlight to the road ahead, and they silently waved their lights back and forth to check for tripping hazards now that words were more difficult to come by.

"But not bunnies, though," Deirdre said to break the silence. "Unless they've dismantled your gender-segregation plan."

"I wouldn't put it past them. They don't care anything about population control."

As they drew closer to the goat barn, with bleating sounds breaking the silence, Micah slowed and used his flashlight to scan the building's exterior. "I thought Derek was never going to go to sleep tonight. 'One more book, puleeze.' Bet it's just because *you* were reading."

"That's a solid toddler imitation," she said, trying not to be flattered.

"I get a lot of practice."

He probably didn't have a lot of adult conversation with just him and Derek living together on the ranch, but Deirdre resisted the urge to ask if he was lonely there. They were finally comfortable with each other again, and she didn't want to mess that up.

"I thought his begging was cute," she said instead, reaching back to his earlier comment. A safer one.

"Parent manipulation 101. How to avoid bedtime."

"I know." She tried to ignore the gooseflesh that peppered her arms over his reference to "parents." He could have said "adults" or "grown-ups," but he'd used the one word that described the role that until now she never knew she wanted.

"But he was trying so hard to stay awake. Those poor little eyelids. So heavy." She smiled into the darkness, remembering.

"As I said before, they have a way of winning your heart, don't they?"

She sensed him watching her, but she didn't dare turn her flashlight on him. She wasn't sure she could trust her response if she caught him staring.

"Bet Derek never had to win you to his side," she couldn't help saying anyway.

"Nope. He made his loud, messy appearance, and just like that—" he paused to snap his fingers "—I was a goner. He became the center of my world."

Emotion swelled in her throat then. Had her own father ever once seen her as the most important person in his life? Or even the top five? Had she ever been more than "the family" for the political flyer or a list of academic accomplishments to brag about at cocktail parties?

Her flashlight caught on Micah as he reached for the baby monitor attached to his belt and peeked at the little screen.

"Is he doing okay?" She hoped that at least one of them was.

"Sleeping like a baby."

They chuckled over his corny joke. She, for one, really needed a laugh. Maybe that would relieve some of the electricity in the air around them and pulsating from her earlobes to her baby toes. Good thing no rain was in the forecast, since one lightning bolt would turn her into a pile of smoldering ash.

She steadied her legs and followed Micah through the staff entrance into the pygmy goat enclosure. But a single brush of his fingers over her jacket-covered arm as he guided her inside sent another round of tingles up to her shoulder and reinforced her warning to stay out of the rain. She drowned out her other suspicion that spending time with Micah in the dark would be a mistake.

Micah latched the door and then flipped a switch. Immediately, the goat barn and the enclosed yard surrounding it were awash with a warm glow from twinkling string lights. If the darkness had seemed dangerous, this magical shimmer doubled down on the risk.

"This is amazing," she breathed anyway because it was. How she hadn't noticed all those lights when they'd visited earlier, she couldn't imagine. "Doesn't exactly look farm-like."

"It's not supposed to, because it's a—"

"Zoo," she finished for him. "But the kids aren't here at night. They'll never get to enjoy all these lights."

"They're part of an idea I cooked up for parents. Maybe a chance for them to leave the kids with a sitter and spend a little time as a couple."

"Date night at the zoo. It has a nice ring to it." Too nice, in her opinion, based on present circumstances and company. The setting was also far too romantic for a place scented with hay, goat and muck.

She crossed her arms and gripped her sleeves, suddenly needing to hold on to something. "You never said why you wanted me to come out here with you now."

If he said, "for a date," she wasn't sure what she would say. Or if there would be any way she could stop herself from tramping across the play yard to throw herself at him.

"I have a job for you to do."

She sighed, her hormones taking a well-deserved beatdown. "Should have known. More free labor."

"I think you're going to like this one." He held up his forefinger in a signal for her to wait and stepped past a stack of hay bales in a protected extension of the building with a gabled roof but open on both ends. When he returned, he carried a black-and-white-spotted baby goat, small enough to fit comfortably in his arms.

"A new baby?" She approached slowly to avoid startling the animal that seemed perfectly content with Micah holding her.

"A *kid*. Or, more specifically in her case, a *doeling*. Our first this season. Since the petting zoo is so new, it's only our second full season. The other does have a few more weeks to go before kidding." He nodded at her strange look. "Yeah, that's what it's called when a goat gives birth. Want to hold her?"

He extended his arms to hand the doeling out to her. Without hesitation, she accepted the transfer. She brushed her fingers over the animal's coat, coarse on top but downy closer to its skin. The tiny goat cuddled against her, seeming to enjoy the attention.

"She's sweet." Deirdre touched the animal's snout, and it nibbled her finger.

"Only a few days old." Micah petted the doeling's head. "In their first few weeks, it's important to get out here and cuddle them several times a day. That way they'll be comfortable around people."

"It's a tough job, but somebody has to do it." She grinned, hugging the goat close so its snout rested just beneath her chin.

"Told you you'd like it. You seem pretty comfortable holding her."

She glanced up, still brushing her fingers through the doeling's coat. "Didn't want you questioning my bravery again."

"Believe me, I would never do that. Richard told me you insisted on having a chat with Kara." He shivered visibly. "She's scary."

"He wasn't supposed to tell you."

Micah answered with a shrug.

"What did you do to her, anyway?" she asked before she could stop herself.

"As a gentleman cowboy, I shouldn't say."

"If it has any bearing on the case, you should."

He met her gaze levelly. "It doesn't, but since you

won't believe me, I'll just tell you that in addition to pushing for a wedding ring, she offered me her kindness—uh, all of it. Since I couldn't see us having a more long-term thing, I politely declined."

"Ouch!"

"I know." He stared at his hands.

"And *kindness*? That's what the kids are calling it these days?" Even she could hear the embarrassment in her laugh. Now, in addition to animal breeding, they were discussing human sex as well.

"I have nothing more to say about that."

He rolled his lips inward, looking more than a little uncomfortable himself. Deirdre found it surprising that he'd said as much as he had. Maybe he'd just been trying to defend his actions, as Brandon would have done, but she sensed there was more to it. Micah seemed to want her to know that he hadn't slept with Kara when he could have had a casual thing with her. That only gave Deirdre more questions. Like why he'd thought she should know and, more importantly, why she cared.

The goat wiggled in her arms. She lowered it to the hay-strewn ground. As the animal took off, probably in search of its mother to feed, Deirdre leaned against the fence, on the opposite side of where she'd stood with Derek just that afternoon.

"Hey, you haven't told me her name."

Micah leaned against the fence next to her and crossed his arms. "I thought you might like to name her."

"Are you serious? Are you sure you don't want to do it? Or Derek? You really want to trust me with that responsibility?"

Micah grinned, getting a kick out of her babbling excitement tinged with insecurity.

"It's just a name." He chuckled and then pushed back his shoulders, pursed his lips and spoke in a low voice. "The mission is yours, should you choose to accept it."

"I don't know." She searched around the pen again for the baby goat that had already located its mother and latched on to a teat. "It's *so* much pressure."

More than that, it felt like a gift. He'd asked her to leave a mark on Harmony Fields, one that would linger there with him and Derek for years after she'd returned to Washington and moved to more high-profile cases than even Maeve O'Leary and her trail of dead husbands. Something to spark their memory of her when she already knew she would never forget *them*.

"Just think for a minute and go with your gut."

"What happens if I come up with something ridiculous?"

"Then Abraham and Mary from over in the rabbit enclosure will be in good company."

"Good point." She watched the animal, drinking greedily, and the long-suffering mother, readjusting its stance every few seconds to maintain its balance. "How about Eleanor Roosevelt?"

He watched the hungry goat for a few seconds and then nodded. "Independent. Outspoken. Eleanor it is."

"Hope you won't expect too much of her," she said. "Those are awfully big shoes to fill."

"She'd eat those shoes, anyway. It'll just be nice having Eleanor here as a reminder—"

As Micah cut off his words, Deirdre couldn't help but to glance over at him, and once she'd met his steady gray gaze, she couldn't look away. She didn't even want to. He must have leaned toward her, as he suddenly felt close. Intimately close. The tip of his tongue darted out to dampen the corner of his mouth, his gaze lowering to her lips. It lingered so long there that her skin tingled.

He was going to kiss her. She could tell herself that she didn't want him to, that it would be an awful idea and a complication to a case with more than enough of those already stuffed in its file, but her thundering heart and sweaty palms revealed that her body and maybe even her heart were completely on board.

Micah leaned forward. Or was it her? But now he was so close that his warm breath tickled her ear, and her heart pounded hard enough to unzip her jacket. Maybe she'd done that, at least in her thoughts, too.

But just when their lips were near enough that their tongues could touch with barely a reach, he stopped his slow lean, his eyes wide, his mouth forming a soft O. "Maybe we shouldn't—"

A sound escaping her throat that she could only define as *desperation* cut off his words, but it was her lips that prevented him from completing whatever he'd been about to say. She pressed her mouth to his, not in one of those delicate kisses like those sweet maidens from the movies she loved but with a hunger that mirrored that of the famished baby goat. Whatever his reticence before, Micah returned her kiss, equally greedy and desperate and wanting.

Deirdre didn't wait for him to dab her lip for permission and instead glided her tongue over the seam of his until he opened for *her*, their mouths mating in a simulation tantalizing enough to make the goats blush. His mustache and beard tickled her skin as he dazzled her mouth and then neck from earlobe to collarbone.

He splayed his hands over her back, their reach beginning at her bra strap, then following the curve of her waist and finally straying to the pockets of her jeans. She wanted more. Needed more.

With an urgency that surprised her, she slid her arms over his shoulders, the muscles she'd only been able to admire before flexing beneath her touch, tendons stretching and ligaments working. Every bit of it was driving her out of her mind.

Even when Micah broke off the kiss to gasp for breath, another of those humiliating sounds of protest escaped her. He smiled against her lips and, turning with her in his arms, leaned her backside against the fence. Then, on an exceptionally deep and delirious kiss, he settled himself against her. All of him.

Her eyes, already heavy with desire, shot open then. An equally shocked Micah stared back at her. They both jumped back as if caught by a monitor in the hall of any high school.

"Sorry," he said before she could form the words.

"No. I'm sorry." She'd definitely started it, but he hadn't exactly fought her off with a shovel, either.

"I don't know what that was," he said, still shaking his head.

Despite her humiliation, she had to turn away so he wouldn't see her smile. If Micah really didn't know what *that* was, there were plenty of animals on the ranch that could explain it to him. He'd been close enough for Deirdre to be intimately aware of his willingness to take that undefinable thing to a satisfying conclusion, but what she couldn't explain was why she hadn't stopped it before it even started.

He cleared his throat, stepping back and giving her a wide berth. "We'd better get back to the house."

"Yeah, we should."

She turned her head, focusing on a pair of goats, already wrestling with their newly emerged horn buds. What were they supposed to do now? Micah seemed to be able to turn off his hormones as quickly as he had the faucet for the goat trough. If only she could shut hers down as easily when her whole body had awakened from its hibernation and had no interest in taking another nap.

They stepped outside the enclosure, and Micah shut off the lights. But just as the space descended back into near darkness, with the only illumination from a few remaining safety lights, a chill tripped up Deirdre's spine. Was it a sound, or were her senses just out of whack after a kiss that made her knees weak? She wasn't sure. But something told her they were not alone.

Micah shifted closer to her, his flashlight's beam directed to the ground. "Did you hear that?"

She touched his jacket sleeve to ask him to be quiet. Like her, he pressed his back to the side of the building, and other than his breathing, he didn't make a sound.

They waited. And listened.

No footsteps. No sounds beyond the bleats from the goats and what could only be the rumble of cattle in the distance. She'd almost convinced herself that she'd imagined it, but as her gaze slid to Micah, her breath caught again. He knew someone was there, too.

He leaned close and whispered again. "By the alpacas."

"Oh, hell, no." Her words came in a stage whisper

at best, but she couldn't help herself. Just as she'd refused to let whoever this was get to Micah or Derek, she wouldn't let them frighten or endanger more of the animals.

She zipped her flashlight in her pocket and withdrew her weapon from the holster. But as Deirdre started to pull away from the wall, Micah reached out an arm like the reflex of a driver shielding a passenger upon impact.

"You can't go out there," he whispered.

"I've got this." She shifted out of his reach as she said it.

"Not alone."

This time she rested a hand on his shoulder. "I'm armed. You're not. You don't know if *he* is."

He shook his head. "You can't—"

"Think of Derek."

Deirdre knew the moment she got through to Micah as he tipped his chin up and leaned his head against the side of the building.

"Trust me. Please," she whispered and then pushed away from the wall.

Praying Micah wouldn't follow, she rushed from one bit of cover to the next. She rounded the rabbit enclosure, barely registering that the animals were skittering about, either hearing or sensing her presence.

Deirdre pressed forward, aware of the danger in looking back. Still, opposing needs pulled her in two directions—backward to ensure she hadn't left Micah exposed to attack and forward so the suspect she believed was there couldn't escape. She'd lost her edge, and there didn't seem to be any way to get it back.

Then, in the open pasture on the far side of the alpaca enclosure, under what had to be the worst lighting of anywhere on the ranch, someone in a dark hoodie appeared to be running with the animals. Or chasing them. They were trying to get away from him, all right, in a bleating chorus of kazoos and panicked circles, their long necks swaying like those of giraffes. Then, one by one, they recognized the missing section of fencing on the southeast side of the enclosure and escaped through it.

"Stop! FBI!" she called out to the only one who would understand.

The suspect looked over, face obscured in shadows and the hood of the jacket. In a movement that could have been a reach for a weapon or an attempt to surrender, the individual covered his or her mouth. A shrill mechanical whistle eclipsed the sounds of even the terrified animals before the one who'd produced the sound sprinted to the mangled section of fencing.

Deirdre raced around the enclosure's perimeter toward the same opening, as though she could halt both the suspect and the stampede. She couldn't get there fast enough. The suspect had too much of a head start. Refusing to concede, she remained in pursuit and followed the suspect into a bank of trees, where branches tore at her sleeves and brambles brought her to her knees. She had to take the risk of holstering her weapon and using the flashlight from her pocket just to get past the brush.

As she finally emerged on the other side, an engine roared to life in the distance. With its lights off, the vehicle—probably a truck—raced down the drive and off the property. Defeated, she returned through the line of trees—and found Micah on the other side, already chasing down the terrified animals.

Though she didn't meet his gaze as she approached, she sensed his disappointment anyway. She'd had the chance to take down the suspect who'd terrified Micah and put his son in danger. But she'd been too busy making out with a witness and forgetting about her responsibility, and, like with everything else lately, she'd failed.

Chapter 11

Micah dropped onto the sofa two hours and a shower later, a mix of frenzied energy and collapse pressing him into the cool leather. Even though his hands were raw from repairing fence wires, and his muscles ached, he should have been more grateful. None of the alpacas had been injured beyond an intense cardiac workout from the ordeal, the newest crime had been photographed and recorded, and the temporary fencing that he and Deirdre had put in place would hold until he could figure out a more permanent solution.

They'd been incredibly lucky. Again. That was the problem. These attacks would never stop until somebody got hurt. Maybe Derek. Maybe him. Or, now, Deirdre.

The woman who'd scared the hell out of him earlier dropped her phone on the coffee table and collapsed on the other end of the sofa. Like him, just back from a shower and dressed in a T-shirt and cotton athletic shorts, Deirdre sat with her damp hair spread across the backrest and closed her eyes, lacing her fingers behind her head. He tried not to notice how amazing she smelled or how soft the skin on her bare legs looked in those athletic shorts or to think about how amazing she'd tasted and felt against his body earlier.

"What a crazy night," she said without moving or opening her eyes.

He had to agree with that. Neither of them could have predicted this evening would include both a kiss in a goat barn that had them walking on eggshells around each other *and* chases of the suspect who'd targeted his family and loping creatures set free to fend for themselves.

Good thing they'd both put a *whoa* on that kiss that would have had him laying her back in the hay with the smallest encouragement. He knew what a bad idea it would be to get involved with the special agent, too. So why were his hands still prickling with a ridiculous need to touch her even now? Why was his body still aching to finish what they'd started? Maybe his moment of panic when he couldn't find Deirdre anywhere, when he'd failed to protect her, too, had messed with his head more than he'd realized.

"Wait." Her eyes opening, she immediately shot a look at the front door. "You checked all the locks, right?"

She pushed off the sofa and started that way herself.

"Hey, stop. We already checked them together."

Finally, she stopped and turned back to him. "We did, didn't we?"

"Twice." Before she had a chance to mention them

again, he added, "As for the shotguns, both are positioned near the doors and ready, ammunition responsibly stored nearby."

"Sounds like everything's fine."

She returned to the sofa but crossed her arms as she sat. Clearly, she wasn't fine—hadn't been since they returned from the petting zoo.

"Are you cold? Want me to make some hot chocolate?"

She shook her head.

"How about a fire?"

She glanced at the fireplace, considering. "Sounds nice, but I don't want to put you to any more trouble tonight."

He shot a glance her way, wondering which part of the evening she'd considered problematic for him, but she avoided looking at him.

"No trouble." At least not this time. He grabbed the remote off the mantel and hit the button, a crackling fire immediately lighting on the grate in the gas fireplace.

Deirdre did look up this time. "You don't have a wood fireplace? Out here on a ranch?"

"I make plenty of fires outside," he said with a shrug. "When I get home, I just want to relax and enjoy a fire."

"It does feel nice."

She sank back again and closed her eyes, but almost immediately, she jerked and sat forward, as if chased from any thought of relaxation. "I still can't get over how fast the alpacas could move," Deirdre said. "Poor things. They were so scared."

They weren't the only ones. As memories of the

not knowing and then the chaos replayed in his mind, Micah shivered. He sneaked a peek at her, relieved to find her watching the fire instead of him.

"I'm just glad we were able to get all ten of them back inside the fence," he said. "I don't know what we would have done if they'd escaped to the other pastures or the road."

She turned to face him then, resting her elbow on top of the sofa and pressing her cheek against her fist, her expression serious. "Well, I know exactly what we would have done. We would still be out there hunting. Until we found every one of them."

He believed her, too. She would have helped him all night. As much as she played the tough FBI agent, she had a soft spot for animals. And for children like his son.

But he couldn't shake the worries and the sense of helplessness that had filled him as she'd left to pursue the suspect and expected him to stay behind.

"If we hadn't gone down to the petting zoo tonight… or if the alpacas had been out all night—" He stopped himself, the what-ifs too frightening to consider.

"But we *did* go. And they weren't stuck out all night."

"How do we know we'll be there next time?"

She held out her right hand, palm up, and then lowered it. "We can't know that. Just as we won't know if the suspect will be armed next time. Or even if a weapon was present tonight but the suspect chose to flee rather than engage. That's why you should have listened to me when I told you to stay back."

This wasn't the first time she'd mentioned it, so he tried to explain.

"Don't you get it? I couldn't just stand there like a coward while you put yourself in danger. What kind of—" He stopped, rethinking since he'd almost said, "man."

"What kind of *person* would I be?"

Her gaze narrowed. "Can we set aside your fragile male ego for a moment? Like I said before, you were unarmed. And only one of us is a trained FBI agent. It's my *job* to pursue suspects."

"My male ego isn't—" After considering those words, he frowned, his whole argument contradicting the claim he'd been about to make. He tried again to explain instead. "And it's my job—my *responsibility*— to protect everything on Harmony Fields."

That Deirdre automatically glanced to the stairs leading to Derek's nursery signaled she still didn't understand that his instinct to shield would extend to her. Or even why it should.

"He's still doing okay?" she asked.

Micah nodded, grateful she'd decided to let the subject go. They would never agree on it, anyway. "Just checked on him. Still sound asleep. I worried he would wake up while we were still out working on the fence."

"That's one good thing."

Leaning forward, he gripped opposite elbows and braced them against his knees. "I only wish I could have gotten a look at the suspect."

"And I wish I'd gotten a *better* look."

He would second that wish. Especially since this suspect had escaped capture. Again.

"But you witnessed him in the act," Micah reminded her. "That's more than any of the other investigators have accomplished so far."

"Fat lot of good it did me." She crossed her arms, sinking deeper into the sofa cushions. "We still don't even know what he wants. And he got away."

"You're saying 'he' now. Are you convinced the suspect is a guy?" He watched her closely, her answer more critical than he was ready to share.

"My vantage point and the lighting were so bad that I can't be certain of much." She pressed her lips into a flat line. "Well, except that the suspect was tall and lanky. You can't shield that behind a darn hoodie like you can hair and skin color."

"So, we're looking for a tall and thin man—or woman—with no specific hair or skin color? Someone who happens to own a sweatshirt."

She gave him a mean look and then shook her head. "So many times I've pressed witnesses to give me more detailed descriptions of suspects. Now I know how hard it is when you really didn't see anything useful. I hate to have to put this description at all in the report to the sheriff."

"At least we can rule out Kara Jackson. No one would ever call her tall and lanky."

He couldn't say the same about Maeve O'Leary, who'd been a Pilates devotee before it ever became a national fitness craze. His rationale for not sharing his ridiculous suspicion was becoming less justifiable by the minute. If the suspect turned out to be Maeve, and something happened to Derek or Deirdre, he would never forgive himself.

"Kara couldn't have run that fast, either."

She sent him a skeptical look. "You still weren't ready to rule her out?"

"I was even before you interviewed her." As for another woman, not so much. "What about the voice? Did the suspect call out to the alpacas?"

Deirdre shook her head. "Not that I heard. Just the whistle. It was so loud that you could probably hear it clear back in Casper."

"I heard it." He swallowed, forcing himself not to shiver again as she was watching him this time. "At first, I thought it was one of the rabbits."

"Rabbits whistle?"

"No, they *scream*. Like a child. But only when they're terrified."

"That's what you thought you heard. And that's why you followed me."

They exchanged a look that said more than words could.

"Yeah."

Deirdre appeared to file away that information as though she could understand, just a little, why he'd come after her.

"I just wish I could have made an arrest tonight." Leaning forward, she propped her elbows on her knees and rested her hands in her palms, sighing. "We could have put an end to all of this. But I dropped the ball."

"You did everything you could."

"Not everything." She met his gaze, her eyes sad. "He, or *she*, is still out there."

"This isn't exactly the life I'd planned to provide for my son, either. One where we're always looking over our shoulders. I'm supposed to make him feel safe."

She smiled then—not the delighted, impish smile he'd come to enjoy a little too much these past few days, but it was something.

"You make your son feel safe and loved every day.

Not every child can say that. You'll also protect him from this vandal or anyone else. If he doesn't already know that, he'll figure it out in a few years."

"You sound like you're filling out my application for Father of the Year." Micah settled back into the sofa cushions, relaxing for the first time since they'd heard sounds outside the goat enclosure.

"I'd better get a pen. You might have a good shot at winning. Can you name any other father who built a petting zoo just so his child and those of his neighbors could spend time with some interesting animals?"

"Hey, I would vote for that guy," he said, chuckling.

Her smile was warm enough to make him shift in his seat. "Me, too."

Deirdre turned in her seat as she had earlier, settling into the listening position with her elbow propped on the back of the couch.

"You know, in all the information you've given me about Harmony Fields and about your life back in New York, you've never told me how you became a cowboy. And how you ended up with all this." She gestured with her free arm to indicate the great room around her.

"I can tell you, but it's not some *Young Guns*–type story. Not Hollywood at all."

She lifted her chin and made a serious face. "I'm prepared to be disappointed but tell me anyway. I really need to hear a boring story. I'm all keyed up after everything tonight. Maybe it will help me get to sleep."

"I'll do my best to be a good sleep aid."

Deirdre shifted on the seat, tucking her bare feet under her, and waited.

"After Dad…you know, I wasn't sure what to do. I only had a few hundred dollars in my savings account that Maeve somehow missed and a few hundred more that I'd just received as birthday presents. Since I could be penniless anywhere, not just in New York, and it was too hard being in a city where everything reminded me of my dad, I bought a bus ticket to Wyoming. I chose it because it was the Cowboy State."

"That's a pretty brave thing for an eighteen-year-old kid to do."

He waved his index finger at her. "Now, don't go calling me brave and messing up my boring story."

"Oh. Of course." She gestured with a flourish for him to continue.

"I know it sounds hokey, but ever since I was a kid, I'd dreamed of being a cowboy. Probably a strange career goal for a kid from the Upper East Side, with an equity fund–manager dad. I didn't even know the difference between Western boots and ropers." He grinned at her then, pleased when she dipped her chin and glanced up at him bashfully over her own boot education.

"Where did you even get a career goal like that?"

"Where else? Westerns. Loved 'em."

Deirdre covered her face with her hands and started coughing.

"You okay?"

"Yeah. Fine." She coughed again. "Go ahead."

"You know, John Wayne, Gary Cooper and, of course, Clint Eastwood."

He narrowed his gaze at her as she cleared her throat again. "You sure you're okay?"

She waved him on.

"So, yes, I wanted to be a cowboy, but I didn't have any idea what one actually did besides ride horses, chase outlaws, impress women. I showed up in Laramie and tried to get a job as a ranch hand."

"I take it you weren't much in demand."

"Not a top candidate. But Doug Blevins, an old rancher who lived not far from here, was looking for some help and didn't mind training a greenhorn from New York City. Even so, it took everyone a while to understand my accent."

"You don't have an accent, as far as I can tell."

"Fifteen years will do that." He tilted his head, studying her. "Getting drowsy yet?"

"Working on it. Would you just tell the story so I can get to my nap?"

"I slept in the bunkhouse at Doug and Marie's place and helped work their land for the next three years, saving money while Doug taught me everything he knew about running a ranch. Then I bought my first piece of property and started my own small operation."

"The ranch that was foreclosed on? How long before you were no longer considered an outsider?"

"I'll let you know when that happens." He chuckled at his own joke. "But seriously, around here, there are some people you will never win over if you weren't born in a ten-mile radius of where they're standing. Good thing there are plenty of others. Once they realized I wasn't going anywhere, they welcomed me like one of their own."

"I can't even imagine what that's like."

"It's nice."

"I bet. Were that rancher and his wife some of the people who welcomed you?" She waited for his nod before continuing. "Do you still get to see them much?"

"Quite a bit, actually. Remember the cook I men-

More to Read.
More to Love.

Get up to 4 Free Books – total value over $20.

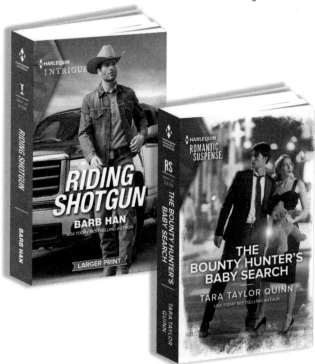

Don't miss out on the newest books from your favorite series!

See Inside for Details

More to Love.
More to Explore.

With more to explore, we'd love to send you up to 4 BOOKS, absolutely FREE when you try the Harlequin Reader Service.

They say that "less is more" — but not when it comes to reading your favorite books!

We know that readers like you can't wait to open their newest book and settle down reading.

We feel the same way. That's why today, you can say "YES" to MORE of the great reading you love — absolutely FREE!

Try **Harlequin® Romantic Suspense** books featuring heart-racing page-turners with unexpected plot twists and irresistible chemistry that will keep you guessing to the very end.

Try **Harlequin Intrigue® Larger-Print** books featuring action-packed stories that will keep you on the edge of your seat. Solve the crime and deliver justice at all costs.

Or **TRY BOTH** and get 2 books from each series!

Your free books are completely free, even the shipping! If you continue with your subscription, you can look forward to curated monthly shipments of brand-new books from your selected series, always at a discount off the cover price! Plus you can cancel any time.

So don't miss out, return your Free Books Claim Card today to get your Free books.

Pam Powers

Free Books Claim Card
Say "Yes" to More Books!

YES! I love reading, please send me more books from the series I'd like to explore and a free gift from each series I select.

Get MORE to read, MORE to love, MORE to explore!

Just write in "**YES**" on the dotted line below then select your series and return this Claim Card today and we'll send your free books & gift asap!

YES

Which do you prefer?

☐ **Harlequin® Romantic Suspense**
240/340 HDL GRSA

☐ **Harlequin Intrigue® Larger-Print**
199/399 HDL GRSA

☐ **BOTH**
240/340 & 199/399
HDL GRSX

FIRST NAME	LAST NAME

ADDRESS

APT.#	CITY

STATE/PROV.	ZIP/POSTAL CODE

EMAIL ☐ Please check this box if you would like to receive newsletters and promotional emails from Harlequin Enterprises ULC and its affiliates. You can unsubscribe anytime.

HI/HRS-622-LR_MMM22

HARLEQUIN® Reader Service —**Here's how it works:**

Accepting your 2 free books and free gift (gift valued at approximately $10.00 retail) places you under no obligation to buy anything. You may keep the books and gift and return the shipping statement marked "cancel." If you do not cancel, approximately one month later we'll send you more books from the series you have chosen, and bill you at our low, subscribers-only discount price. Harlequin® Romantic Suspense books consist of 4 books each month and cost just $5.49 each in the U.S. or $6.24 each in Canada, a savings of at least 12% off the cover price. Harlequin Intrigue® Larger-Print books consist of 6 books each month and cost just $6.49 each in the U.S. or $6.99 each in Canada, a savings of at least 13% off the cover price. It's quite a bargain! Shipping and handling is just 50¢ per book in the U.S. and $1.25 per book in Canada*. You may return any shipment at our expense and cancel at any time by contacting customer service — or you may continue to receive monthly shipments at our low, subscribers-only discount price plus shipping and handling.

▲ If offer card is missing write to: Harlequin Reader Service, P.O. Box 1341, Buffalo, NY 14240-8531 or visit www.ReaderService.com ▲

NO POSTAGE
NECESSARY
IF MAILED
IN THE
UNITED STATES

BUSINESS REPLY MAIL
FIRST-CLASS MAIL   PERMIT NO. 717   BUFFALO, NY

POSTAGE WILL BE PAID BY ADDRESSEE

HARLEQUIN READER SERVICE
PO BOX 1341
BUFFALO NY 14240-8571

tioned?" He waited for her nod before continuing. "That's Marie. And the neighbors who watch Derek sometimes? Doug and Marie. And the neighbor who made the quilt you thought I was destroying?"

"Let me guess. Marie?"

"You're good at this game."

Deirdre stood up from the sofa and stepped closer to the wall of windows. "I can see how you started now, but I still don't understand how you were able to move from broke cowboy to rancher to über-successful rancher, all in just fifteen years."

"First, fifteen years is a long time. The second part dealt with determination. I kept my head low, worked my tail off and reinvested profits from livestock sales back into the ranch."

"And the house, of course." She leaned her head back and stared at the woodworking on the great room's ceiling.

"That was mostly Leah's project. I was still living in the old house, located right here, when I met her."

"I wondered how she fit into all of this."

He shook his head, recalling the memory of color swatches and chaos over signs of success that hadn't mattered much to him. "Don't get me wrong—I love this house. It's amazing. But I really liked the old house, too. I would probably have stayed in it another ten years if she hadn't suggested that we needed a bigger place to make Harmony Fields look like a *real ranch*."

"As opposed to the *pretend* one you were living on before."

"I thought the same thing," he said, rolling his eyes.

"I wondered if you got to make many of the decorating decisions for this place. Some of it, well, just doesn't seem like you."

Micah slid a glance her way. Deirdre had only been here a few days. She couldn't know him that well, and yet she seemed to see him more clearly than Leah ever had.

"I got to have an opinion on some of it." He shrugged, smiling. "Okay. Not much."

"Like the guest room?"

He shook his head. "Or the paint colors for the master bedroom and the nursery. The architect, the builder, Leah and the interior decorator she insisted on did most of it."

"And did a great job mostly."

He glanced around. Some choices he should have expressed stronger opinions about, and some, like that ridiculous pecan range hood cover, he should have nixed for the showy extravagances they were.

"Wait." He pointed to the fireplace and the sofas and the accent chairs by turns. "I chose those stones for that wall myself. And I picked out all of this furniture."

"My two favorite things in the whole house."

Micah would have wondered if she was joking if she weren't stroking the sofa arm like she would a cat. Or him, his thoughts added without permission.

"Mine, too." But he didn't look at her as he said it, worried he'd be too tempted to touch her the way she had the soft leather.

"Do you have any photos of the original house? I bet it was nice."

"Well, 'nice' might be a stretch, but it was comfortable. Homey."

"A nice place to raise a family," she said before he had the chance.

"Yeah." The bookshelf in the corner drew his attention. Some of the photo albums, including his wedding album, had been destroyed by the vandals, but he'd filled the new shelves with some that had been relegated to a back bedroom before.

"You know, I might have photos of the old house in one of those books. You sure you want to see them?"

"Only if they'll make my bedtime story even more sleep-inducing."

"I'll do my best." He crossed the room to the bookshelf and pulled out a couple of albums, including one filled with Derek's baby pictures. Then, as an afterthought, he grabbed the single scrapbook that included photos of his life back in New York. He carried them all back to the sofa and piled them on the coffee table.

"What are all these?"

"I'm not sure which book they're in." He gathered the first and started flipping through pages.

As if she recognized this delicate invitation into his past, Deirdre sat back, folding her hands and waiting instead of reaching for a book.

One of the books contained only construction photos for the house, as his late wife had documented every step from demolition to framing to closing in to near completion.

Deirdre scooted closer to him so she could get a better look at the photos.

"If she recorded the whole process, why are there no pictures of the house before they tore it down?"

"I asked her that," he admitted. "I also wanted to know why she'd print out all these photos that she took on her phone. She wasted a ton of printer ink to make this album."

"Maybe she was just excited to build her dream house and wanted to record every step in the process."

"Maybe."

Leah hadn't been nearly as enthusiastic about recording the milestones in her pregnancy, he realized now. She'd refused to let him take photos of her, saying she didn't want any record of her looking so fat. In retrospect, that truth offered a prediction of what would take place later.

"Not a single photo of the old house?" Deirdre asked as Micah closed the first album and set it aside.

"Nothing yet, but I'm sure there has to be at least one somewhere."

Despite that he probably wouldn't find it there, he couldn't resist selecting a newer book next.

"Are those Derek's baby pictures? Let me see." Deirdre scooted closer again, this time so close that their legs nearly touched, as she took hold of one side of the album.

This book recorded his son's life from those first messy moments while the obstetrics nurse cleaned up his tiny red body. There was even a photo of Micah holding the baby next to Leah in the hospital bed— after she'd applied her makeup and fixed her hair, of course.

"You have a beautiful family," Deirdre said automatically and then shifted on the cushion next to him. "I mean, Leah was pretty."

"Yes, she was," he managed in what he hoped was a normal voice. No matter what had happened after that, the statement was no less true.

He continued turning pages, with most images featuring Derek alone, lying on a play mat looking cute, sitting in a highchair, his face painted with birthday cake, being coaxed to touch one of the first arrivals at the petting zoo. Micah could be found in some of the photos. Leah was in far fewer, but he'd printed all of those, since they would be the only things his son would have to remember his mother.

Deirdre had a sweet comment to make about each one, excited as though she'd never seen a baby picture before. Her words touched him in the way that all parents love to hear that others think their babies are beautiful, but there was something more to it. Something tender.

"Oh my gosh, that boy is so cute. How could you ever be upset with this sweet little guy?" She pointed to a photo of Derek with a bowl of mac and cheese that he'd dumped on his head.

"I believe we've discussed the baby-puke moments." But he couldn't help grinning. "Anyway, you said you couldn't coo."

"I wasn't cooing."

"That was definitely cooing."

Deirdre crossed her arms and pushed out her bottom lip in a pretend pout. "And if it was, he's not here to hear me, so it doesn't count."

"Whatever you say." He set the book aside and reached for the third album.

"What's in this one?"

"Just some old photos," he said vaguely. "If the old house isn't in this one, I don't know where the pictures would be. And they're not on my phone anymore."

But a few slipped out the moment he opened the cover. "Here they are."

He shuffled through the small stack, showing Deirdre the interior and exterior of the three-bedroom bungalow that had only had room for two.

"These are the photos that Marie took and gave to me. She's all about still using a traditional camera and film." After closing on the property, he'd been so proud that he'd brought Doug and Marie by for a tour.

"It's really nice." Deirdre pointed to the photo of the tiny living room with a big picture window. "And you're right. It does look homey."

He didn't know why it made him so happy that she could see that, but it did. After setting the stack on the table, he flipped to the next page of the book.

"The rest of these pictures are of my life back in New York."

Deirdre met his gaze then and dampened her lips. "But I thought you said there aren't any—"

"There aren't," he assured her. "Truth is, I'm lucky to have any photos at all."

Micah flipped through the pages in what felt like a crowbar pulling open a sepulcher.

"This is my mom, Tonya," he managed, despite the thickness in his throat.

"She was beautiful. You look like her."

He blinked several times, trying to hold back emotion, but Deirdre's gaze felt warm on his profile.

"Are you saying you think *I'm* beautiful?" He'd meant it as a joke, but when he glanced her way, Deirdre's cheeks pinkened prettily. Her reaction pleased him more that it should have, and if he were honest with himself, he would admit that he thought the same about her. "If you think I look like her. You need to see a photo of my dad."

They exchanged an awkward look since she'd probably already seen pictures of murder victim Len Perry. But he continued flipping through pages anyway, surprised to find that, like in Derek's album, most of the photos were of him alone, not with his parents. Finally, he came across a shot of him and his father near Castle Garden in Battery Park. From his age and their forced smiles, he could only guess that his mother had taken it.

He pulled back the plastic covering, peeled the photo from the sticky adhesive and handed her the print.

"You're right. You do look like him. Much more here than in the photos we already had of him."

He forced himself not to think about what pictures they did have, since one of them was probably postmortem. "You're saying that because we're photographed together."

She studied it through squinting eyes and then shook her head. "I think it's more you both look so sad in it."

"But we were smiling." It unsettled him that she'd picked up on the truth that most would have missed. She'd never known his father beyond a weathered case file. But she knew him, he realized, his legs feeling so unsteady that he was glad they were seated.

He accepted the photo back from her and stared at those long-ago faces.

"We both know that anyone can smile in a photo, but it doesn't always mean the people in them were *happy*."

"Guess you were right about that one. Mom took it from her wheelchair. You can tell by the odd angle. Dad and I put on our brave faces, but we must not have been all that convincing. That was the last outing we had as a family before she died."

"I'm sorry."

She wore a solemn expression, as though she regretted being right.

"I'm not. It was a good day." Though his throat filled again, he added, "I'm glad we got to spend it together."

"I'm glad, too."

He turned the pages silently, hoping to find more that Deirdre would want to see but pretty sure he wouldn't. His father had never been a fan of being in front of a camera, even on good days. Neither remarked on the awkward middle school pictures, the team photo from JV basketball and the random selfie that offered no explanation why his thirteen-year-old self had thought that printing it out was a good idea.

On the pair of photos of him with a birthday cake, Micah stopped, his breath catching.

"That's my eighteenth birthday party. I'm there." He pointed to himself next to the cake, looking as uncomfortable as he always had around Maeve. "And Dad's over there."

He indicated a slightly out-of-focus image of his father applauding, his elbows lifted at shoulder level.

"What about her? Can you see her?" Deirdre leaned over him, partially blocking his view of the photo. "She didn't take the picture, did she?"

He bent closer, examining it, and then shook his head. "No, but she's not in it, either. Well, she is, but…" He pointed to the hand in the corner of the image, cutting the cake.

"Of course, she would be the one with no face in

the picture but holding the knife. She probably tried to avoid the camera."

Micah couldn't stop shivering. He didn't even try to tell himself Deirdre hadn't noticed as she pulled back from the photo album, her gaze narrowed. Though he turned the page and tried to act natural as he peeled apart two pages stuck together with that photo-destroying adhesive, he braced himself for her barrage of questions. He was still hiding something, and if she didn't already know it, she at least suspected. Finally, he pulled the two pages apart.

"Is there something about—" Deirdre gasped and pointed to the book.

He followed her finger to the photo album lying open on the page that had been between the two glued together. His breath froze in his throat.

His father and the woman who would murder him stared back at them from a souvenir wedding chapel photo, complete with an Elvis impersonator and a heading that read, We Got Hitched in Vegas.

Chapter 12

"Well, *Viva Las Vegas*."

Deirdre managed to avoid clenching her teeth when she said it but couldn't keep it up afterward. "I thought you said you didn't have any pictures."

After all the things they'd shared in the last couple of days, including that kiss that still hung over them like a pair of huge, puckered lips in the corner of the room, he'd been lying to her all along. He'd just humored her to get help finding who'd been targeting his family. But if he ever aspired to try a career off the ranch, she would suggest acting. He feigned shock really well. For the longest time, he didn't even close his mouth. When he did, he swallowed visibly and then lifted his gaze from the photo album, looking like he'd seen a ghost. *Bravo!*

"I *didn't* have any."

His voice sounded strange, as though his own words

didn't make sense to him, but she refused to buy what he was selling.

"It's not a good idea to lie while the evidence is staring us right in the face."

He had the nerve to glare at *her*.

"Believe what you want, but I can tell you that until this moment, I didn't know this photo existed. I wasn't even at the wedding. I'd hoped no photos existed from that day."

Strange how she wanted to give him the benefit of a doubt, wanted this to be an accident and not a lie. Had her father and ex-husband taught her nothing about the risk in trusting men?

"Then how do you explain how it got in your photo album?"

Micah raised both hands and lowered them. "Your guess is as good as mine."

Then, lifting a brow, he flipped back to the birthday-party photos. "You know, I've never seen those pictures before, either."

"You didn't put them in the book?" The tiny hairs on the back of her neck lifted as she realized he might be telling the truth.

"Would have been hard to do, since I didn't know about them."

He met her gaze as though daring her to accuse him of lying again. Then he shook his head, his expression pinched.

"You don't think…?"

"That Maeve would have put them there? Doubtful." She'd considered it herself but immediately dismissed it. "She doesn't seem like the sentimental type. And since she probably planned to have a different identity not long after that wedding day, she wouldn't have wanted photos of those nuptials floating around."

"I don't mean her." In the party photo, Micah brushed the tip of his forefinger over the image of his father, the plastic covering separating it from his touch. "I mean *him*."

"I can see the party pictures, but why would he put his wedding photo in *your* album?"

Micah wasn't listening. Nor was he focused on the photo that most interested her. Instead, he pulled back the plastic film over his birthday photos and slid his finger under each of them as though performing delicate surgery. When both shots were free, their four corners curling toward their centers, he flipped the first one over. He appeared disappointed with the adhesive residue he found on the other side.

"What were you expecting? The date stamp?" That made sense since photo shops used to print the month and year on the back of developed pictures.

"It's probably nothing."

But his breath hitched as he turned over the second image. Deirdre leaned closer, trying to get a better look. Someone had written in script on the back of it.

"What does it say?"

He handed her the photo and let her read it for herself.

You see, your party was as wonderful as I told you it would be. Ariel does love you. Pretty soon you'll love her as much as I do. Love, Dad

"Wow. I'm sorry."

He accepted the photo back from her and lowered it facedown on top of the book.

"Why did you think to look there?"

"It was just something Dad did. After Mom died, he started leaving notes for me. In my backpack. Inside the refrigerator. Under my pillow. He must have found it easier than talking about feelings, and he wanted me to know he was there for me."

"That's sweet. It probably helped during that shaky time after he met Maeve."

As she waited for an answer that didn't come, her stomach felt queasy. "Don't tell me he stopped writing the notes after he started dating her."

He cleared his throat. "Okay, I won't tell you."

"I'm really sorry, Micah."

"I never received any sort of note from him after that. Until now." He pointed to his father's clear handwriting. "I hate that I'm a thirty-three-year-old man with a kid of my own, and it still matters. This was his last message to me—ever—and it was still about *her*."

He spat the last word, and his shoulders curled forward as though he were eighteen again, feeling all the pain and betrayal for the first time.

"I'm so sorry."

Micah gave her a side glance. "You're going to have to stop apologizing. Even about losing the suspect. And the other thing. You didn't do anything wrong."

"You know I did. In addition to everything else, I came here and forced you to dig up a past you wanted to forget."

Her gaze lowered to the photo again. They'd finally located a decent image of Maeve O'Leary—this time purporting to be Ariel Porter Perry—and though the photo would be great for use with facial-recognition software, she couldn't bring herself to even ask him for it. Because of her, he'd found the note that had to be like losing his father all over again.

"I'm really—"

He lifted a hand to stop her from apologizing again. "Don't be. I never looked at those albums. If you hadn't urged me to look back, I might not have found this stuff for *another* fifteen years."

"Your dad's promise that you would one day love his murderous wife?"

Deirdre winced over her harsh words even though resentment against the senior Perry lingered like a hard rock in her stomach. Micah only offered a sad, closed-lipped smile.

"Not that. I could have waited a few more decades before seeing that message. I'm talking about this."

He turned to the page with the wedding photo, peeled back the plastic and loosened it from the adhesive. Though he flipped it over to check the back, this time he found only residue.

"You wanted *that*?"

"No, but you do." He handed it to her. "And I needed it as a reminder of Las Vegas."

"Because your dad thought you would one day want memories of his wedding?" Deirdre stared down at the smiles of the deceitful bride and the vulnerable widower she'd targeted.

"The picture reminded me how much Maeve loved Vegas. Remember? You wanted to know about her favorite places. And whether my dad planned to or not, he just helped in maybe locating his murderer."

"So she liked Las Vegas," Deirdre said evenly.

He nodded as though he'd just given her the address of Maeve O'Leary's hiding place.

"She talked about Vegas all the time, like it was heaven or something. There would be plenty of places to hide there, don't you think?"

"Thousands. But it's something." Though she'd tried to sound upbeat, his frown told her she'd failed.

"That's not helpful at all, is it?"

She shrugged. "From what I've read, about thirty million tourists visit that city every year. I bet a lot of people go there to disappear."

"So, it wasn't helpful." He tapped his fingers to his forehead several times in quick succession, as though trying to shake information loose. Then he pushed back his shoulders. "But this will be. The other place that Maeve loved was Greenwich Village. I don't know why I didn't think of it before. She visited there constantly. The population has to be smaller than thirty million, right?"

Deirdre lunged for her phone and did a quick search. "Just twenty-two thousand."

"Do you think she could be hiding somewhere in the Village?"

"Maybe." She stared down at her phone, regretting what she would have to say next. "It's something, anyway. Enough that I need to check back in with the team."

Micah glanced down at his watch. "You're going to call them this late? If it's nearly eleven o'clock here, then in New York it's—"

"Almost one." She clicked through her series of contacts until she found a listing for Sean Colton.

"If you call your cousin now, you'll just wake him up and make sure someone else has trouble sleeping tonight."

"You're right." She set her phone aside. "But first thing in the morning, I need to give the team an update. This is the best lead we've had in a while."

"Since learning about my dad? And me?"

When Deirdre shrugged, Micah grinned. "Well, it's about time for that hot chocolate. Want some?"

She nodded. It wasn't as if she would be able to sleep anyway now that she had both a photo and at least one solid clue about where to locate Maeve O'Leary.

Once Micah had crossed to the kitchen, she reached for her phone again and stared down at Sean's contact information. Sean probably wouldn't mind being awakened in the middle of the night if she'd arrested Maeve and located Humphrey Kelly, but this information didn't come close to that.

Deirdre crossed and uncrossed her legs as a thought that had been niggling since they'd discovered the photo settled bluntly in front of her. Once she reported in with the information she'd located in Wyoming, the team would rightly expect her to be on the next plane to LaGuardia to join their search of Greenwich Village. Micah probably expected her to go, too, now that she had the information she'd come for, whether she'd fulfilled her end of the bargain or not. She still had to prove herself to the FBI, after all.

How was she supposed explain to any of them her need to stay at Harmony Fields a little longer? Well, she didn't care what she had to say to them. Someone was still out there targeting Micah and Derek. She had to convince the team to let her stay until the suspect could be stopped.

Micah shouldn't have been surprised to catch Deirdre searching the wedding photo for more answers when he returned with the hot chocolate, so it shouldn't have bothered him that he did. He'd bargained for her help with the investigation on the ranch while he'd still believed he could offer her no valuable information. Now they were even. She'd come to Harmony Fields searching for pictures and other details, and nothing could keep her here now that she had them.

He shook away his annoyance as he set the mugs on the table, reminding himself that he didn't want her to stay. Deirdre blinked and looked up as if only then realizing he'd returned.

"Thanks." She pointed to the chocolate concoction with whipped cream on top and then glanced down at the photo again. "Maeve O'Leary is a beautiful woman. Just like you said. They both look so happy and in love." She paused to set aside the photo and collect the mug instead. "It was a lie."

"Only one of them was lying," he said.

She nodded, her eyes wet. Something squeezed inside his gut. Like him, Deirdre understood intimately the pain of betrayal, but her empathy for his father touched his heart, surprising him.

He took a sip of his drink and returned it to the table. "I wonder how many other photos Maeve owns that look just like that one. Only with different grooms."

"None is my guess," she said. "If she planned to marry and murder more husbands, she wouldn't want any photographic evidence around for police to track her."

"You mean, if police were even smart enough to recognize that the guys' deaths weren't accidental."

"Good point." She lifted her mug to her lips and took a sip. "Even so, if not for your dad tucking that photo into your album, which just happened to have cheap, sticky pages that stuck together and hid it from Maeve, we wouldn't have any evidence at all."

"So, you're saying I'm *lucky*?" Even the word tasted acidic. Nothing about this whole situation could be called that.

Deirdre set her mug aside and then turned on the sofa to face him.

"I would never say that about your life then. What happened to you was tragic. But now?" She paused and gestured to the balcony upstairs, through which his son's closed bedroom door was visible. "You have to admit you are downright blessed."

"Sometimes your bad luck follows you no matter where you go."

As soon as the words were out of his mouth, Micah regretted them. Did he want her to ask questions? Did he need her to know the one thing he'd spent so much time and effort hiding from all his friends here?

He stared at his hands, gripped tight, but he couldn't seem to loosen them. Though she didn't speak, he could feel her gaze on him. Intense. Unwavering. And seeing right through the decorative wall he'd built around the ugly truth of his life.

"When are you going to tell me?"

Looking up, he found her watching him just as he'd predicted. "What are you talking about?"

She leaned toward the coffee table and flipped the photo of his father and stepmother facedown. Then she turned back to him. "What really happened with your wife?"

His throat tightened, the distance between wanting to tell her and really forming the words long and expanding.

"I've already told you all about her."

"There are a few things you didn't explain. Like why you got rid of her clothes so quickly. Why there are no photos of her in this house, except for one album. And why you throw your wedding quilt on the ground for picnics."

He shook his head to make her stop, but she only peppered him with more questions.

"Why did you mention to me about people who think only of themselves? People who don't care who they leave behind." She paused, pressing her lips together. "And why aren't you constantly telling your son about his mother, so he grows up knowing that she loved her family?"

"Because she didn't!"

His words were loud and felt as if someone had ripped them from his throat. Deirdre stared back at him with wide eyes, her mouth slack.

"You wanted to know." Leaping up, Micah stepped to the fire to warm his hands. He spoke to the flames rather than to face her judgment or, worse, her pity.

"Now do you see why I haven't spoken about it? It doesn't help anyone to agonize over things no one can change."

"Talking about it might help *you.*"

"What are you, my counselor or something? I was doing fine before you came here, asking questions and opening old wounds." He glanced over his shoulder, confirming the pity, and something else. Something he couldn't define.

"Were you really? Fine, that is? Don't you think it's finally time that you told someone?"

He considered her words as he stared into the flames,

which were far more under control than his life lately. Then, with a sigh, he returned to his seat.

"Leah was already planning to leave when she died," he said before Deirdre could pose another question.

"I'm so sorry."

He shook his head, not wanting to hear her platitudes or allow them to stop him now that he'd started.

"It didn't matter that she had a six-week-old baby. She was already packed. The accident happened when she'd gone into town to pick up a rental truck for her stuff. She lost control of her car and hit a tree."

Deirdre looked stricken, just like all those mourners at the funeral home who'd come to offer their condolences. Only, she knew the truth.

"It was what it was." He focused on his hands in his lap. If he planned to get through this discussion, he had to avoid looking at her again.

"Did her choice to leave come as a surprise to you?"

Despite his plan, he shot a look her way. "Why are you asking—"

"Was it?"

He shook his head.

"Did you love her?"

"I thought so. She was my wife." He waited for her to ask another question, but when she didn't, he finally answered. "Yeah."

His throat tightened as anger and hurt wound together, as they always did when he allowed himself to really remember Leah.

"I thought we shared this vision," he explained. "We would build Harmony Fields together, raise a family and make a difference in our community. It turned out she just liked the idea of being a successful rancher's wife. The land. The house. Kind of ironic that she hated living here."

"It's not for everyone."

He narrowed his gaze at her. "You should know."

"Did it get better after she got pregnant with Derek?"

"If anything, it got worse. It wasn't what she'd signed up for." He blinked away the memories, many of which had charitably passed in a fog. "And then the house was suddenly filled with the stress of a newborn, and she wanted out."

"You hid all this from your neighbors?"

"Leah was already gone. What good would it have done for me to malign her character at that point? We were already in mourning and had enough to deal with. She hadn't filed for divorce yet, and no staff were working at the house at the time, so I tucked the boxes away until after the funeral. Then, when I did donate her stuff, I drove to Cheyenne."

"Why go through all that trouble? You crafted this alternate story because your wife left you?"

"No." He shook his head. "You don't understand. I didn't do it because she wanted to leave me. It was because she left *him*."

"And she planned to divorce *you*."

"Yes, she did. She also said she wouldn't be leaving empty-handed."

"No prenup?"

"You'd think I would have learned from my father's experience. But no. I would have lost the ranch if we'd divorced and been forced to split everything."

"She didn't say anything about child custody?"

Her wary expression told him she already knew the answer.

"In all her threats, she never once suggested that she wanted custody of her son. What kind of person leaves her own child?"

"Apparently, a lot of people do."

Micah held his hands wide. "Now do you see why I kept this information to myself? I didn't want anyone to know. I didn't want *my son* to know."

"So the idea of abandoning a kid didn't catch on with all your neighbors and upset the delicate social order in all of southeastern Wyoming?"

He shook his head, scrunching his face and mouthing the word *what*. "No one needed to know that Derek's dad was ridiculous, just like his grandfather."

"What are you talking about?"

"Are you trying to say you don't see the similarities between the two stories? They're exactly alike."

"No, Micah. They're not." She shook her head hard for emphasis. "The circumstances are completely different."

"My father and I both married women who made fools of us. I don't want Derek to be ashamed of me like I was—" His words broke then, but the truth lay open in the air between them.

"Of him," Deirdre finished for Micah, shaking her head. "Your father was taken in by a black widow. And you were unlucky enough to have a wife who realized too late that marriage and motherhood weren't for her. The situations weren't the same."

"But I *knew* better," he insisted. "I'd watched Maeve sink her manicured nails into my father and then twist and turn them until she got her way. Still, I came across a woman just like her—one who found my bank account more attractive than me—and I let her do the same thing to me."

"You're conflating two situations that have nothing to do with each other. Whether Maeve took advantage of him or not, your dad was a grown man. He was responsible for his own decisions, and, unfortunately he *chose* a woman over his son.

"You're *nothing* like your father." Deirdre leaped up from the couch and whirled to face him.

Micah stood as well, Deirdre's words feeling like an easy way out, an escape he didn't deserve. "You didn't even know my father."

"But I know *you*." She crossed her arms, lifting her chin, daring him to argue. "I know you put your child first every time. When Derek grows up, he'll only be proud to be your son."

"You think you know me…"

"I know you," she repeated, her gaze never leaving his. "And if your wife didn't know how infinitely lucky she was to have you in her life—"

Deirdre never had the chance to finish what she'd been about to say, as Micah shot forward and pulled her to him, firm strength against an equal match, hearts pounding with the same frenzied pace. At first, she stared up at him in shock, but then the corners of her mouth softened in welcome, and he crushed his lips to hers.

Chapter 13

Deirdre braced herself against an incoming tide as she absorbed Micah's kiss that tasted of desperation and, maybe, relief. She recognized that he was probably just grateful for the things she'd said about him, but his arms felt so good around her, his body so tempting pressed against hers. She couldn't help but to join him in the frenzy.

Her hesitation earlier now feeling like someone else's life, in some distant reality, she claimed his mouth, reveling in the pressure and texture of his lips. She brushed hers over his once, twice and then a third time before settling in deep. Quickly, she discovered she wanted more, craved it with a breathlessness and heat that eclipsed the flames still dancing in the fireplace. Tonight, even just kissing Micah Perry would not be enough.

A fleeting appeal for caution stole through her

thoughts, but she hurled it aside. She didn't want to be careful this time, chose to ignore the clash between what she wanted and what she deserved. On this one magical night, she would show him how amazing he was and how much she wished they were different people. Ones who stood a chance of winning the lottery and ending up together.

She slid her hands up his arms and over his shoulders, reveling in the flex of his muscles beneath her touch. Once her fingers reached their destination at his nape, she fitted herself to him, convex to concave, demanding strength to welcoming softness. Micah pressed her to him as well, his effort and the ineffective masks of their cotton shorts leaving no questions about the depth of his desire.

They kissed with the urgency of the last dance at a bar closing forever, each touch a gift, each taste a memory. Though she grew light-headed, she still protested with a groan when Micah slid his mouth away from hers, and they both gasped for breath.

"I love your sounds," he breathed against her neck and then moved on to adore her earlobe.

"That's a compliment I've never received before." Her desire-roughened voice might have embarrassed her another day. Now she didn't care.

As Deirdre initiated another fevered kiss, she pressed her thigh to his and walked him backward the few steps to the couch. Micah stretched out on the leather, his head on a throw pillow, and reached out to her. With a wicked smile, she braced herself over the length of his frame and lowered to him in slow, halting steps.

Impatient, he reached up and jolted her elbows,

causing her to land with her full weight on top of him. She buried her face, laughing against his cheek.

"Oof." He winced and then chuckled. "That was supposed to be a smooth move."

"It was. Really." She propped herself up on her elbows again.

"Thanks for protecting my fragile male ego."

"Thought you didn't have one of those. Don't worry. I've got your back." She glanced over her shoulder and down the length of their perfectly stacked bodies. "Or front."

"Front is good."

He gave her one of those smiles that made her heart pound and her body warm in all its secret places. Then, when Micah's expression became serious again, ice poured uncomfortably over those same spots.

"Is this a good idea?" he asked.

"Probably not."

"Only probably?"

She leaned her forehead against his. "*Absolutely* not."

He cleared his throat. "But do you still want to…?"

For a few seconds, she pretended not to understand what he was asking. Then she grinned. "Oh, hell, yeah."

"You took the words right out of my mouth."

He found another way to keep those lips busy, lifting up and pressing his mouth to hers. She followed him back to the pillow and returned his kiss as if it were her first but one she was determined to perfect. She strained against him. Wanting. Needing. Demanding.

She gulped air when she reluctantly lifted her head. "Do you, uh, have…something? I mean, I'm on the pill, but, you know, nowadays I can't afford to take any sort of risk."

Deirdre frowned. She sounded as nervous as a teenager who'd never been in this position before. The nervous part, that was real.

"Kitchen."

Kitchen? She lifted off him, and he sat up, brushing back his hair that already stood every which way. When he was finished, he hurried from the room.

After several seconds of rustling and drawer slamming, he returned to the great room, carrying a small box of condoms.

She watched him over the back of the couch. "Did you just pull those out of your junk drawer?"

He shrugged, grinning. "Lucky they were there, too. Right beneath some AA batteries, a box of broken crayons and a package of pacifiers with just one left in it."

"Sexy."

"What can I say? I'm a responsible single dad. Not a saint. The junk drawer has a baby lock on it, too, so I guess we can call this *supersafe* sex." As he rounded the end of the sofa, he hesitated. "I mean, if we're still going to do this."

"You never know." She cleared her throat and then managed to add, "I might lose interest if you keep dawdling."

"Can't let that happen."

He hit the wall switch as he passed, leaving only the fireplace and a small lamp in the corner to cast light and shadow about the room. When he sat next to her, he immediately started tracing a line of kisses along her throat. As he dipped his thumb and forefinger just beneath her T-shirt collar and traced mesmerizing lines along both her collarbones, Deirdre closed her eyes and all but swooned.

"There's a four-poster bed in that room if you'd like to relocate." He pointed to the closed door that led to the main-floor master suite. "Great new mattress."

"And leave one of your favorite pieces of furniture?" Trying to look more confident than she felt, she smiled and brushed her hand slowly over the leather.

"It's about to become my all-time favorite," he said.

He took her mouth again in an exquisite kiss that reignited her passion until she squirmed next to him, trying to move closer. When he reached for the hem of her T-shirt, she yanked it over her head herself, but then she glanced down and covered her plain sports bra with crossed arms.

"Let's just pretend that's something lacy and feminine."

"Why would we need to do that?" He gently peeled her hands away from her chest and then tried to slide one of the bra straps over her shoulder. "Everything I'm dying to see is right here."

"You'll never see anything if you try it that way." She chuckled, took a deep breath and pulled the vise-like contraption over her head.

Micah didn't even touch her. He followed the lines of the newly exposed skin down the slope of her neck, over the curves of her breasts to the dip of her waist with only his gaze, and yet her skin tingled and warmed as though he'd touched her everywhere. Loved her everywhere. If he didn't do just that, and soon, she would ignite like the log in that gas fireplace.

"I knew you'd be perfect."

He breathed the words, close to her neck but still without the contact she craved.

"I'm not—"

"You are to me."

His words were like magic, setting free something inside her, opening locks and smashing shackles. She pressed herself to his chest and claimed his mouth, drawing in his gasp and then following his movement as he smiled against her lips.

She bunched up his T-shirt and slowly exposed the chest and taut belly that even his tight work shirts had failed to properly predict. He reached back with both hands and ripped it over his head. Unable to hold back any longer, she splayed her hands over his chest. Micah chose that moment to touch as well, first with gentle, exploring fingers and then with purposeful hands, capable of breathtaking finesse.

Her hands found a mission of their own, working at the waistband of his shorts until Micah stopped what he was doing, stood and stepped out of them along with his briefs. Another of her sounds must have escaped as her gaze followed his lines of work-earned strength and masculine virility. Of broad shoulders, tapered waist and powerful thighs. All backlit by lapping flames. He grinned back at her knowingly. Then he drew her to her feet and peeled away the last of her clothing.

When they both stood fully naked, Micah drew her against him and kissed her slowly, luxuriously, in no hurry despite the obvious insistence of his body. He backed her to the sofa and waited as she stretched out, but when she reached up to draw him to her, he held up a forefinger, asking for a delay.

He made the wait worth her while, bending first to

press an openmouthed kiss to the inside of her ankle. Then he started a journey northward, sharing delicious attention in some spots along the way and ignoring the pleas of others until she wiggled and squirmed. Finally, he edged Deirdre onto her side and stretched alongside her, giving her access to him as well. Her passion building with each sigh, each shiver, Deirdre joined him in fervent exploration, first with hands, then lips and tongue. She wanted more. She needed all.

"Please!"

"Well, you did ask nicely." Micah grinned as he sat up and made quick work of putting on a condom.

He glanced back at her over his shoulder. "You're sure about this?"

"You're still asking?" She gestured, indicating all that had already taken place on the sofa. But at his serious expression, she nodded. "Yes, I'm sure."

He shifted then and braced himself above her, waiting. "You said you couldn't take a risk. But everything about what we're doing here is one of those. The biggest risk of all."

She knew he was talking about more than sex. More than two consenting adults borrowing each other's bodies and seeking momentary relief. He referred to complications when everything about their fledging relationship was so blanketed with them that there should have been caution signs posted all around them.

She couldn't think about that now. Not if she planned to be in the moment. To experience all of it, even if it would be just this once. After another nod from her, Micah brought them together in one slow shift. They began to move, first slowly, then with intention, then with desperation. Deirdre fell first, her release both blissful and bittersweet. Micah followed soon after and buried his whiskered face against her neck.

For a long time, the only sound beyond their labored breaths was the crackle and pop of the fire. But as Micah shifted away and slid on his shorts to dispose of the condom, the thoughts that Deirdre had been pushing aside gathered inside her, determined to be heard now.

Micah was wrong. Sex wasn't the biggest risk between them, beyond the crapshoot physical relationships always presented. The gamble was that one of them would let it go too far, let a search for pleasure and relief become something more. Would make the mistake of falling in love. If that was the biggest risk, she worried that for her, it might already be too late.

As Micah pulled his T-shirt over his head and started for the stairs, he had to remind himself not to run. That was ridiculous. He'd never been one of those awkward-morning-after guys, who tiptoed out before their intimate partners had barely made it through the afterglow. But something about what had just taken place between Deirdre and him felt different.

He should have known it would be a mistake to go to bed with Deirdre, even if technically they'd never made it close to anything with a mattress or sheets. Just kissing her should have been enough of a warning. Even then, all he'd been able to think about was finding another chance to taste those lips. But more than that, he should have known that having sex with Deirdre Colton would rock his world and make him desperate to repeat that act anytime and anywhere she liked.

Just the possibility that she could have the kind of

control over him that Maeve had had over his father scared the hell out of him. Why had he even started something with her, knowing there was no possible future in it? She belonged in Washington, and Wyoming was his home. Nothing could erase those seventeen hundred miles between them. Until now, that had been just fine by him.

When he reached the landing, he couldn't resist looking back at her, though he'd promised himself he wouldn't. Though her back was to him, she still appeared dejected, her shoulders dropping, her head hanging, as she pulled her T-shirt back over her head. She had to assume that he was rejecting her right after making love with her, but why wouldn't she believe that? He'd practically leaped off the sofa the moment their breathing returned to normal, and his excuse about checking on Derek sounded as weak then as now.

His mouth went dry as she pulled the shirt down so far that it nearly covered her shorts. He hated that she felt the need to hide now, after he'd already seen and sampled all her beauty beneath those layers of cotton, but he couldn't tell her how those images were burned in his memory. Or how he'd run because he was scared, not that he didn't want her. Hell, from now on, he would probably be turned on every time he saw a sports bra at the store, since it would remember him of her creamy skin beneath hers.

He shook his head to dispel the images but couldn't help sneaking another peek at her. Though he caught her watching him, she shifted her gaze to the fire and then grabbed the remote to shut it off.

"Is Derek okay?" She made a show of crossing to

put the remote on the mantel instead of looking over at him again.

"I haven't checked yet. I'm going now."

"Oh. Right."

Deirdre shook her head, signaling he wasn't the only one who felt discombobulated after what had just taken place between them.

"I just wanted to make sure he's all right," he said.

She nodded, but her gaze flicked to the video baby monitor he'd left on the coffee table. He could easily have checked on his son that way, and they both knew it. At least she didn't point it out.

He continued up the stairs and down the hallway, needing to put a little distance between them. From the stark look on her face, he could only guess that she needed it, too. Beyond that she thought he was rejecting her, Deirdre had to wonder what she would tell her team when she called them in a few hours. He might have been a rancher who'd slept with an investigator, but she was an FBI special agent who'd had sex with a witness.

If only his feelings about what had happened between them were as easily definable. He'd known that Deirdre was only in Wyoming temporarily. She hadn't even planned to spend one night when she'd first arrived. She hated everything about this part of the country and the ranch, and yet he'd let himself become involved with her anyway. Worse even than his history with Leah had taught him nothing, but he'd let her get close to his son, too.

Outside Derek's room, Micah paused, rubbing his forehead. Derek would forget about her. Kids were resilient that way. But Micah wouldn't forget. He wouldn't even be able to cuddle Eleanor Roosevelt in the goat enclosure without thinking of her. As for that couch, he would never be able to sit on it again without seeing Deirdre lying there.

He carefully turned the knob and opened the door and stared into the darkened room. With the only light coming from the hallway, he could barely make out Derek's bed, the toy shelves, the dresser and the rocking chair. Glad he'd remembered to pick up his phone, he pulled it from his shorts pocket and clicked on the flashlight app.

He didn't want to awaken Derek, but he had to get a peek at him, maybe sneak an extra good-night kiss. After everything that had happened since they'd put Derek to bed—first the trespasser and then everything with Deirdre—Micah just needed to watch his little boy sleep. He hated that he was there for his own needs, not his son's. Deirdre was wrong about him: he didn't put Derek first.

Still, he was already there, so he crossed the room to Derek's bed, holding the light low so it didn't shine on the boy's face. Derek looked so sweet, sleeping as he always did on his back with his fisted hands above his head. Micah brushed the little boy's hair back from his face. After Deirdre left in a few hours, it would be just the two of them again. Maybe it would be hard for him to return to that, but he could be more focused on protecting Derek from the suspect targeting them.

As he bent down to drop a kiss on the child's head, his gaze caught on something that looked white against the dark headboard of Derek's big-boy bed. Micah redirected his light on what turned out to be a piece of paper taped to the headboard. He ripped it off the wood and brought it closer, aiming the flashlight app at it. He stiffened as he read the words, blood freezing in his veins.

Leave Wyoming or the kid is next.

Chapter 14

Deirdre stood at the bar in the kitchen, taking her first sip of the chamomile tea she'd spent fifteen minutes trying to locate, when she heard Micah tromping down the stairs. She barely had time to brace herself before he rushed into the kitchen.

"Good. You haven't gone to bed," he said.

She set down her mug to avoid spilling it and raised her right hand to signal for him to stop whatever he'd been about to say. "Look, I'm tired. Can we just skip the postmortem for now? It's been a really long night, and I get that everything was a big mistake, but I'm not ready to discuss it."

Rather than to look away as she'd expected him to do under these awkward circumstances, he pinned her with a look she couldn't quite define.

"That's not what I want to talk about."

Deirdre wrapped her hands around her mug. "I'm

not in a good place to talk about anything else, either. I'm just going to drink this tea and—"

"Well, you'd better get in a good place. And fast."

He produced a piece of paper. Holding it by the corner, he set it on the counter next to her.

"What's this?" Something telling her not to touch it, she leaned closer to it and read. Her chest tightened as though she'd been the one running from upstairs. "Where did you find this?"

"Taped to the headboard of Derek's bed."

She shot a look to the stairs and then back to Micah. "He's been in this house?"

He didn't have to answer. His ashen coloring and overly bright eyes did it for him.

"Any idea when?" She started working out the timeline in her head.

"Well, *that* wasn't in his room when we put him to bed."

"So, sometime between seven thirty and—" she paused to glance at her watch "—just after 1:00 a.m." Hours that had included a sweet interlude in the petting zoo, the chase of a vandalism suspect, an alpaca roundup and whatever they could call what had happened between them on Micah's sofa. Her gaze drifted into the great room all on its own, but when she jerked it back, she caught him watching her, his eyes cold.

"Yeah, someone got *to my son* when I wasn't paying attention."

She squeezed her eyes shut and opened them again, her stomach feeling like a rock. While her thoughts were flitting to all the unimportant matters, he'd stated the succinct and critical truth. This was about Derek. Nothing else mattered, and if she hadn't been off her game from the moment she'd arrived at Harmony Fields, she would have recognized that.

"He isn't hurt, is he?" She started away from the counter to go check for herself.

"Wait." He didn't say more until she stopped and turned back. "He's fine. He's sleeping."

Then he gripped the edge of the counter, his knuckles white, and tucked his chin, closing his eyes.

"He's okay," she blurted. "You just said it yourself. No one hurt him."

"But they could have."

"The baby monitor." She pointed to the great room, where the device still rested on the coffee table. "You had it with you the whole time."

The look he gave her made her squirm, and not in a good way.

"I wasn't watching it all the time." His gaze flitted to hers and away. "As long as the suspect was quiet and didn't wake up Derek, I would have had to get lucky to check the monitor in time to catch the intruder."

"We weren't that lucky." She included herself in that responsibility because she shared it now. Micah might have felt guilty for failing to shield his son, but she'd been with both of them on the ranch, and the invader had gotten past her as well.

"We know it wasn't at eight thirty." Micah watched the moving hands of the ornate, analog clock on the wall that separated the kitchen from the great room. "The suspect was too busy chasing alpacas to be up here at the house."

Deirdre shook her head. "We don't know that for sure. We still haven't determined if we're looking for just one suspect."

He paced to the sofa and back to the bar. "Another one could have been here at the same time."

"And though I heard a vehicle drive off, that doesn't mean he or she couldn't have parked just down the road and backtracked to the house."

"While we were busy tracking down a bunch of terrified alpacas." He tilted his head back, his jaw clenched, and jerked both hands out, fingers splayed. "He was in here with my *son*!"

"I know, but we have to try to stay calm. We have to think this through." She didn't even mention that the suspect could also have been in the house during the time that they'd been preoccupied in the great room. That would have been too much for him to bear. Or her.

"How do you expect me to stay calm?" He continued to pace, his words coming in that same staccato clip. "I've done everything I was supposed to do. I've reported every incident to local police. I've even traded everything I know about my stepmother for your help, but we're no closer to finding answers than we were before."

"We can't let him win." She tried to look calm, but her skin was the only thing keeping her from flying apart, just as he was.

Micah stopped then, turning his whole body to face the counter, where she still stood, trying to appear in control. Finally, he gripped his forehead.

"You're right." He took several deep breaths and returned to the bar stools. "What do we do now?"

"First, we call the sheriff's office." She pointed to the note. "How much have you touched that thing?"

"Just by the edges."

"That's good." She pulled out her cell phone and

dialed the direct line for the sheriff's office, though at this time of night the dispatcher would answer it just like the emergency line.

"They can still dust for fingerprints," she said while she waited for it to ring. "They might find something."

"Unless whoever wrote it did the same thing you did or wore gloves, like in all the other incidents."

Deirdre scowled at the phone until she heard the click as the call became active.

"Albany County Sheriff's Office, what is your emergency?"

She paced into the great room and filled the dispatcher in on the basic details, noting she didn't believe the suspect remained on the premises.

"A deputy is on his way to take the report," she told Micah when she returned to the kitchen.

She reached up to touch her hair, which had to be a nightmare by now. Crossing to the sink, she wetted her hand and brushed her fingers through it. Then she finger-combed it into semblance of order and tied it in a ponytail, using the band she kept on her wrist. Micah must have gotten the idea, too, as he stepped to the sink and used some water to wet down his hair as well.

Deirdre took a few steps back, giving him a wide berth. "One thing the deputy will want to determine is how the suspect gained access to the house."

He sighed. "The alarm system I'm supposed to have installed is on backorder. If it had already been installed, we would have heard it all the way from the petting zoo and maybe farther."

"Only if you set it. A lot of homeowners have a system and then forget to arm it."

"I'll never forget to do it," he said as seriously, as if he were taking an oath.

She believed him, too. He'd put up with more than anyone should have to from the trespasser on his property.

"I still don't understand how the intruder got in *again*," he said. "We replaced the locks after last time."

"I have a theory on that one." She led him through the kitchen and down the stairs to the lower level, stopping at the slider. Sure enough, the operational side of the door appeared closed but had only been propped over the open space. "One of the oldest tricks in the book."

"But it had a broom handle in it." He pointed to the piece of wood, exactly where it should have been.

"That trick is a myth, unfortunately. At least for some sliders, where it only takes a simple screwdriver to pop it off the track."

He blew out a frustrated breath. "I'll remember that for the next time someone breaks into my house."

She met his gaze directly then. "Let's hope this is the last time."

He did his best to put the door back in the track and then tromped back up the steps after her. She moved back to the bar and sat on a stool.

Micah stood on the other end but didn't sit. "Wait. You said *first* before. What else do you recommend I do?"

Deirdre pointed to the closed door of the bedroom where he'd invited her to join him just an hour before. "Then you start packing."

"What are you talking about?"

She pointed to the letter, still on the counter, the

piece of tape at the top holding it in place. "I think you should do what it says."

"What do you mean?"

She nodded. "Whoever wrote that wants you to leave the state. I think you should do just that. Get out of Dodge."

"Then what was all that earlier about not letting him win?" He planted his elbows on the counter and rested his angry face atop his fists. "I am not leaving Harmony Fields. No one is going to drive us from our home. Harmony Fields is my legacy for my son."

"Nobody's forfeiting a legacy here. It's just a few days away to give law enforcement a chance to do their job." Since he was still shaking his head, she pulled out her trump card. "You'll also be removing Derek from what has become a dangerous situation, and I know you'd do anything to keep him safe."

He glared at her, but he pushed back from the counter and crossed his arms. "In this grand plan of yours, who's supposed to take care of the livestock and the petting zoo? And, for that matter, where exactly are Derek and I supposed to go?"

Deirdre lifted a brow.

Micah pointed at her and started backing away. "Oh, no. We are not going with you to New York. That's an awfully convenient solution for you, anyway. Almost like you planned it."

This time Deirdre crossed her arms. "You really think I created a hoax threat to Derek just to make you fly to the East Coast with me?"

He sighed and shook his head.

At the clang of the doorbell and the sound of pounding to go along with it, Micah crossed to the door. "That didn't take long."

But instead of the deputy, Sheriff Guetta stood on the decking outside the front door, his frown deeper than Micah's.

"What are you doing here?" Micah stepped back and let the sheriff inside.

Dressed in a nylon sweat suit, its jacket zipped over what appeared to be a pajama shirt, Richard stomped through the house to the bar where Deirdre still sat.

"My dispatcher thought I might be interested in this one myself," he groused. "I assure you, I wasn't."

Micah rolled his eyes. "And yet you're here."

Richard sat on one of the bar stools and drummed the countertop. "It's looking like déjà vu, too. So, give me an overview here. I didn't love getting pulled out of my beauty sleep."

Micah and Deirdre took turns filling him in on the details—at least the ones he needed to know. The sheriff listened, asking an occasional question and sometimes jotting down something in the tiny notebook he produced from his zippered pocket.

"Now Special Agent Colton believes that Derek and I should go with her to New York to follow up on a lead for *her* case."

"It's the most reasonable idea." She frowned at Micah before focusing on the sheriff. "Just for the weekend. The ranch hands can take care of the livestock and the petting zoo. Your department could keep watch over Harmony Fields, maybe even sending a deputy to patrol the property a few times a day.

"Then, in New York, I'd like to take Micah to Greenwich Village just to see if there's a place that sparks some memories. Maybe a specific place that Maeve O'Leary might have mentioned."

"You see?" Micah said, gesturing to her. "It sounds like a crazy idea. Not to mention self-serving."

Richard spun in his chair to face him. "You know, I'm inclined to agree with her."

Micah's eyes widened. "You're what?"

"It's a reasonable plan, Micah. One that will keep your son—and you—safe. I'll put Sheriff's Deputy Greg Martin on the assignment."

"Greg's a good guy, but—"

"Micah," he interrupted, "it's time for us to take care of this, once and for all." He brushed his hands as though the matter were settled. "I don't know if taking down a serial killer could be considered self-serving, either."

"Since you've decided to gang up on me, fine. I'll go. At least we can get Derek out of danger." He focused on Richard alone. "You're right. We need to get this over with. It has to stop."

Micah dug through his junk drawer and handed Richard a spare key. "Here. For the deputy."

"What about this?" Richards pointed to the note on the counter. "Who has touched this?"

"Just me. And just the corners," Micah told him. At the sheriff's direction, he produced a paper lunch bag from the pantry to put it in.

"Great." Richard clapped his hands once. "I'll text you Greg's contact information, so you can stay in touch over the weekend. Now, I don't know about you, but I have a bed calling my name."

"Thanks, Sheriff Guetta," Deirdre said. "I'll be checking in with my team, and we'll be on the first flight we can book tomorrow."

When the sheriff waved away her comment with a brush of his hand, she braced herself for whatever he would say next. Maybe he wouldn't be her ally on this, after all.

"You can call me Richard," he said after a few seconds.

"Thanks."

As he stood up from his stool, the sheriff leaned his head back and chuckled. "I sure would like to be a fly on the wall for this little trip of yours. You two are a hoot."

"Thanks, Richard." Micah patted the lawman's back harder than was necessary and then led him to the door.

Richard glanced back just as Micah reached for the latch. "Oh. I need to have a few words with the special agent. Just police stuff."

His gaze narrowed, Micah gestured for Deirdre to take his place. "I'll just be in my room. Packing."

He crossed to his bedroom, went inside and closed the door.

Despite her trepidation, Deirdre stepped to the door and waited. "Yes?"

"Just wanted to wish you luck that you find some great leads on your trip."

"Thank you." She tilted her head and narrowed her gaze.

Richard grinned and lowered his voice. "Also wanted to give you the heads-up that your T-shirt is inside out."

"Oh." She glanced down, her cheeks burning, and then cleared her throat. "I wear it like that sometimes."

"I bet you do. Cheers." He grinned as he opened the door, stepped outside and closed it.

Deirdre glanced over her shoulder to ensure that Micah was still in his room, then yanked off her shirt and righted it.

If even a stranger had been able to pick up on the fact that something had happened between Micah and her, how would they be able to keep it from a whole team of investigators in New York? Particularly a whole team of Coltons.

Crouched behind one of those excessive outbuildings, the spectator nearly cheered as the rental car carried the rancher, the kid and their guest from Harmony Fields. But despite the change in circumstance, it remained important to stay low and stick to the plan. Still, it was a moment for celebration. Micah Perry was finally running scared.

After all the little events taking place around the ranch—so much work for so little reward when damage could be repaired in a matter of days—who knew that it would only take a note placed close to a sniveling two-year-old to make the cowboy run for the hills? It was just a threat, mostly. Placed during that perfect time while the rancher and the lady chased alpacas in that ridiculous petting zoo. The kid wasn't the target—at least not the original one. Collateral damage was always a problem.

The rancher had needed a wake-up call, anyway, since he'd been spending too much time trying to get *into* the pretty investigator and not enough time planning to get his ass *off* the ranch.

Now that the rancher had abandoned ship, it would

be important to observe his next steps. The spectator couldn't begin to tell him what a mistake it would be to return to this place that wasn't his. If they could stay gone, they would get to continue to enjoy breathing in and out and the steady thump of their heartbeats. But if he'd only gone for reinforcements, some promises would just have to be kept. The kid would be the first to go.

Chapter 15

Micah followed Deirdre into the low-lit New York hotel restaurant the next evening, as out of place as she must have felt when pulling her rental car onto his ranch several days before. He'd paired his dress boots with khaki trousers and a fitted navy dress shirt and left his hat at home, but he still couldn't shake the feeling that everyone was watching him and wondering about the cowboy who'd strayed too far from the ranch.

He shouldn't have worried about standing out, though, when the most beautiful woman in the room carried his son through its center, drawing every eye as she passed. Including his. She wore the same incredible jeans as the day he'd met her. Same boots, too, though tonight she appeared as though she belonged in them. The creamy blouse with the strappy thing under it could make any guy long to see what was beneath those layers, but now that he knew all that promise, he was in a worse position. He could think of nothing else.

Micah shoved away his hazardous thoughts as he'd been forced to so many times during their drive to Casper and then on their flight to LaGuardia. On his first trip back to New York City since he'd buried his father, and with an even more perilous situation unfolding back home, he couldn't spend the whole weekend only thinking about her. Wanting her. Wishing things could be different. The little boy cuddled against her shoulder served as a neon sign, a reminder that he wasn't the only one who could be hurt if he got that wrong.

The waitress took one look from them to Derek and then led them to a booth in the back of the restaurant. Discrimination against child patrons aside, she couldn't have chosen a worse place for them with its privacy offering an automatic intimacy that he, for one, didn't need, and the battery-powered candle reminding him of the blaze in the fireplace the night before.

Deirdre shot a look at the same candle and then busied herself, sliding Derek into the wooden highchair that the waitress had positioned at the end of the booth.

"You're good at that," Micah told him once she had latched the buckle.

"He's just taking pity on me and making it easier."

She sat and immediately used her phone to scan the QR code for the menu, signaling that he wasn't the only nervous one.

"Sorry that he insisted on you carrying him."

Derek had thrown his head back the moment Deirdre stopped by their hotel room to collect them for dinner, insisting that "Dee-Dee carry me." Micah hated that he'd given in *again*, but an impossibly extended travel day could have stretched even longer.

"You kidding? He's been a trouper all day. From rental cars to airplanes. Even on that scary taxi ride from the airport. He didn't scream once on the plane, which I thought was a requirement for anyone under three. So if he's a little grumpy now, I'll cut him some slack."

She set a napkin in front of Derek, reached in her purse and poured a few oyster crackers onto his tray from the little bag that had been a lifesaver all day.

"I don't remember seeing that shirt back at the ranch." Micah winced. Now she knew he'd noticed.

Deirdre crossed her arms as if to cover her top. "I didn't have many choices in my suitcase that would work here, since I didn't get a chance to make a stop in DC. Heck, I don't even *have* a suitcase. Just that duffel from Gary's."

"Told you it would come in handy."

She rubbed her hands up and down the see-through material that covered her arms. "I paid entirely too much for this in the hotel gift shop. It was the only one I could find, though. I'll have to pick up a few things tomorrow."

"It looks great… I mean…fine. Not much call for muck boots and Henleys in your job here, I would imagine."

"Or flannel," she agreed. "You're not wearing any tonight, either."

He shifted on the wood bench. "Thought we would be meeting your team here."

She set her phone aside. "I told you what Sean said when I called him with updates about Las Vegas and

Greenwich Village. It wasn't stuff I needed to tell him in person."

"Oh, I remember. But what about the photo?"

"I just took a picture of it with my phone and then texted it to the team."

"Right. Technology." He couldn't have sounded more ridiculous and apparently hoped for a world record for moronic comebacks. For an escape, he pulled up the QR code and pretended to read the menu.

"Depending on what we find in Greenwich Village tomorrow, maybe we'll meet with them after that," she said. "He was a little curious why I would bring a witness with me to New York, so I had to explain about the situation on the ranch."

"You didn't tell him about Richard coercing you to help with the investigation, did you?"

She lifted a brow. "I told you that the whole team is in law enforcement, right? So, I presented all information on a need-to-know basis."

They exchanged a look that hinted on additional details the team had no business learning about, and then she went back to studying the menu on her phone. In the low light, he couldn't tell if she was blushing, but his cheeks and neck had to be the color of the ketchup bottle.

Then she looked up. "Wait. You got dressed up just to meet my team?"

He blinked over her quick return to the earlier subject and glanced down at his shirt and khakis.

"Possibly." He could have argued that the team also happened to consist of her cousins and brother, and he felt the pressure to impress them, but he'd dressed tonight for one person alone. It irked him that both of them knew it.

He considered pointing out that she'd gussied up, too, even purchasing a new shirt for dinner, but that just could have been because she wanted to look presentable in the city. Even if he knew some intimate details about her past and had had a decent introduction to her body, the truth was that he knew little about Deirdre's life on the East Coast. At a minimum, it had to be far more glamorous than the one he led on the ranch.

Though he continued to pretend to study the menu, when the waitress returned, he hadn't read anything beyond the words *appetizers* and *main courses*. He took a risk, based on the condiments on the table, and ordered a hamburger and fries and an IPA for himself and a grilled cheese and milk for Derek. With his luck, the restaurant would be vegan. Deirdre added a burger and a beer to the order, confirming his gamble.

When the food came, they ate as though someone had set a timer for them to clear their plates. Micah hadn't even realized how hungry he was until the food arrived, and he had to force himself to take breaths between bites. Even Derek got over his grouchiness long enough to shove the triangles of sandwich that Micah cut for him in his mouth.

"It's probably strange for you being back here after all these years," Deirdre said, finally taking a break and wiping her lips with a napkin.

"It does feel like all the people are headed to different places, and they all expect to get there this instant, no matter who they have to step on or drive over to make that happen."

She chuckled at that, sitting back and appearing to

relax for the first time since the waitress had put them in the corner. "Remind me not to take you to Times Square while we're here."

"You forget that I was born here," he said and then shivered as he imagined all that humanity squeezed into that square between Broadway, Seventh Avenue and Forty-Second and Forty-Seventh Streets. He shook his head. "Funny how that never bothered me when I was a kid. It was home then, I guess."

"I'm sure it was different."

He shrugged. "I'm just not used to *so many* people anymore."

"You mean because there are eight million across the five boroughs and closer to two million in Manhattan alone?"

"Doing random info searches again?" At her nod, he added, "Did you know there aren't quite six hundred thousand in the whole state of Wyoming?"

"I looked that up, too," she said with a smile.

He handed Derek a fry and then watched as his son jammed the whole thing in his mouth.

"On the ranch, if you choose to, you can spend a few days without seeing a single other human being." It could also get awfully lonely there, but he didn't tell her that, since Harmony Fields would be emptier when he and his son returned there without her.

"Feeling a little homesick?"

Something, anyway. "I guess so."

"Well, you won't have to deal with that for too long. You've already got a return flight on Sunday night. I'm not sure how long I'll have to stay in the city before returning to DC."

"Don't you mean *home*?" He squinted, trying to remember if she'd ever referred to the place where she lived that way.

She straightened. "Of course, home. What did you think I meant?"

Though he didn't answer, she shifted again. "Living in the city—here or Washington—isn't better or worse than the rural Northwest. You have to know that, since you've experienced both. They're just different ways of life."

He couldn't help but to grin at that. "You sure seemed to think the East Coast was superior when you first arrived at Harmony Fields."

"I apologize for whatever I said that day. I was a stressed-out traveler, and you weren't exactly the most cooperative witness."

"Guilty."

They'd both had preconceived notions about each other. They nibbled fries and finished their beers, probably remembering their first meeting far differently.

He watched her for several seconds and then dived into the subject they really needed to discuss. The one they'd tiptoed around all day, careful to add extra space and avoid a misstep.

"You know, at some point we need to talk about what happened between us back in Wyoming."

She crossed her arms and tilted her head. "Must we?" Then her shoulders drooped. "I know we should. And we will when the time is right. Is it okay if that isn't tonight, while we still have so much to deal with over the two investigations?"

He nodded, though he doubted that she would find a right time to discuss it.

"Did you get a chance to talk to Deputy Martin?" she asked, quickly changing the subject.

"Just three times," he admitted. "I talked to Rob and Kevin, too. All the ranch hands assured me that the cattle and the petting zoo animals got their dinners just fine, no one has burned the place down yet, and there have been no escapees."

"So, a pleasant day on the ranch, then. I take it you've never taken a vacation away from Harmony Fields before."

"Ranchers don't get vacations. At least not spontaneous ones and not without a huge support system." He set the last bite of his burger back on the plate instead of eating it. "This isn't a vacation, either."

How many times would he need to remind himself of that?

"Guess not." She sipped her beer and set it aside. "You never told me what the deputy said."

Stop calling me so often. Well, maybe he wouldn't share that. "No signs of trespassing or damage yet," he said instead.

"Did he check inside the house or just the perimeter?"

"Both, as well as all the outbuildings. He used the key I left with Richard and said he'd walked through all three levels each time and hadn't seen anything out of the ordinary."

"How would he know what was ordinary?" She pointed at him with a French fry.

"I asked him that, too. But he only kidded me about the note I left on the table in case there were any visitors while we were gone."

"You left a note? You didn't tell me that."

He stared down at his plate, swishing his own fry through the leftover ketchup. "We were so busy packing the bags and the car seat and the rest of the stuff for Derek that I didn't get the chance to mention it."

She gave him a dubious look and waited.

He shrugged. "I just told them to take whatever it was that they were looking for and to leave us the hell alone."

"What if what the person wants is the ranch?"

"I don't know what I'll do. I just know that it has to stop before someone really gets hurt. Or worse."

As if they'd timed it, they both shot a look to the highchair. The child he'd sworn to protect sat with his chin tucked to his chest, his head bobbing in sleep, a chunk of grilled cheese still grasped in his hand.

"I won't let anything happen to him."

At Deirdre's promise—which she shouldn't have made, since she wasn't even working on his case anymore—Micah turned back to her. She tilted her chin, and something fierce and determined flashed in her too-shiny eyes. A surety filled him that hadn't been there even a minute before.

Whatever else he didn't know about Deirdre Colton and how many questions still lay between then, on this commitment she'd made, he absolutely believed her.

Deirdre stopped just past noon the next day and bent her head back to stare up at the pattern of square carvings inside the opening of the massive marble Washington Arch. Now at the north gateway to Washington Square Park, just past the two statues of George Washington on the arch's piers, she and Micah took a moment to breathe. Even after traipsing around Greenwich

Village all morning, past cute brownstones and mom-and-pop pizza joints, they still hadn't seen anything that reminded him of Maeve O'Leary. Her neck and back hurt, and she wasn't even carrying Derek in the backpack the way that Micah was.

"Don't tilt too far back or you'll fall over," he said.

Next to her, Micah somehow still stood upright with Derek and the backpack pressing down on his shoulders. At least he'd had a break an hour earlier when she'd helped him slide off the flannel he now wore knotted around the carrier's waist strap. The sun and low-seventies temperatures in Manhattan felt much warmer without the Wyoming wind.

"And don't you look up at all, or you'll fall over and squish him."

"Sound advice."

Since father and son should have been wearing matching Yankees baseball caps, and only Micah had his, she searched the ground for the smaller hat in the pickup game they'd been playing for the past two hours. She plunked it on the child's head, but he immediately pulled it off again by the bill.

"Why don't you just put in that pocket on the bottom."

After she'd done as he asked, Micah pointed through the arch to the plaza, with dozens of New Yorkers surrounding the fountain at its center.

"Are we going in?"

"Might as well," she said. "You probably need a break, anyway."

"Is that you volunteering to carry the backpack for a while?" He grinned over her and waggled his eyebrows, causing the cap to lift and lower on his forehead. "I know how much fun you had last time."

"Not a chance."

He shrugged. "Had to give it a shot."

"I won't fall for that again."

As they stepped into the wide circular plaza area, Micah slowed and looked around, appearing as if he were mining his memories at the same time. "I remember coming here as a kid."

"With Maeve?" she said hopefully.

He shook his head. "With my parents. And then with Dad after Mom died. That was still pretty new the last time I was here."

He pointed to One World Trade Center, with its mirrored exterior and towering spire, visible from the park.

Despite the spectacular and poignant view of the building with the memorial, constructed after the tragedy of September 11, she sighed.

"I suppose it was expecting a lot for me to think we could just walk around town and you would suddenly see a place that sparked a memory with Maeve in it."

"We had to give it a shot," he said.

With slumped shoulders, she led him deeper into the park, away from the fountain, which would be a draw for Derek. At one of the benches positioned along the path, she helped Micah remove the backpack and freed the toddler from the harness. After a quick diaper change, she lowered the child and started a game of chase, giving his dad the chance to stretch his neck.

Just as Deirdre caught Derek for the third time and swung him in a circle, her arms crossed over his chest and tiny feet swinging out like a propeller and squeals of delight filling the air, her phone buzzed in her pocket. She rested Derek's feet on the ground, the child immediately taking off again, and pulled out the phone.

When she read the words on the screen, she froze. "What is it?"

Micah was suddenly next to her, the boy he'd caught on his way to her giggling and bent over his arm.

"It's from my cousin Eva to the team group text thread." She flashed screen to him and then read it again herself. "She wanted to let us know that someone tried to kill Ciara Kelly today."

"That's terrible." After a few seconds, he added, "Now who's Ciara Kelly?"

Deirdre had been typing a return message, asking for more details, but at his question, she jerked her head up, blinking. Of course he wouldn't know that part of the story. He knew little of it, and yet he was still there helping.

"Ciara is Humphrey Kelly's wife. Originally, she was questioned in the case since they'd only been married six months when he disappeared."

He tilted his head. "Another black widow?"

"Not this time. It's pretty complicated, but she's no longer considered a suspect. Their marriage turned out to be one of convenience so that Ciara could inherit the money from her grandmother's will and use it to pay for her own mother's cancer treatment. It looks like Maeve has somehow convinced Humphrey to go along with her plans."

Deirdre didn't realize that her words were coming faster and faster until Micah shook his head, his eyes wide.

"I said it before," he said as he carried his son back to the bench, where he'd left the backpack, "but—"

"The truth is better than fiction," she finished for him. "Yeah, I know. And, again, you have no popcorn."

She waited for him to make a joke, but he only stared back at her, straight-faced.

"Now this Ciara is a victim, too? What happened?"

As she returned to the bench to help him with the backpack, she glanced down at her phone again, waiting for it to buzz and provide her with more answers. When it sat frustratingly silent, she had to resist the temptation to shake it. Finally, she looked up at him.

"Apparently, I won't be receiving any more details right now. All I know so far is that sometime today, a driver in a small, dark car tried to run Ciara down. My brother has been assigned to watch over her until Humphrey and Maeve are apprehended."

Micah had just snapped the backpack harness over his son's shoulders and turned away so Deirdre could lift it onto his back, but at her words, he whirled to face her again.

"Couldn't that be a long time? Do you really think you're that close to catching Maeve?"

"Well, it would be awfully coincidental if someone other than Maeve or Humphrey or at least one of their accomplices made an attempt on Ciara Kelly's life today."

"You said before that you don't believe in coincidences."

"I still don't." She let that sink in as she lifted the pack onto his shoulders. "We believe that Maeve and Humphrey are somewhere in this city right now."

"Then we'd better get back." Micah snapped the buckle and walked several steps. "Are you coming?"

"But we still haven't found any place Maeve would have frequented."

"I'm doubting that whatever I would have to say would have any impact right now."

He kept walking, so she fell into step beside him as he hurried toward the arch and the park's exit.

"You're probably right." She didn't try to hide her disappointment. Even if she knew she was being selfish, she still needed for her lead to be the one leading to Maeve's whereabouts and arrest. Otherwise, after everything, she still would have nothing to take back to the bureau at the end of her *vacation*.

"Your team probably needs to get together to strategize, too."

This time, she simply nodded but glanced over and caught him watching.

"I know you hoped to close this case yourself, but you might have to settle for just being part of the *team* that finds this missing psychiatrist and brings down a serial killer."

"That has to sound ridiculous to you."

He shook his head but walked even faster, forcing her to jog to keep up, even with the extra thirty pounds on his back.

"We all have our motivations for what we do. For me, I've been waiting fifteen years for Ariel Porter Perry—or Maeve O'Leary or whatever name she's going by today—to face any sort of justice for murdering my dad."

Deirdre shook her head, her stomach queasy with the truth of her self-centered mission. "I'm sorry. That was so insensitive of me to—"

He shook his head until she stopped talking so he could finish.

"If there's anything I can do to speed up that process that will put her in prison for the rest of her life," he said, "I'm ready to do it."

Chapter 16

Micah wasn't sure why he'd even suggested that they take one more look around Greenwich Village, attempting to find spots they hadn't crossed the first time, before hitting the West Fourth Street–Washington Square subway station. He couldn't remember seeing Maeve anywhere in that area, anyway, and even if something had sparked a memory, he didn't really want to help Deirdre right now.

Had he ever met a more selfish person? Someone who had less trust in others? Even when they were this close to catching his stepmother, Deirdre really believed that saving her FBI career by being able to take credit for stopping a serial killer was more important than actually putting one behind bars.

He tightened his jaw, but that only reminded him that his neck hurt after carrying Derek all day. His shoulders hurt. And his back hurt. In fact, it would be easier just to say that every part of him felt as if he'd been run over by a truck and save himself time in describing it.

On his back, his son only added to the tension by choosing this moment to sing his new favorite song, which sounded something like, "Dee-Dee, Dee-Dee, Dee-Dee, Dee-Dee," forever and amen.

"You don't have to keep looking," she said. "We can just go back to the hotel. The team's already trying to set up a meeting."

Micah didn't answer. The least she could do was be honest with him—this was about her. It had always been about her. He'd thought behind the walls she'd built to protect herself from those who'd hurt her, there was a tender, kind and giving person inside, but he'd been wrong. The other day he'd told her that some people couldn't think beyond the length of their own wingspan. He just hadn't realized that he was talking about *her*.

"Just a little longer," he said finally.

He couldn't hold out too long, or Derek would miss his nap, and it would be a really long night.

"I'm sorry."

"So you've said." He continued scanning the area as they passed, redbrick brownstones with fenced patios, walk-ups with probably incredible views, cast-iron lampposts and trees planted right into the sidewalk.

"I mean it."

"Good to know."

"You can't forgive me for needing to be the one to make this arrest?"

He could. That was the crux of it. He could, and he wanted to, and she didn't damn deserve it. If he needed a reminder that he was just like his father, she walked next to him, the best and worst thing that had happened in his life in years.

"Okay. I give up."

He'd meant the search, not giving in to her plea for forgiveness, but even as he said it, something farther up the street caught his attention. Though he'd been sweating all day while carrying an extra thirty pounds on his back, a chill skittered up his spine. The shiver started inside him and worked its way out.

"What is it?" Deirdre asked, her eyes wide.

Without answering her, he rushed up the street and stood in front of the eight-story Art Deco–style building with metallic-gold reliefs that looked like the scales of justice. The place dripped of money and class—the first, the thing Maeve always craved, the second, something she'd never had.

"This is it! I remember now."

"The Village Historical Hotel?" she asked, reading the sign.

"Maeve loved this place." He tipped his head up slightly to get a better look at the more pronounced penthouse floor with a balcony. "What's not to like? A five-star hotel. The priciest in the whole city. I never saw her here, but I remember her talking about it in this dreamy voice. She said she would live here if she could."

Deirdre leaned close and spoke in a low voice. "She wanted to *live* here?"

He nodded.

"We've got to go," she whispered. "Now." She linked her arm through his and rushed him down the street.

"What's going on?" He spun around and pointed back to the building. "Why are you doing—"

Realization dawning, he stopped and looked from Deirdre to the hotel and back. "You don't think—"

She shrugged. "I don't know. But if she is there, she can't see you standing on the sidewalk in front of the place."

"You're right. We need to get out of here. You have to get back to your team."

Micah hurried to the corner and turned north in the direction of the subway station. He was still reluctant to help Deirdre, but that didn't seem to matter anymore. After all this time, after all the things she'd done or might even still be doing, he might be able to help take down Maeve O'Leary.

Deirdre took a deep breath later that afternoon and pulled open the door to the A Grind Above coffee shop on the Upper West Side. As nervous as it made her to meet in person with the team for the first time, the fact that she would have given anything to have Micah there with her bothered her even more.

How was she supposed to pull back from him when she couldn't do anything these past few days without wondering what he would think about it or wishing she could share it with him? The worst part was that this time Micah truly deserved to be there. Even if he was clearly frustrated with her, without his help that day, she would have nothing new to report to the team.

The place was as busy and loud as Eva had predicted it would be in the group chat, but Deirdre still found her four cousins squeezed around a table in the corner, compostable coffee cups in front of them. Although they had some general resemblance, their varying hair colors from Cormac's dark brown and Liam's dirty blond to Eva's dark red, plus a full range of eye colors, made it tough to pinpoint. Had Deirdre not already known that they were siblings, she wouldn't have guessed it. Still, compared to her and Aidan, they were all practically identical.

Sean, both the team leader and the oldest brother on that branch of the Colton family tree, noticed her first and waved her over.

"Sorry I'm late," she said, resting her hands on the back of the one empty chair. "I had a hard time figuring out the subway map."

"You're lucky to have a place to sit. We had to fight off a bunch of poachers," Liam, the ex-con–turned–NYPD informant, said with a grin.

Sean, the detective from the NYPD's Ninety-Eighth Precinct, rounded the table to greet her with his hand outstretched. "I keep forgetting that you're not from New York."

He must have thought better of shaking her hand, as he pulled back and then gave her the awkward hug of a distant cousin. Deirdre forced herself to keep a straight face. Working with relatives was difficult enough without family being little more than strangers.

Eva, the rookie cop and the youngest of the four, pushed a paper cup to the spot they'd left for her. "Hey, Deirdre. I got you a latte. Hope that's okay."

"It's great. Thanks." It gave her something to do with her hands besides wring them.

She appreciated that Eva and the twins, Cormac and Liam, waved instead of standing for another round of uncomfortable greetings.

"Well, let's get started." Sean rested a manila folder on the table and leaned his elbows on it rather than open it. Despite all the conversations taking place in the coffee shop, he glanced around to see if they would be overheard and kept his voice low. "I really appreciate all of you coming together so quickly. I'd expected to schedule a meeting while Deirdre was in town, but because of these new developments involving the attempt on Ciara Kelly's life, we need to change our timing and format a little."

He pulled his phone from his pocket and propped it against the decorative canning jar filled with coffee beans at the table's center. "Because his role has changed, Aidan will now be joining us by video call."

Sean clicked the call button, and her brother's face appeared on the screen.

"Hi, everyone," Aidan said. "Checking in from the Kelly home. All is well. The victim received no injuries and is resting comfortably. Because Maeve O'Leary has been named as a person of interest in today's incident, and she remains at large, I will stay with Mrs. Kelly, pending further instructions from the team."

"Thank you, Aidan," Sean said. "Now, let's have Deirdre fill us in about the discovery she made today in Greenwich Village."

Deirdre cleared her throat, suddenly more nervous than she'd ever been for any report in the DC field office. "In addition to providing us with a photo of our suspect that I shared with you for identification and facial-recognition purposes, witness Micah Perry has offered other critical information about Maeve O'Leary, a woman he knew under the alias Ariel Porter Perry. Maeve, who was Micah's stepmother, is wanted for questioning in the suspicious death of his father, Len Perry."

Sean gestured in a circular motion. "And today you discovered…?"

She crossed and uncrossed her legs. "Micah had suggested that Maeve spent a lot of time in Greenwich Village, so he and his toddler son accompanied me to New York with the hope that he could identify places where Maeve enjoyed spending time in the Village. Places where she would possibly hide."

"And you found a good lead, right?" asked Cormac, the private investigator who regularly worked with the NYPD and the DA's office.

"We did. The Village Historical Hotel seems to be a solid path for us to follow. Micah was able to recall that Maeve loved the hotel. She once even said she would live there if she could."

"Well, that's something," Aidan called out from the phone.

Deirdre shifted in her seat but covered it by taking a sip of her latte. She didn't need any feedback from her sibling with far more experience in law enforcement than she had.

Liam leaned closer to the rest of the team. "Do you think that this whole time we've been searching for Humphrey and Maeve, they've been living high on the hog at the Village Historical Hotel?"

"Maybe," Deirdre said.

"If he's still alive, that is," Eva chimed.

"There is that," Liam agreed.

Sean frowned at his sister and brother by turns. "It's a solid premise. One I think we should definitely check out."

"Best we've had so far," Cormac noted.

Sean held his hands up, taking control again. "I

think we should set up some careful surveillance of the property, both inside and at the perimeter."

Eva raised her hand. "I volunteer for inside. Carmine and I could use a night out, and from what I've heard, the Village Hotel has an amazing restaurant—its bar has all this rich, dark wood and even tin ceiling tiles."

"Sure you and your detective boyfriend will be able to focus on something besides the romantic decor?" Cormac asked, earning a mean look from his sister.

"You're not going to get to expense this dinner, either." Liam, who since his release from prison ran a juvenile awareness program with the Ninety-Eighth Precinct, pointed to their older brother. "Tell her, Sean. You don't have the budget for that, do you?"

"Thanks for the input, Mr. Always Play by the Rules, but I wasn't going to ask to expense it," Eva said.

As much as Deirdre appreciated knowing that hers wasn't the only family where sibling rivalry played a part, she didn't have time for it now.

"Aren't we talking about stopping a black widow here?" she said in a low voice. Then, when she had everyone's attention, she added, "Micah and I should be there, too. He's the only one of us who's ever seen Maeve in real life. The one most likely to be able to pick her out, even if she's in disguise."

Deirdre's chest tightened, and her palms started sweating as she waited for them to respond. Could they see straight through her to know that she and Micah had been far more involved than any special agent and witness should be?

"He's also the only one Maeve could recognize," Liam pointed out. "He's not in law enforcement, either."

"Don't you think that's a good thing?" Deirdre said.

"We all don't want to look like we're on a stakeout, do we? Micah's a really smart guy. He won't mess it up. I would think that any of you who participate would need to be in disguise, anyway. Didn't you say Humphrey knew your family well? I'm the only one that *he* wouldn't recognize."

"What will you and Mr. Perry dress up as?" Aidan called out from the phone. "A couple on a date? A married couple? Maybe one with a kid?"

Deirdre straightened in her chair. What was her brother's problem? Was she more upset that he was making those comments to question her professionalism or that he had come awfully close to the truth?

"We would never involve his son in the matter, Aidan. That's out of the question. But don't you think pretending to be a couple is better than, I don't know, declaring, 'Hey, I'm an FBI special agent staking out the place'?"

Her cheeks and neck burned. She didn't bother fooling herself into believing the other members of the team didn't notice. Hopefully, they thought it was indignation over her brother's words and not her inappropriate relationship with the witness himself.

"She's got you there, buddy," Liam said with a laugh. "Sounds like they're doing some great training down there at Quantico."

Eva crossed her arms and studied her cousin. "Why didn't you bring Mr. Perry with you tonight? Especially after he's been so helpful to you, providing information for the case."

"Like Liam pointed out, he's not in law enforcement."

"But haven't you already involved him in the case?"

It felt as if she were a hostile witness in a criminal

case. Only instead of one attorney or legal team, five different investigators were pelting her with questions, plenty of which it might not be in her best interest to answer. But since this one was more benign that most, she decided to answer it in an abbreviated fashion. If anyone asked her to take a polygraph test, she would fail with flying colors, focusing so hard on telling as little as possible of the truth.

"Yes, he's been helping me, in exchange for my assistance looking into a series of crimes on his property, Harmony Fields Ranch. Someone has been targeting his property, his animals and now him and his son."

Cormac tilted his head. "Do you think it's possible that those crimes could have some connection to those we're investigating here?"

She'd never considered it before, but she immediately shook her head. "Of course not."

"Even though Maeve is a suspect in his dad's death?" Cormac pressed.

She shook her head again. "The only connection is that Micah was dealing with the fallout from the escalating series of vandalism incidents and, now, personal threats when I arrived to interview him about Maeve O'Leary."

"Awfully nice of you to help him out with his case," Aidan called out from the cell-phone peanut gallery.

Deirdre lowered her gaze to the phone. If she could get by with *accidentally* dropping the call, she would do it instantly. "Anyway, Micah agreed to come with me to New York because of a direct threat to his son there. He's probably back in his hotel room dealing with the sheriff's office right now."

Sean gripped the edge of the table and waited for the

team to turn back to him. "Enough chatter. We need to take Humphrey and Maeve O'Leary into custody, and this is the best lead we've had so far. Deirdre's right. Perry has the best chance of being able to identify Maeve, particularly if she and Humphrey aren't together."

"So, you want me to make a reservation?" Eva asked.

Sean nodded. "For two." He turned back to Deirdre. "You can make a second one for you and Perry."

Cormac gestured from himself to his twin. "What are we supposed to do?"

"Glad you asked." Sean pointed at Cormac. "You'll be part of my surveillance team, posing as a package-delivery driver." He turned to Liam. "And you're a jogger, running through the neighborhood and checking out behind all the buildings."

"How come I always get the dirty jobs?" Liam asked.

This time Sean smiled. "Got to keep you in shape, to keep up with the kids in the juvenile program."

"What about Derek?" Deirdre asked.

Eight pairs of eyes stared back at her with confusion. Even Aidan was quiet for once.

"You know. Micah's son. We can't leave him back a the hotel with a bottle of soda and the remote."

Sean nodded. "I'll get one of the officers at the Ninety-Eighth Precinct to give him a tour and encourage him to choose a career in law enforcement."

"What if he wants to be a rancher like his dad?"

"Just giving him options." The team leader grinned. "So, we're set, right?"

Sean's siblings all made affirmative sounds and cleaned up their coffee cups and napkins to prepare to leave. Deirdre made the same sounds, but she wasn't close to set. She might have volunteered Micah's services in participating in what amounted to a sting, but she hadn't asked him if he was willing to do it.

This would be more than just asking him to stir up old ghosts by walking up and down the streets of Greenwich Village, looking for something that sparked a memory. Now she had to convince him to not only pretend to be on a date with her—which he probably wouldn't be too happy about after the way she'd left things earlier—but also risk seeing the devil who'd murdered his father face-to-face.

The unusual ring of a video call interrupted Deirdre two hours later as she bent close to the hotel bathroom mirror to apply mascara. Her already-unsteady hand jerked, creating imaginary lashes up the side of her eyelid. Grabbing a makeup-remover cloth, she marched out to the hotel room desk, where she'd plugged in her phone.

When Aidan's name flashed on the screen, she considered not answering. He'd rarely called her before, never by video, and this wasn't a good day for him to start. Only with her luck, he would probably call Dad and give him another reason to be disappointed in her.

She tapped the button, and Aidan stared back at her, his black eyes narrowing.

"What is it? I'm kind of busy." She brushed at the makeup smeared on her eyelid.

"I can see that. What's all over your eye?"

She stopped wiping long enough to give him a dirty look. "What do you need? I have to be ready in twenty minutes."

"For your big date with the cowboy?"

"You know it's not a date." She frowned at the screen.

"Of course I know it's not. The question is, do you?"

"I don't know what you're talking about."

But because she did, and he didn't appear to be ready to let her off the phone, she carried it back into the bathroom, where she'd spread cosmetics all over the counter. The wig and the glasses she would need to wear rested next to the sink. She propped the phone against the backsplash and grabbed her tube of mascara.

"Say whatever you need to and be done with it so I can get off the phone."

"You should be careful, big sister. It's all kinds of unprofessional for you to get too close to a witness. And you're already in enough trouble with the bureau."

She bristled over his accurate review of the situation, but that didn't stop her from shooting back. "I get it that you're this law enforcement expert after nearly a decade with the US Marshals Service, but I'm not 'too close' to Micah Perry."

She kept her gaze on the mirror as she lied, her hand shaking more than it had earlier.

"I heard how you spoke about him during the meeting. I *know* you. I'm your brother."

"Clearly, you don't know me that well, and you're my *half* brother." As soon as the words were out of her mouth, she regretted them. She was becoming defensive and mean.

After a long pause, he spoke again.

"Okay, then, I *half* know that you're lying and have become involved with a witness. To what degree, I'm not sure. And I *half* know that you could be messing up your career."

She didn't bother trying to argue with him. "Don't you think you should be focusing on taking care of our witness?"

"*Mrs.* Kelly is safe. She's in her kitchen, cooking dinner. I'm doing *my job* just fine."

Deirdre picked up the phone from the counter and stared at his face. "Good to know. I have to go now."

But before she could cut off the call, her brother got in a parting shot.

"I just hope you know what you're doing if you're *taking care of* Micah Perry."

Chapter 17

Eva sighed as she stared at the man sitting across the table from her at the magnificent bar inside the Village Historical Hotel the next evening, even if he couldn't keep a straight face when he looked back at her and had avoided it for the past few minutes. So much for combining a romantic dinner with Carmine DiRico with a little police surveillance.

A least Carmine didn't have to wear a disguise since, as far as they could figure, Maeve O'Leary had no way to know him, and Humphrey Kelly had never crossed him while serving as an expert witness in court. He looked like the same dark, beautiful NYPD detective who'd been her partner for a brief time and her pretend husband for a few days in an undercover operation and now had promised to be her love for life.

She, on the other hand, had to look like an escapee

Morticia Addams with that ridiculous black wig against her pale skin. How was she supposed to blend in when even the man who loved her most couldn't look at her without laughing?

Across the room, Deirdre sat alone at a table, waiting for her "date" to arrive. She had a spinster-librarian thing going on with her hair tucked in a light brown wig, arranged in a bun, reading glasses riding low on her nose. The combination was designed to help cover the wireless earpiece/microphone that kept her in contact with the team members in the surveillance van outside. Deirdre didn't really have to be in disguise, since neither suspect would recognize her, so Eva had to give her cousin credit for being a team player. Someone might ask her about the Dewey Decimal System, but at least she wouldn't have to deal with someone inquiring about her kids, Wednesday and Pugsley.

After taking a sip of her Shirley Temple, she patted her hair again and settled her purse where she held her weapon in her lap.

Carmine turned back to her, his smile practiced and benign. "Please stop playing with your hair. It doesn't look too bad."

She returned his loving look. "This should serve as your reminder never to lie to me in our marriage. You're a lousy liar."

"Noted. Now, how come you got the best seat? I wanted the door-facing seat."

He didn't have to mention that there wasn't a police officer alive who felt comfortable with his back exposed to anyone entering a room or building.

From her seat, she could see not long the heavy wood-and-glass doors that separated the bar from the lobby, the whole bank of elevators and more beautiful doors that led to the outside. "Because this time, Detective, I get to pull rank on you. I'm the member of this investigative team. You're my arm candy."

"I'll try to remember my place."

She winked at him, knowing she would have his support and firepower, if necessary, from the weapon tucked in his ankle holster, should she need it.

"I'm thinking this whole plan might be a wash," she whispered, reaching out to touch his fingers on top of the table.

"Did anyone on the early surveillance team catch even a glance of either of the suspects?"

Eva shook her head. "We still don't know if they're even staying here, and as much as Deirdre talked up her superwitness, Micah, he hasn't even shown up."

She focused as the exterior door opened, and Micah, with spiky bleach-blond hair and a close-trimmed dark beard, sunglasses covering his eyes, strode inside. And she'd thought her getup was bad. He would probably have to shave his head to get rid of that style.

"One superwitness, present and accounted for," she said.

Sure enough, the visitor crossed to the table where Deirdre sat and took the seat next to her for the better vantage point, immediately tracing kisses down her cheek to justify the cozy seating arrangement.

Deirdre stiffened as she caught Eva watching the display, her hands gripped in front of her, eyes blinking too much.

"Mark my words," she whispered to her future husband. "There's something more to that story than play-acting."

"Ah, you're just happily coupled, and now you want everyone else to be the same." He reached over the table to caress the back of her hand.

"Maybe. But mark my words anyway."

She glanced from the lobby to the exterior door and then back just as the elevator doors opened. A couple stepped out and crossed into the bar, heading to a table away from the windows. Her breath caught in her throat.

Humphrey. The height and weight were the same. He obviously wore a disguise—a prosthetic nose, strong-framed glasses and a wig as bad as hers—but she would have bet her life and those of all three of her brothers that the man heading to that table was the same one who'd supported them after their father's death.

"That's Humphrey. I know it," she whispered to Carmine, who had to nod and continue to face her since he couldn't afford to take the chance of turning to look. "He's in disguise, but I'll never forget his kind eyes."

He did reach down to scratch his calf, just in case.

Eva was tempted to rush, to demand to know why Humphrey, who'd once seemed like such a good man, someone she and her brothers had relied on, had turned out to be just another criminal. One who'd manipulated her and her brothers to suit his own needs.

She took the signal from Carmine to watch and wait. They'd taken this long to track down Humphrey, believing that he was a victim. Now they just needed to wait for the perfect time to take him down.

Micah's insides shook as he sat so close to Deirdre, touching her as he'd longed to so many times in the past two days. Kissing her neck and watching her pulse beat in her throat. Hearing her breath hitch. Feeling her nervousness, even before her tongue darted out to dampen her lips.

All of it was for show.

He had to be in this spot to be able to see guests entering the bar, and the only way he could justify that cutesy seating arrangement was to pretend he couldn't keep his hands off her. Whether invention or truth. He tried to fight it, to make it just as much a work of fiction as their days on the ranch had apparently been. Perfect yet finite. A long drive that led only to a brick wall.

So, why even at this awful, inopportune time, did her pull remain so strong? At first, he'd said no to this theater performance. He'd even asked her why she needed him now when she'd insisted on pursuing the vandal alone the other night. But she'd said this time was different. That he was the only one who'd seen Maeve close enough to still identify her in disguise. It was just like the other night, when he'd wanted to talk about what had happened between them. To make sense of something he couldn't let go of no matter how much he hyperextended his hands. Like with everything else, she'd made it on her terms. When the time was right. *Her time.*

Still, when she'd come to him for help, he couldn't deny her, even knowing she only wanted it for herself. He'd given in. Just as he suspected he always would with her.

He was just like his dad, after all.

Deirdre cleared her throat and whispered, "Please."

She didn't even say what she was begging for. That he would touch her more? Or never again? His body and maybe even his soul longed for the former, but he suspected she'd requested the latter. She touched her ear to indicate the earpiece/microphone and watched him out of her side vision. Even if she wanted to, she couldn't answer him now.

But he was tired of asking. He would give her that space she craved soon. And then he would walk away. Or drive, really. Then fly. Back home, he would have the chance to lick his wounds, heal and thank God that Derek was too young to remember what Micah could never forget.

"Do you see Eva?" she whispered and then gestured with a tilt of her head to the table across the room.

Micah caught sight of the black-wigged woman that he assumed was her cousin, but the couple that Eva watched at one of the tables drew his attention. Though both of them were in disguise, just like he was, he ignored the guy completely. Only the woman mattered. Micah tried not to stare, but a roaring sound filled his ears and heat welled in his chest, stretching and spreading, until it was all he could do to remain seated and not leap up and throw the jacket that Deirdre had borrowed for him to the floor.

It was Maeve O'Leary.

This was the same woman, the one who'd waltzed into his family and stole first his father's good sense and then his life and then moved on with impunity to destroy other families.

Did she really think she could hide behind that ridiculous, short-blond wig with all those bangs across her forehead? She'd made the mistake of not covering her eyes. Those despicable, frigid eyes. He would never forget them for as long as he lived.

He glanced over at Deirdre and nodded, signaling both his positive identification of his stepmother and that the time had come for her to signal those in the unmarked police van outside, Liam, Cormac and Sean among them.

Suddenly, the air in the room changed. Maeve and the man, who he could only assume was Humphrey Kelly, stood and started toward the door.

"Signal," he whispered to Deirdre.

But her head was already turned. "H and M, on the move," she said in a low voice to her microphone.

In Micah's peripheral vision, Carmine and Eva came to their feet. As she turned back from passing along the message, Deirdre stood as well, her gaze moving from the perimeter of the room to the exit, and he followed her lead.

As Maeve and Humphrey continued toward the door, Humphrey darted nervous glances at Eva. The man recognized her, too.

The rest happened so quickly that Micah wasn't certain what took place first.

"Stop! Police!" Eva called out, her firearm aimed at the couple.

At what felt like the exact same time, Maeve yanked a girl of maybe six from a table where she sat with her family, positioned the terrified child in front of herself and held a gun to the little blonde head. The low murmur of voices around them became shrieks and cries as guests dived under the shiny wood tables.

At Maeve's signal, Humphrey sidled next to her, at least having the decency to appear anguished at the events taking place around him.

"Drop your guns or the kid dies," Maeve called out.

Guns, plural? His ears reverberating with the sound of that shrill voice that he hadn't been forced to hear for fifteen years, Micah shifted his gaze from side to side. Carmine and Deirdre had their weapons trained on Humphrey and Maeve as well, but, like Eva, they bent to lower them to the ground.

Instantly, Maeve backed out of the restaurant, using the child as a shield, Humphrey at her side. They darted through the lobby and out the door, where they faced off with police and the rest of the team. Carmine and Eva grabbed their firearms and raced after them, Micah and Deirdre right behind them.

Just as they reached the sidewalk, Maeve forced a driver from a running black four-door and leaped inside, Humphrey sliding into the back seat. Then she pushed the little girl to the sidewalk, slammed the door and pulled into traffic. As one police officer rushed to grab the child and return her to her family, the others climbed back into the van. Carmine and Eva squeezed in with them, but there didn't appear to be any more space.

Deirdre shot a frustrated look back to Micah. He looked back and forth for options.

"Micah, Deirdre, over here." Sean stood inside the open door to his unmarked patrol car.

They ran over to him. Deirdre leaped in the passenger seat, while Micah slid in back. Sean peeled out after the van and flipped on his lights and siren.

Micah pressed his face to the center section of the window partition that separated the front seat from the back and spoke through the little square holes. "Can't you go faster?"

"Are you and I seeing the same traffic here?" Sean

asked, keeping his focus on the road. "Could you do me a favor and put on a safety belt? I'm Sean, by the way."

"Oh. Right." He scooted over to the door and clicked the belt. "I'm Micah. But could you—"

"He's going as fast as he can," Deirdre said.

But she seemed to be rocking in the seat, as anxious as he was. Micah closed his eyes, nausea and hopelessness welling in his throat. It was their one chance to stop Maeve O'Leary, and they were letting her get away.

They wound through the city, chasing the van that pursued the stolen vehicle. Soon they were out of Manhattan on Interstate 87. Then the interstate became county routes, and the busy city streets transformed to open expanses, rolling hills and then jutting mountain peaks, all of it eventually becoming hidden behind a mask of night.

"Why haven't they stopped them?" Deirdre pointed to the police van ahead of them on the two-lane road, the car already having vanished over the hill ahead. "Why haven't they—"

"I don't know," Sean said with a sigh. He shook his head. "I have no idea what's happening up there."

Deirdre couldn't blame him for being frustrated. She'd probably asked some variation of that question each fifteen minutes of the past ninety, and Micah had slid a few similar queries in between hers, interspersed with his own through long bouts of silence. But Sean had to know that they were as frustrated as he was. They'd been so close to arresting Maeve, to finally getting justice for Micah and for the Maeve's other victims, and now every mile they drove seemed to make that less and less likely to happen.

She pulled the earpiece she'd worn earlier and held it out where her cousin should have been able to see it in his peripheral vision. "I can try to contact—"

Sean shook his head. "You can't even get a decent cell signal out here. I wouldn't count on Bluetooth."

"Wait."

Micah stuck his head against the partition again. "What's going on?"

"Something's happening now." Sean leaned his head as if that would help him to see around the van with its flashers on. "They shot out the tires."

"They waited all this time to do that?" Micah said.

Sean didn't answer, but Deirdre was with Micah on that one. They could have taken that action several counties ago.

Their driver pulled to the side of the road, opened the door and drew his weapon. "Stay here."

"I'm not staying here," she said, but he was already gone. Deirdre opened the door and pulled her pistol from the holster. She glanced at the man in the back, where arrest suspects usually sat, memories of a different night and a different risk making her chest tight.

"You stay here."

She didn't wait for his answer—she closed the door and rushed to catch up with the others.

The disabled car now rested abandoned on the side of the road, and police were using rechargeable search-lights to scan the area for the suspects. They didn't have to look far. No more than one hundred feet from the road, Maeve stood with her weapon pointed directly at Eva. Humphrey shifted next to her, appearing nervous and upset.

Deirdre stepped over to Liam. "How did this happen?"

"Eva had it under control, but Maeve threatened to shoot Humphrey if she didn't put down her gun."

"You mean shoot her next meal ticket?"

"Never said she was thinking rationally," Liam said.

Out of the corner of her eye, Deirdre caught Micah joining the group gathered by the van.

She slipped over to him. "What are you doing here? I told you—"

"No way I'm staying in the car and letting you—I mean *any of you*—handle this alone."

Her throat tightened with just the idea that she'd let Micah put himself in danger to identify Maeve earlier, and now she was doing it again. But arguing with him didn't seem to make a difference. "Could you at least stay behind the folks with the weapons?"

"Will do."

She could relate to Carmine's fear when he jumped out of the van, carrying a bullhorn to reason with the suspect holding the woman he loved, but Cormac wrestled it away from him before he had the chance to speak.

"You don't want to do this, Maeve," Cormac called into the bullhorn. "There's no way out. You don't want to hurt someone Humphrey cares about, do you?"

Eva stood with her hands up, bravely facing the woman holding the gun on her. But Humphrey appeared nervous, shifting from one foot to the other.

"Maeve, honey, please don't do this," Humphrey said, needing no bullhorn to be heard.

"Shut up, you ridiculous, weak man!" She'd glanced over at him but jerked her head back as Eva lunged, trying to reclaim her weapon. "Get your hands back. You know I'll shoot."

Maybe it was because they all knew she could— and probably would—that Sean rushed in that moment, weapon in hand. He placed himself between his little sister and the woman threatening to kill her.

"Laying down your life for a friend seems pretty cool until you really have to do it." With a laugh, Maeve aimed and fired.

Only she'd missed Humphrey's movement before. He leaped out, putting himself between Sean and the gun. The bullet struck him right in the throat.

"You idiot!" Maeve shouted at him as he bled out on the ground.

With tears in his eyes, Sean sat on the ground with his mentor, holding his head in his lap. "You lost your way, but I always knew there was good in you."

Humphrey gasped and attempted to speak, but he only gurgled, the air streaming from his lungs for the last time.

Chapter 18

As the others crowded around Humphrey, delivering first aid that would relieve no pain and waiting for the ambulance that would serve as a hearse, Micah scooted through the group to the target that drew him far more—Maeve. Yes, he felt bad that she'd had the chance to take another life, but the time had come for her to account for one earlier on her hit list. The chaos had to be to blame for the fact that though she was no longer accessorizing with a .22 pistol, she didn't yet have a pair of matching bracelets on her wrists, and she hadn't been secured in the back of Sean Colton's patrol car.

That lucky truth didn't appear to be lost on Maeve, either. Now outside the beam of the spotlight, she inched closer to an area where it would be easier for her to make a break for the woods. Good thing that darkness benefited him, too, even if he shivered with revulsion just stepping this close to her again.

"Well, if it isn't Mommie Dearest."

Maeve jerked her head to look over at him, though she wouldn't be able to see his face. He fixed that problem by awakening his phone and turning that soft light on himself.

"Micah?"

"Are you seeing a ghost, *Maeve*? Or would you still prefer me to call you Ariel?"

She chuckled into the darkness, having recovered from the surprise. "It was a pretty name, wasn't it? Len Perry's son, all grown up. How long has it been? Twelve years?"

"Fifteen. Seems as if you'd have more vivid memories of your murders. Becoming too many to recall?"

"You always did have such an imagination."

He flicked on his flashlight app and flashed it over to all the law-enforcement personnel still gathered around the most recent victim.

"You saw that yourself. It was an *accident*."

"Tell that to the judge."

"Guess I'll have to."

She sounded sad, but if that emotion was authentic—he didn't hold his breath on that—she regretted only her potential loss of freedom.

"I have one question for you, and the way I see it, you owe me one."

"I don't owe you anything, but I'll give you a gift, since I never really gave you one at your party."

"I want to know *why*." To his shame, his voice broke on the last word.

"Why did I marry your father?"

He gritted his teeth that she'd purposely misunderstood his question, but her answer made him shiver anyway.

"A lady needs things. Pretty things. It was just wonderful that your father wanted to provide so well for me."

"Then wherever he is, I'm sure he's happy knowing that his son wanted to give you something, too—a new address, where you'll live for a long, long time."

The sound of approaching sirens drew everyone's attention and gave Maeve a chance to make her break for the woods. In the hours that followed, the team and other officers combed the woods, but without the help of tracking dogs, they couldn't locate her. She was gone.

Deirdre could barely keep her eyes open by the time Sean dropped Micah, Derek and her back at their hotel at well past midnight. The extra stop at the Ninety-Eighth Precinct to pick up Micah's son made it even later. At least the child had been in good care there, as they'd found him fed and asleep on the sofa in the captain's office, with an officer nearby, when Micah had gone in to collect him.

Besides his thank-you to that officer and to Sean when he left them, Micah had barely spoken during the whole trip back from rural New York.

She glanced over at him as he carried Derek down the hall to his hotel room, his expression showing the wear of a long, exhausting night.

"Do you want to talk about the conversation you had with Maeve?"

He shook his head as he used the key card to open the door. "I don't want to talk about *anything* tonight."

"Just tonight?"

Micah shrugged, confirming her suspicion that he might never want to share anything his stepmother had said before she'd escaped, though she suspected the team would want to interview him about it. She hated that he would be forced to discuss it, since it was obvious that whatever he'd learned had done nothing to salve his pain.

"Are you ready to fly out tomorrow?" She glanced at her watch. "I mean, later this morning."

This time he answered with a shrug, but he didn't protest when she followed him into the room. Other than the portable crib stationed in the corner, his room looked just like hers.

Micah laid Derek on the spare bed, changed his diaper and put on his pajamas, saving the bath for the morning. The toddler whined when his father brushed his teeth, but he snuggled right into the crib the moment Micah lifted him inside.

"Well, I guess this is goodbye," he said when he looked up at her again.

A rock immediately settled in her belly, and her eyes and nose burned. "Maybe we can meet for coffee downstairs before you leave."

He shook his head. "There won't be time. I thought Derek and I would grab breakfast at LaGuardia before our flight takes off."

She swallowed against the lump forming in her throat. "Sounds smart."

Micah grabbed two bottles of water from the mini-fridge and handed one to her before opening the second. He sat on the end of the extra bed.

"I'm sorry Maeve got away. I know how important it was to you that you would get credit for arresting her."

"That's not—" she began and shrugged, lowering to sit next to him on the bed. He was right about her selfish agenda, but that didn't matter anymore. It hadn't worked out how anyone on the team had planned it. Maeve had escaped, and Humphrey was dead. They'd tried to stop a black widow from killing again, and they'd failed.

"Whatever happened, I'm still grateful to you for helping us to locate Maeve and Humphrey. So thank you. Maeve will try to go underground to avoid capture now, but the team is even more determined to bring her to justice."

"You're welcome," he said. "It's too bad that your cousins lost their friend, but maybe Humphrey's act at the end helped to restore their faith in humanity. They're lucky that way."

She narrowed her gaze at him, his words confusing. Was he hinting that she'd contributed to his loss of belief in others?

"It will be good that you can finally get back home, where you can focus exclusively on your own situation so you can figure out once and for all who's been targeting the ranch." She paused to open the water bottle and take a long drink, her throat suddenly dry.

"Until this weekend, I thought it might be Maeve."

Deirdre had just lifted the bottle to her lips, but at his confession, she drew in a sharp breath and choked on the water. She coughed into her elbow several times, eyes watering. "Maeve?" she managed.

Suddenly, a few things made sense. "That's why you kept asking if I thought the suspect could be female, isn't it? That's what you were hiding, too. But you didn't put her name on the list of possible suspects. Why?"

"It felt like a ridiculous theory, so I didn't want to tell you. That my stepmother could have gotten low on funds from her most recent husband, somehow learned that I'd become successful with the ranch and then come to take everything from me again." He shook his head, smiling. "It sounds outlandish now, but I just couldn't shake it."

"Do you still believe it?"

He shook his head. "I don't think so."

"I wish you would have told me then. If you had, I would have helped you to see that she was an unlikely suspect—for the crimes on the ranch, at least."

"Why do you say that?"

"She's a black widow. She uses sex and the promise of love to control the men she targets and make them not question while she gains control over their assets. To come after you—a stepson who already suspected her—wouldn't be her modus operandi at all. You wouldn't have your blinders on around her.

"More than that—" she paused, gesturing with the closed water bottle "—you wouldn't have been a good mark for her, because your assets are tied up in the ranch. In the land. The equipment. The livestock. Even the petting zoo. All of that would have to be liquidated, which takes time, and Maeve likes to cash out and vanish right after her victims die."

He nodded, lowering his head. "You're right. I

should have told you. Then I could have let it go, so I could focus on more plausible theories."

"I think the answer is far less complicated than you first thought. Probably someone closer to home. Some who wants the ranch itself and not the money from selling it off."

Micah sat quietly, appearing to consider her words. "I bet you're really good at your job," he said finally.

She scoffed at that. "Tell that to the special agent in charge in DC." But warmth spread in her chest at his little offer of praise. "Did you hear any more from Sheriff Guetta or Deputy Martin today?"

"That's the thing. I really haven't. I've been trying not to call Richard since he put Deputy Martin in charge, and Greg has stopped getting back to me. I haven't heard from him at all since Friday night."

"Is it possible that you were bugging him too much with all the texts?" The way the hairs on the back of her neck lifted suggested there might be more to it than that, but she didn't want to overreact when Micah was already worried.

"I don't know. Maybe."

She glanced at her watch and then calculated the hour, even in the Mountain Time Zone. "It's a little late to call Richard tonight, but if you don't hear from the deputy by morning, you could call the sheriff before your flight."

"That sounds like a good idea. I'm sure everything's fine, anyway. The ranch hands have checked in. Cattle are doing great. Kevin even texted me photos of Harriet Tubman and Booker T. just so I would know that the petting zoo crew is getting the best care."

"Not Eleanor?"

She expected him to smile like she still did when she thought of the doeling. He didn't.

"There haven't been any incidents since we've been gone," he said. "None. So, I'm sure everything's fine." Then he nervously scratched his neck.

Of course he was worried. He'd spent the weekend helping her to chase a vampire in New York City while pretending that his own problems wouldn't still be waiting for him when they returned home. And the last thing he'd seen before they'd left the ranch was a threat against his only child.

Leave Wyoming or the kid is next.

Cold fingers of dread traveled up her arms as she recalled the note, leaving a trail of gooseflesh. She couldn't send them back to Harmony Fields without her.

"You know, I still have a few days left before I'm expected back at the DC field office."

His gaze narrowed. "What are you saying?"

"I think I should come back with you."

Immediately, he shook his head. "It's not your responsibility."

"I promised I would help you figure out who was targeting the ranch, and I haven't upheld my end of the bargain."

"We both know it wasn't really a bargain," he said. "But thanks anyway."

"Well, after everything you've done here, I still owe you."

"You've helped a lot already. You spent hours running around the ranch, looking for clues. You even interviewed my not-quite-stable ex."

"Really—"

"You don't owe me anything."

Her knees felt weak as Micah ushered her toward the door. Her heartbeat raced. He was dismissing her, and she couldn't let him do it.

"Micah, please."

Instead of responding this time, he watched her, waiting.

"This is about Derek. If something happens to him— or you—and I could have done something about it, I will never forgive myself."

He appeared to consider for a few seconds and then nodded.

"What does that nod mean?"

"Guess you need to get online and book your ticket. Get ready for another vacation out West."

Something about the quiet on the ranch struck Micah as odd the moment that Deirdre pulled the new rental car up the drive the next afternoon, past the barn and the outbuildings to the house. The vehicle's windows were closed, so it wasn't really a sound. More a heaviness in the air, pregnant with foreboding. It didn't make sense. Nothing was out of place. The cattle still grazed on the fields in the distance. The doors on all the supplemental structures appeared to be closed, if not locked.

Not for the first time, he was relieved that Deirdre had decided to return with him to Wyoming, but there was no way he would tell her that. He was still trying to figure out what had been in that decision for her, and though he hadn't figured it out yet, he was certain there would be something.

"We're probably overreacting," he said, trying to

convince himself of that fact. He hadn't been away from the ranch in years. Maybe other people felt the same type of uneasiness when they returned home from a trip.

Deirdre shut off the ignition, and as she looked through the windshield and side and rear windows at the same scenery, her gaze narrowed.

"We don't know that. We still haven't heard back from Deputy Martin. When I texted Sheriff Guetta, he agreed with me that it was a bad sign. He said he would send someone else to check on the place."

"I don't like the idea that Deputy Martin is out of contact, either, but Richard could already have sent another deputy by. We won't be receiving a report card showing all the places they checked."

She frowned down at her phone. "But a text telling us they've finished would be nice."

"Maybe Richard just hasn't gotten around to sending it yet."

"You're probably right." She looked around once more, then opened the car door. "Let me take a quick look around at the outbuildings, and then I'll come back and check the house. You two stay here for a few minutes. By the time I get back, we'll probably have the all clear from Richard. I'll let you know when I receive it."

"Sounds good."

He separated the spare set of farm keys from his house keys and handed it to her. She gave him the key fob for the rental so he could crack open the windows.

Micah waited, trying not to worry as Deirdre headed into the first building, her weapon drawn. She was trained for this work, he reminded himself. Competent.

"Want out," Derek called from the back seat.

"I want out, too, buddy. But we have to wait for Miss Deirdre."

Derek kicked his feet. "I go with Dee-Dee."

"You get to go with *me*, but we have to wait just a few more minutes."

Deirdre emerged from the first building about a minute later and continued on into the second, about twenty-five yards from it. She didn't stay there long, either, but when she reappeared again, she gave him a thumbs-up with her free hand.

"Good news, my man. She received the text from Richard. Now you and I can go in the house."

While Deirdre continued farther down the drive to the last of the outbuildings before the main barn, Micah climbed out of the car and opened the back door to un-buckle Derek's car seat. Figuring he could bring in the luggage later, he started up to the house with son riding piggyback. He chose the first-level slider rather than the front door upstairs, so he would get a look at the amount of work necessary to fully repair that entrance. He would put it on his to-do list for the week to make an appointment with a door company. Then he would check back in with the alarm company to finally get an installation date.

Switching his son from his back to his hip, he in-serted the key into the sliding door lock and opened it. From his first step inside, he sensed that something was different. With another look from the bar to the entertainment room, Micah flipped on the stairway light and started up the stairs.

"You're going to love getting to take your nap back in your big-boy bed today."

Derek shook his head. "No nap."

"Yeah, you slept a little on the airplane, didn't you?"

"Airplane. No nap."

"How about we talk about this after lunch?"

At the top of the stairway that led into the kitchen, Micah froze behind the closed door and listened to the difference he'd sensed downstairs becoming clear. It was the sound. Like voices, or music or something. Had he forgotten to turn off a Bluetooth speaker when they'd left for New York? Would the speaker even work when he'd taken his phone with him on the trip?

He reached for the doorknob and turned. A house that didn't look anything like the one he'd left greeted him on the other side. A sink filled with dishes. Wadded paper towels, frozen-pizza boxes and an open peanut butter jar with a butter knife still protruding from its center covered the counters.

"What the…" He closed his mouth and then held a finger to his lips to signal for Derek to stay quiet.

Micah stepped through the doorway and glanced back and forth, relieved to find no one in the kitchen. Had someone been squatting in his house while they were out of town? Could it have been the deputy, who had a key? Had he stopped communicating with him in favor of spending a weekend in a free vacation house, complete with a stocked refrigerator?

Cautiously, he rounded the corner and stepped into the great room. More of the same greeted him in that massive room—garbage and empty food containers littered the coffee table, and laundry and discarded shoes had been strewn on the floor. The source of the sound, Micah's seventy-two-inch flat screen, sat with its power still on, some reality TV show with bikinis and tropical sunsets covering the screen.

Micah's scalp prickled. His gaze lowered to the cherubic little boy in his arms, the child he was supposed to protect. He started backing out of the great room. Whoever the squatter was, he could still be in the house, and he might not be willing to give up this prime getaway location without a fight.

What had he been thinking, bringing Derek back into the house without at least having Deirdre check it first? Had the signal she'd given him from the driveway even meant that she'd heard back from Richard, or had she only been indicating that the outbuilding was clear?

He moved quietly, watching for movement around him. They needed to reach the lower level, and then he would find Deirdre outside. Just as they'd joined together to locate Maeve in New York, they could face this intruder together as well.

As Micah spun around at the bar, the basement door in sight, a man that he could only describe as a human grizzly bear stepped into his path. With linebacker shoulders and eyes as wild as his beard and mane of hair, neither of which had seen a barber or a bottle of shampoo in weeks, the man planted himself between Micah and the door to the basement.

But nothing about the guy was as terrifying as the shotgun he had aimed right at Micah and his son.

Chapter 19

Deirdre closed her eyes and lowered her chin to her chest after closing and locking the third outbuilding, where everything appeared perfectly in order. Just the barn and a quick look around the house and then she could collapse inside, knowing she'd kept Micah and Derek safe. At least someone was thinking of them, since it was clear that local law enforcement had fallen down on the job. She lifted her head, holstered her weapon and pulled her phone from her pocket to check the screen in case she'd missed the vibration from a text.

No missed calls. No texts. She sighed. First Deputy Martin, and now Sheriff Guetta was MIA as well.

"Some kind of friend you are." She scrolled through her contacts to the listing for Richard, ready to tell him just what she thought of him. Then she reconsidered. Micah was as exhausted as she was and probably dying to get the all clear to bring his son into the house. It wasn't fair for her to make him wait any longer than necessary.

She tucked her phone away and withdrew her weapon again. With a quick glance back at the rental car, she pulled open the heavy barn door.

The putrid, unmistakable smell of death hit her before she took a step inside. She gasped, squeezing her eyes shut and pressed her lips together to fight back the overwhelming need to retch. They'd wondered what had happened to the deputy. Now she knew. Her dominant hand shook so badly that even her support hand probably wouldn't be enough to steady it if she needed to fire, but she had to do this. Micah and Derek were counting on her. She couldn't let them down.

Pulling her long-sleeve T-shirt's collar up over her nose and mouth, she stepped inside the barn and flipped on the LED bay lights. Like Micah had told her, most of the stalls were empty, since the horses spent most of their time out in the pasture, but she still had to open each door and peer inside. A man she assumed was Deputy Martin, from his black uniform, lay slumped in the stall at the far end of the barn, a gaping hole in his chest, a crimson puddle of dried blood spread on the hay all around him. From the look and the smell, he'd been there awhile.

Deirdre started toward the door. She needed to reach the car and get Micah and Derek off the property immediately. But as she passed the tack room, she couldn't help but peek inside. Another deputy, probably the one she'd asked Sheriff Guetta to send, had collapsed against a saddle rack, still sitting up, his head slumped forward. As a cry escaped her lungs, she rushed over and checked for a pulse. When she found nothing, she swallowed. The blood and the condition of the body told her he hadn't been there long.

This time she rushed all the way out, wiping blood on her pant leg as she went. She ran faster, second-guessing herself with every step. Should she have taken them to safety the moment she'd entered the barn? Should she have refused to take them to the ranch at all until the threat was eliminated?

Her lungs ached from the exertion by the time she reached the car. She pulled open the door. "We've got to get out of here."

A sharp cry escaped her as she realized she was alone.

The massive house ahead of her, the one she'd found so beautiful only days before, looked like a trap now. But Micah and Derek were inside. She knew it. And they weren't alone. For her, it might be suicide to rush in, but she had no choice. The man and the child she loved needed her. Now more than ever.

After dialing 911 to report the murders and making a promise she intended to break, saying she would wait for backup, she rushed over to the house. As she moved from slider to slider on the lower level, hoping to find one that was unlocked, heavy footsteps pounded on the decking above her.

"Oh, officer," an unfamiliar voice called out. "We're up here."

More stomping continued until Micah came into view on the deck stairs, Derek in his arms. A burly-looking man walking closely behind them held a shotgun to Micah's head.

At the bottom of the steps, the man turned Micah

to face her. The rancher had a tight expression, but he held his son tight, as though he could protect him from gunfire with his own body. Her pulse hammering, her breath coming in short gasps, Deirdre positioned her weapon between her dominant hand and her support hand and aimed.

"I wouldn't do that if I were you," the man said, chortling. "It'll get so messy when I have to shoot them both. Do you know how big a hole a shotgun can make at short range?"

Because she did, she lowered her weapon.

"Now, that's a good girl," he said. "Why don't you go ahead and drop that on the ground?"

She did as she was told, keeping her hands away from her body.

"That's much better. Now, you're law enforcement, too, right? I heard FBI."

She nodded.

"Well, I would like to report these trespassers. They broke into my house, and I think they should have to pay for doing that."

"*Your* house?" Even with a gun to his head, Micah tried to look back at the other man. "It isn't your—"

When Micah stopped himself, the man chuckled again.

"You're the Beckett boy, aren't you?" Micah said. "You're Willie Beckett's son."

The hairy guy grinned. "Took you long enough to figure it out. But I'm not a boy anymore." He shifted his gaze to Deirdre. "We haven't been introduced. I'm Josh. This squatter has been living on my ranch and in my house. That doesn't seem fair, does it?"

Deirdre studied him, recalling the story Micah had

told her when he was coming up with a suspects list. "Didn't your dad lose the place to—"

"Foreclosure?" Josh said. "That's what the bank called it, but it's really stealing a man's land and his dignity. My dad had a heart attack over it when the bank took it."

He used the shotgun to hit the side of Micah's head. "Then this guy stole the place right out from under my dad."

"I'm sorry your dad lost the land, but that parcel was only ten acres. I've bought hundreds since then. Harmony Fields isn't the same ranch at all."

"My house was right here." Josh gestured to the new structure.

"It was, but this house is five times as big as the original one," Micah said.

Deirdre shook her head at Micah. He needed to stop arguing with Josh. A man who had nothing to lose was the worst opponent.

"I don't care what you did to dress it up. This is *my* house and *my* ranch, and I'm not leaving," Josh said.

"Do you plan to kill us to keep it?" Micah asked him.

Josh laughed again. "You act like that's hard to do. Ask your friend Deirdre what happened to the deputies who were nosing around in my business while you were gone."

Micah looked pale. "*Deputies?*"

Deirdre held up two fingers. Micah shivered visibly.

"It's too bad, really," Josh said, shaking his head. "You could have made it easier on yourselves. I gave you so many warnings. So many opportunities to walk away with your lives. Now you won't get to go at all."

He flicked off the safety on his pump-action shotgun and racked it. "I need you to give me all your weapons and your cell phones. Or this poor little guy…well, you know."

Deirdre tossed her phone his way and then took a few steps forward and kicked her weapon in his direction. Micah gave him his phone as well, but as he turned, Josh ripped Derek away from him anyway.

Immediately, Derek shrieked.

"No. You can't take my son."

The other man smiled. "I can do whatever I want to do. I'm the one with the gun."

Deirdre took a few slow steps forward, her hands steepled as if in prayer. "Please, Josh. It doesn't have to be this way. I know you'd never want to hurt a child."

"Of course I don't. I'm not an animal."

"I know you're not." She took a few more steps. "Just let us go. We'll disappear. You'll never have to see us again."

He shook his head then. "You make it sound so easy."

"It can be. Really."

When he glanced down at the toddler, Deirdre lunged for him. His reflexes quick, Josh squeezed the trigger. Fire immediately burst across her shoulder, burning, searing. It stole her breath away. As the image of Micah tackling the other man to the ground, where he hit his head, and Derek rolling away from them went in and out of focus, Deirdre fought. But soon oblivion was too appealing, its greeting a sweet escape from the pain.

From somewhere far away, she heard a little boy call out, "Dee-Dee hurt."

* * *

"You're going to be fine. You're going to be fine. You're going to be fine." Micah repeated the words to Deirdre like a mantra as he drove her in his pickup to the clinic outside Laramie. He said the words mostly because he didn't know if she would be okay, and he didn't know what he would do if she wasn't. Already, the blanket wrapped around her shoulder was turning redder by the minute. He was driving as fast as he could. He prayed it would be fast enough.

"Where's Derek?" she asked when her eyes popped open for a fraction of a second.

"He's okay, too. Richard's wife has him." He wasn't sure whether she heard him or not as she faded in and out of consciousness.

Several patrol cars from the sheriff's office had arrived at the ranch just as shots were fired. Micah had briefly knocked Josh Beckett unconscious, but he came to just as one of the deputies snapped handcuffs on him. He would get his trip to jail by way of a stop at the hospital so he could be examined for a concussion injury. The man deserved a lot less, in Micah's opinion, but in the United States, he was still considered innocent until proven guilty.

"Come on, Deirdre, fight." The words squeezed him from the inside out. "Fight for us."

He'd never realized until that moment just how much he wanted them to be an *us*. Would he lose her just when he'd finally realized she was the only person who could make his life and Derek's complete?

When he reached the clinic, medical personnel immediately prepped her in the small, barely adequate emergency surgery center. In the hallway, as a nurse attempted to roll her into surgery, she stopped and stared down at Micah's hand where he squeezed Deirdre's fingers in a vise grip.

"Please, Mr. Perry, you're going to have to let Deirdre go."

The next afternoon Deirdre awoke in her semiprivate room at Ivinson Memorial Hospital in Laramie—truly private now, because she didn't yet have a roommate. She blinked several times as the image at the end of her bed shifted in and out of focus.

"Micah? Is that you?"

"Yeah. I'm here."

She tilted her head, studying him. "How long have you been here?"

"Other than when I had to get Derek settled at Doug and Marie's and when I had to go back to feed the animals, I've been here ever since you were transferred in."

"You need to go home, then." She adjusted herself against the pillows and winced. "You need to get some rest."

He leaped up from his chair and was at her side instantly. "Are you okay?"

"I'm fine," she assured him. "You heard the doctor. My shoulder is going to heal great. After some physical therapy, I should have full mobility. I'll even be able to go back to work."

"That's great."

"Wow. You might want to curb your enthusiasm on that one."

"I'm sorry. It's just that…"

"That what?" she asked when he didn't finish.

He drew his chair over to the side of the bed. "I don't want you to go."

She swallowed. Those were at least some of the words she'd longed to hear from Micah, and now that he'd spoken them, she realized that they didn't make a difference.

"You don't know how much I'd love to stay."

"So *stay*."

His voice broke on the last word, and her heart fractured with it. Wanting something didn't make the impossible possible.

She pressed her lips together and then shook her head. "I can't. I have to go back to work. And even if I didn't have a job I love in another state, it would never work between us."

"Why not? I…uh…love…you."

"Love shouldn't be that hard, Micah. It should be effortless. Joyous." And him telling her he loved her should have made her feel wonderful. It only hurt— more than her shoulder, with far less promise of healing.

Instead of answering, he reached for her hand over the top of the hospital bed's bars. She knew she should pull away, but she gave herself the gift of that moment. It would be so easy to settle for so little now, but she couldn't let herself. Even she deserved more.

"Have you ever met two more wounded individuals?" she said, after the silence stretched long. "I will spend my life chasing my parents' approval when I know in my heart that I matter so little to them. I will beat myself up, trying to prove I'm worthy. Trying to prove the unprovable."

"You don't need to chase anything." He rubbed the back of her hand with his thumb.

"I know that here." She pointed to her head. "If only I could see that here." Her fingers moved to her heart.

Deirdre shifted her hand so that their fingers laced. "And you. I don't think you realize how much your father hurt you while you carried the guilt from not being able to protect him. Now you go through life waiting for people you love to be like Maeve was with him. To put themselves first and you last. I can never measure up to that test. No one can.

"But it's worse for you," she said. "You believe that allowing yourself to really love someone would make you weak."

"You're wrong."

But she could see in his eyes that he knew she was right.

"I love you, and I love Derek. So much. I wish what you're able to give me would be enough." She shook her head. "I want more."

He nodded and stood. Then he leaned over the bed bar and pressed his lips to hers. It tasted of him and tears that she had yet to cry. It tasted like goodbye.

Chapter 20

Deirdre sat in a straight-back chair in her DC apartment a week later doing the necessary exercises that would help her pass the physical to return to active duty. Every day the repetitive stretches to gain full range of motion became a little easier, but she cared less in equal increments about their results.

When her phone rang with the ringtone for a video call, she frowned. The cell was clear across the room. She let it go to voice mail, but thirty seconds later, the whole series started over again.

She wasn't at all surprised to see Aidan's name on the screen when she picked it up. He'd been calling that way a lot lately. She'd started looking forward to those calls, too. She touched the button, and his face appeared on the screen.

"Ever thought that a person might be busy?"

"Why? Were you busy?"

She shook her head, smiling. "Not really. Just want to know if you ever thought about it."

"I'll try to keep it in mind," he said. "How's the PT going?"

"Fine."

"And your life is?"

"Fine."

"Have you talked to him?"

"Who?" She kept her expression bland, but shivers climbed her arms, signaling she was still alive, after all.

"Are you going to call him?"

She propped the phone on the table and crossed her arms so that he could see them. "Aidan, why are you asking me all this? You're the one who gave me the lecture about how unprofessional it was to become involved with a witness."

"I stand by those words, too."

"Well, good. Glad we have that settled."

"I told you that as a US marshal. As your brother, I have to ask you if he's worth the headache."

She shook her head. "I don't know."

"Is he?"

She didn't even have to think about it. "Yeah."

"Then I guess you're busy with some things to think about, so I'm going to go now."

"You're ridiculous, little brother."

He grinned into the screen.

"And Aidan?"

He lifted a brow and waited.

"Thanks."

Though Deirdre startled at the sound of the buzzer outside her apartment building, she wasn't surprised to hear it. Aidan had called to clear the visit, since he would be in Washington for the day and wanted to stop by to see for himself how her shoulder was healing. She couldn't help feel a little jumpy, since her brother had never visited her apartment before, but it was more than that. She had a confession to make.

There was a difference between knowing that the son wasn't to blame for the favoritism their father showed him and actually admitting out loud that she blamed Aidan for it. She wanted to apologize for that and tell him about an important decision she'd made. This adulting business wasn't easy.

She hit the buzzer without speaking to him, even though he would give her a hard time for that reckless move as soon as he made it up the stairs to her apartment. Then she crossed to the door and waited for him to knock.

"I know. I know," she said a few minutes later when she opened it.

Micah stood in the hallway, his hands gripped in front of him. "Hi." He cleared his throat. "Know?"

She shook her head, her hands shaking so badly that she had to stuff the good hand in her pocket. At least the other remained hidden in its sling. "Never mind. Uh… What are you doing here?"

"I wanted to talk with you." Softly, he added. "Is that okay?"

"You came all the way here to do that? You could have called."

"You've been rejecting my calls."

He was right about that, she acknowledged with a shrug. She hadn't gone the extra step of blocking him, but she'd pushed away the hurt that came with each of his calls by tapping the "end" icon to reject. Even now, she wasn't ready to talk to him, wasn't ready to face all she'd felt when she'd walked away, but she couldn't close the door in his face. Not in a million years.

"How did you know where I live?" she managed finally.

"Aidan."

She pursed her lips. Her little brother needed to learn to stay out of matters that were none of his business. "He's been extra helpful lately, hasn't he?"

"Yeah, I know."

Deirdre narrowed her gaze, wondering what she didn't know, but he didn't offer more, and she wasn't ready to beg, so she waved him inside. He carried in a duffle bag and set it next to the door. Did he plan to stay? Did she want him to?

"Where's Derek?"

"He's at Doug and Marie's, getting spoiled."

She nodded, still having no answers. "Would you like some coffee or tea?"

"Coffee's good."

As nervous as he appeared, she was tempted to recommend against caffeine, but she led him to her sofa and went to put on a pot.

Minutes later, she carried out mugs of coffee one at a time, using her good hand. After both were in place on coasters on the coffee table, she sat at the other end of the couch. "You said you wanted to talk?"

He took a sip and set his mug aside. "I wanted to tell you that Eleanor Roosevelt misses you."

"Sorry to hear that."

"And Jane Austen and Anne Frank and Alexander Hamilton."

"Apparently, a lot of pygmy goats miss me."

"And Derek." He dampened his lips and then stared straight into her eyes. "But mostly me."

She blinked as her heart squeezed, contorted. "I've missed you, too. But you have to know it isn't—"

"Enough? I know."

Her pulse pounding in her chest, Deirdre folded her hands and waited. Would he say something that would change everything? Could anything make that much of a difference? And if he offered no more of himself than he had in Wyoming, would she still jump at the chance?

"It's just that you left your muck boots in your closet in the ranch house," he said.

Deirdre lifted a brow. "I know. I thought someone else might be able to use them."

"They're yours. I brought them for you." He paused, clearing his throat. "And I was hoping that you'd let Derek and me stay with them."

Her breath hitched. "You still don't get it. This was never about *location*. Well, not completely. It's more than that."

"I know," he said, his eyes damp.

"Then I don't understand."

He rested his elbows on his knees and positioned his chin between the V formed by his hands. "I never told anyone everything that Maeve said to me when I caught up with her."

I figured you would tell when you were ready. But what does that have to do with this? With us?"

"Everything," he said, tucking his head and shifting

his shoulders. "She only said why she married Dad. Not why she killed him. But the two reasons were the same. She said, 'A lady needs things. Pretty things.'"

"So, we were right. It was about money all along."

He nodded. "You were right about me, too. And my dad. I've spent a lifetime expecting everyone to fail me. Then I keep them at arm's length, so they can't. I never leap. Not really."

"I don't understand. How does this make any—"

"But then there's you," he rushed on before she could say "difference." "After all the pain and betrayal you've faced, you still put yourself out there." He lifted his head and met her gaze. "You're still open to love. You have hope."

"Wh-what are you saying?" She thought she knew, but he was going to have to spell it out for her. And if he spelled differently, she would die.

"We can't let Maeve win." He immediately shook his head. "No, it has nothing to do with her. Not anymore."

Micah scooted closer to Deirdre on the couch and took her hands. "I was sleeping through life until you pulled that rental up the drive of the ranch and shook me awake. Now I can't imagine my life without you in the center of it. I'm in love with you. I've fallen for the agent who breaks the rules."

"But is love enough?" Her voice cracked as each word felt as if torn from her soul.

"It can be. It *has* to be. You said you love me, too." He squeezed her hands. "I'm ready to leap, Deirdre. No waiting for the other shoe to drop. No holding back a piece of me. I'm all in. I'm all *yours*."

He appeared to search her eyes. When she didn't—*couldn't*—answer, he kept talking, his words coming in a nervous rush.

"I can sell the ranch so that Derek and I can move here. You'll have the chance to get your FBI career back on track, and I'll have exactly what I want. I'll be here. With you."

For the longest time, words wouldn't come. What did a person say when everything she'd ever wanted was packaged with a bow and set right in her hands?

He finally slid his fingers away and then crossed and uncrossed his arms. "Are you going to say anything? Do you want me to leave?"

She shook her head.

"Could you at least tell me which question you're answering with that shake?"

She smiled. "I don't want you to leave."

Micah puffed up his cheeks and blew out a breath. "That's good. That's very good."

"But I don't want you to move here, either."

He sighed. "Why not?"

"When my superior at the bureau contacted me about my return date, I realized I no longer had anything to prove there. My heart wasn't in it. I fell in love with a cowboy from Wyoming and with his son and the land and the animals that are so much a part of who he is. I want to be there with him."

"Anyone I know?" he asked with a grin.

He scooted close and pulled her to him, careful not to press against her sore shoulder. His kiss, though, wasn't gentle at all, filled with both desperation and hope. Her whole body came alive under the spell of his lips. But most of all her heart.

When he finally pulled back, she pressed her forehead to his and gasped for breath.

"When do you want to make this big move?" he asked.

"Whenever you're ready."

"Oh, I'm ready." He kissed her deeply then, with a longing that was both familiar and still new. Then he smiled against her lips and set her back. "Richard's going to love this. He's always been Team Deirdre."

"Could have fooled me."

He raised his index finger. "There's one other thing— Marie said no rush or anything, but when we're ready, she'll make us our own wedding-ring quilt. She did make me promise something."

"What's that?"

"That we won't throw it on the ground." He grinned. "We'll only keep it on our bed."

"Then can you put in a special request from me?"

"Sure. What's that?"

Deirdre offered him a smile that promised they would be happily distracted for the rest of the day. And then some. "Could you ask her to get started on the quilt right away?"

The investigative team had to schedule its next meeting entirely by videoconference since even an in-person plan to meet halfway between New York and Wyoming seemed a little excessive. Using her brand-new personal laptop, Deirdre joined the meeting from the downstairs office at Micah's house that she was still trying to get used to calling Micah's, Derek's and hers.

She smiled at the camera where she was one of the six tiles in the videoconference.

Sean took the lead, as he always did.

"Obviously, we are all saddened by the loss of Humphrey and more determined than ever to apprehend Maeve O'Leary," he said. "We won't let her slip through our fingers again.

"We all need to do our parts to track down any information about Maeve's other victims."

Deirdre raised her hand then.

"Yes, Deirdre," Sean said.

"Since I'm technically not in law enforcement anymore, I would be happy to resign from the team, if that's what all of you wish."

"I'm not in law enforcement," Cormac said.

"And, technically, I was on the wrong side of the law," Liam chimed in.

Sean grinned. "So all in favor of having Deirdre leave the team, raise your right hand."

No hands showed.

"And all those opposed?"

There were six votes that time.

"The noes have it," Sean said. "Now, Aidan wanted to give us an update."

Aidan waved at the camera. "Hi, everyone. I just wanted to let you know that since Maeve O'Leary remains at large, I have moved Ciara Kelly to a safe house as a precaution."

"Does Maeve have any reason to come after Ciara now that Humphrey is dead?"

Aidan raised both hands. "We don't know for sure. We have no idea whether she'll risk coming after Ciara for revenge when she has nothing to gain but satisfaction, but I would put nothing past Maeve O'Leary."

Cormac nodded. "We've all learned the hard way not to underestimate Maeve."

"Also, I can tell you that Ciara Kelly is hiding something. I feel like it's something big. And I'd know a secret anywhere."

* * * * *

Get 4 FREE REWARDS!

We'll send you 2 FREE Books plus 2 FREE Mystery Gifts.

FREE Value Over **$20**

Both the **Harlequin Intrigue®** and **Harlequin® Romantic Suspense** series feature compelling novels filled with heart-racing action-packed romance that will keep you on the edge of your seat.

YES! Please send me 2 FREE novels from the Harlequin Intrigue or Harlequin Romantic Suspense series and my 2 FREE gifts (gifts are worth about $10 retail). After receiving them, if I don't wish to receive any more books, I can return the shipping statement marked "cancel." If I don't cancel, I will receive 6 brand-new Harlequin Intrigue Larger-Print books every month and be billed just $6.49 each in the U.S. or $6.99 each in Canada, a savings of at least 13% off the cover price, or 4 brand-new Harlequin Romantic Suspense books every month and be billed just $5.49 each in the U.S. or $6.24 each in Canada, a savings of at least 12% off the cover price. It's quite a bargain! Shipping and handling is just 50¢ per book in the U.S. and $1.25 per book in Canada.* I understand that accepting the 2 free books and gifts places me under no obligation to buy anything. I can always return a shipment and cancel at any time by calling the number below. The free books and gifts are mine to keep no matter what I decide.

Choose one: ☐ **Harlequin Intrigue**
Larger-Print
(199/399 HDN GRJK)

☐ **Harlequin Romantic Suspense**
(240/340 HDN GRJK)

Name (please print)

Address   Apt. #

City   State/Province   Zip/Postal Code

Email: Please check this box ☐ if you would like to receive newsletters and promotional emails from Harlequin Enterprises ULC and its affiliates. You can unsubscribe anytime.

> Mail to the **Harlequin Reader Service:**
> **IN U.S.A.:** P.O. Box 1341, Buffalo, NY 14240-8531
> **IN CANADA:** P.O. Box 603, Fort Erie, Ontario L2A 5X3
>
> Want to try 2 free books from another series! Call 1-800-873-8635 or visit www.ReaderService.com.

*Terms and prices subject to change without notice. Prices do not include sales taxes, which will be charged (if applicable) based on your state or country of residence. Canadian residents will be charged applicable taxes. Offer not valid in Quebec. This offer is limited to one order per household. Books received may not be as shown. Not valid for current subscribers to the Harlequin Intrigue or Harlequin Romantic Suspense series. All orders subject to approval. Credit or debit balances in a customer's account(s) may be offset by any other outstanding balance owed by or to the customer. Please allow 4 to 6 weeks for delivery. Offer available while quantities last.

Your Privacy—Your information is being collected by Harlequin Enterprises ULC, operating as Harlequin Reader Service. For a complete summary of the information we collect, how we use this information and to whom it is disclosed, please visit our privacy notice located at corporate.harlequin.com/privacy-notice. From time to time we may also exchange your personal information with reputable third parties. If you wish to opt out of this sharing of your personal information, please visit readerservice.com/consumerchoice or call 1-800-873-8635. **Notice to California Residents**—Under California law, you have specific rights to control and access your data. For more information on these rights and how to exercise them, visit corporate.harlequin.com/california-privacy.

HIHRS22R3

HARLEQUIN
PLUS

Try the best multimedia subscription service for romance readers like you!

Read, Watch and Play.

Experience the easiest way to get the romance content you crave.

Start your **FREE TRIAL** at
www.harlequinplus.com/freetrial.